The Bakken Blade

A Zeke Traynor Mystery

Enjoy! Jeff Siebold

Jeff Siebold

Book cover design and interior formatting by Tugboat Design

ISBN-13: 978-1-7336387-1-5

ACKNOWLEDGEMENTS

The author wishes to acknowledge Elizabeth Bruno, his editor, for her helpful comments and attention to detail. And, the author also wishes to again acknowledge Deborah Bradseth of Tugboat Design for her excellent creative work.

ALSO BY JEFF SIEBOLD

Zeke Traynor Mysteries

Lilac and Old Gold

Bluegrass and Crimson

Ardmore Green

The Crisp Poleward Sky

Dedicated to Karin. Always an adventure with you!

CHAPTER 1

Randy Cunningham drove his 2005 Honda Civic across the Little Missouri River on the Four Bears Memorial Bridge, heading home from work. It was just after seven in the morning, and he was tired, yawning loudly after the long night shift.

There's no action after two AM, he thought to himself. *Don't know why I take the third shift. Only ones come in the casino are Indians, and they're lousy tippers.*

For two years Randy had been a dealer at the Four Bears Casino located on the Fort Berthold Indian Reservation across the Little Missouri River from New Town, North Dakota.

It was just turning dawn outside, the opposite of twilight, and he kept his headlights on as he approached New Town, and further on, his home. Well, his present home, a single-wide trailer in a trailer park east of town with muddy dirt roads and heavy equipment parked between the trailers. Most of his neighbors were oilmen.

Randy yawned again, shook his head hard, and turned on the radio to keep himself awake. It probably wasn't a great idea to have stopped for that boilermaker after work, he decided. He decelerated as he approached New Town, careful to stay legal. He couldn't afford a speeding ticket, let alone a DUI. He was already behind in his child support, and he didn't need more trouble.

The Civic eased into town a few moments later as North Dakota Highway 23 became Main Street in New Town. Ahead Randy saw flashing lights stopped on the side of the road and what looked like two cop cars. He made a quick decision and turned south on 89th toward the railroad tracks, then east on 2nd Street. He could take this route and circle around the cops. The turn took him into an industrial area across from the tracks, deserted at this hour. Still, he drove carefully.

Old metal and wood industrial buildings, equipment yards and junkyards full of abandoned vehicles were to his left. On his right were the railroad tracks, and just beyond them, giant storage silos used to load the trains. He was aware that street-lights were rare in this area of town. He looked at his watch. He'd be home in five minutes. He looked at the tracks again.

And then he saw it. Sitting on the tracks, sort of slumped, was the gray looking form of a person.

Randy slowed a bit, just to be sure the person was alright, whoever it was. Maybe a drunk, or a homeless person. There were a few in the area, some who rode the rails and dropped in and out of town. He stopped his car.

There was no movement from the direction of the tracks. It was eerily quiet and still. Randy looked around, but there was no one else, no other car or person in sight. He hesitated, rubbed his eyes, and looked again. The lump on the tracks had not moved.

Reluctantly, he pulled to the side of the road and shifted his Civic into park. He leaned over and took the flashlight from his glove compartment and tried the switch. The bulb lit up. He shook his head once, then opened the car door and walked toward the slumped figure.

* * *

As he approached the three sets of tracks running parallel he was overpowered by the metallic odor the light breeze blew his way. His mouth tasted like pennies, and as he drew near, he could see the lump was indeed a body. It was the body of a woman. She was naked and facing away from him, her shoulders rolled forward and her head bowed down. She was looking at the ground.

"Ma'am?" Randy called. "Ma'am, can I help you?"

As he stepped closer he smelled the deep rich odor of blood. He shined the flashlight at the figure. She was gray and cold looking in the morning light. Her black hair was in disarray. And there were small rivulets of liquid running down her back and arms. He moved closer and played the flashlight over the woman's back.

Suddenly Randy realized that the woman was dead. And at the same moment he saw that she was skinless, that she'd been flayed. He turned and vomited violently.

* * *

"I believe it's the backlash they're concerned with," said Clive Greene.

Zeke Traynor sat across the table from him at The Alibi restaurant, one of Clive's downtown D.C. favorites. It was an easy walk from their Pennsylvania Avenue offices.

"A Native American woman is four times as likely to experience sexual abuse," said Zeke, "than a woman who doesn't live on a reservation. In some ways, it's a travesty."

Dressed in chinos and a coral linen shirt with rolled sleeves and beige Allbirds on his feet, Zeke was in full casual mode.

"How would you possibly know that?" asked Clive, biting the end of pork sausage from his plate of bangers and mash.

Zeke sipped his Black and Tan. "Just did some reading when I heard about the case."

Clive nodded. "Ah, yes, the eidetic memory. Sometimes I forget, you being so…uh, normal in other ways, you know?"

Zeke smiled. "And two-thirds of the violent crimes on the reservations weren't prosecuted last year. The prosecutors seem reluctant to take the cases."

"It's the responsibility of the FBI, you know, to police the reservations. And the Federal Prosecutors. It may not be exactly what they're trained to do."

"So they hired you?" asked Zeke.

"It's a sore spot," said Clive. "They need better results, but, well, the reality is that there are typically no federal offices on the reservations. Most of them are hundreds of miles away."

Zeke nodded.

"The tribal councils, well, the feds say they don't have much power," Clive continued.

"The maximum sentence they're allowed to impose for any crime is three years," Zeke contributed, absently. "Even for murder." He shook his head.

"This is a particularly heinous crime, and they've hired us to consult, to keep the focus on it, to be sure the crime is solved," said Clive. He shoveled a forkful of food into his mouth.

Zeke nodded. "Or be their scapegoat if it doesn't work out quite right," he added.

"Well, sure, that," said Clive. "It goes with the territory."

"What do we know about the crime?" asked Zeke.

"Order another Black and Tan, and I'll tell you."

* * *

"So from what they can tell, the woman has had a rough go of it," said Clive. "She dropped out of high school in her sophomore year and has been on food stamps and welfare programs ever since. Three children by the time she was eighteen. Last year she moved out of her family's rented home and moved in with her boyfriend. Into an apartment over near New Town, North Dakota. According to her mother, this was the third boyfriend in three years."

"Also a Native American?" asked Zeke.

Clive nodded.

"What's her name?"

"The girl? Her name was Jenny Lakota. She was a member of the Sioux tribe in western North Dakota," Clive replied.

Zeke waited.

"She was killed with some sort of knife," Clive said, flatly. "Apparently she'd been at a local bar, the Salty Dog in New Town. The FBI said the Reservation Police were called in when a fight broke out. The FBI checked, but the local police officers said there was no sign of her there at the bar when they arrived."

"Where is this?" asked Zeke.

"The Fort Berthold Reservation," said Clive. "It's not the largest reservation, but law enforcement is undermanned there. Not enough of a police presence since the oil boom."

"I imagine that many of the Tribal Officers quit to work in the oil fields," said Zeke. "Average oil field job pays over $79,000 a year."

Clive nodded, thinking. "Yes, that's right, the police there are called the 'Reservation Police Tribal Officers.' I'd forgotten."

"How did it happen?" asked Zeke.

"Apparently she left the bar when the police were called and found her way to a mobile home that was parked over by the elementary school a few blocks away. May have gotten a ride from someone. Some roughnecks, the oil kind, were in the trailer, already engaged in, eh, well, let's say they were getting a leg over."

"So she was raped?"

"According to the officers, she probably was. Possibly by several mingers."

"And then she was killed," Zeke said. "With the knife you mentioned?"

"She was found the next morning on railroad tracks next to the grain silos on the outskirts of New Town. It was a casino worker who found her when he was coming home from work. The casino is west, across the Little Missouri River."

"That's pretty open country. Not much cover," said Zeke.

"Right," said Clive. "The area's mostly barren land with some small, gentle hills. Agricultural. She was closer to town, though."

"How was she killed?" asked Zeke.

"Someone flayed her. Stripped her skin off. She bled to death or died of shock, not sure which one. I saw the pictures. Gruesome," said Clive, suddenly done with his meal. He pushed the plate away.

Zeke shook his head slowly.

"It's a high profile crime, you know. In an area where the feds and the tribes seldom see eye to eye," added Clive.

"It's horrific," said Zeke.

"I'd like you to take point on this one," said Clive. "They're expecting you in North Dakota the day after tomorrow."

"Tomorrow's the pawnshop action. After that I'll head to New Town."

* * *

"It's after six," said Clive Greene, standing abruptly. "Time to go."

Clive was tall, aristocratic and British in his worsted wool suit and rep tie. His tan moustache and hair were trimmed to perfection. He was in his Washington, D.C. office at the head of his conference table and surrounded by his A-team.

"I'll man the communications," said Sally, the youngish blonde sitting next to him. She had a slight figure and a wispy voice and was the best researcher in the industry despite her penchant to imitate Marilyn Monroe.

Kimmy, ex-Mossad and deadly, was also employed by Clive's organization, The Agency. She sat restlessly across the table from Sally, fidgeting, her legs crossed under her in the chair.

"Let's do it then," said the fourth person in the room, Zeke Traynor. He stood and smiled at Kimmy, his slate blue eyes complimenting his longish blond hair and making him look anything but deadly.

They exited the office single file and moved quickly to their respective stations, Sally to her computers and Clive, Kimmy and Zeke to the operations area of the building.

* * *

Fifty minutes later, the three agents were parked across the street from an unassuming retail store in a one-story strip mall of indeterminant age. Clive was in the driver's seat, and Kimmy sat next to him. Zeke was sprawled casually in the backseat. It was dusk.

The store looked like a resale shop, with odd musical

instruments, rifles and televisions displayed in the front window. There was a striped curtain behind the display. On the floor, several open suitcases of unknown age held pots and vases filled with green plants and red and yellow flowers. There were bars on the windows and on the adjoining glass door. A sign in the window read, "Cassidy's Pawn, We Buy Guns," and beneath it, "A Pawn 4 All Store." An "Open" sign hung on the door.

"Squint a bit and it looks like a money laundry, doesn't it?" asked Clive.

Zeke smiled and Kimmy nodded as she bounced in the seat. Kimmy was just over five feet tall and weighed about a hundred pounds. She was dressed in a bright flowered skirt and a loose white blouse with three-quarter sleeves and breast pockets.

"They close at 7:30 PM today," Clive continued, repeating a fact from the briefing. "Just a few minutes, now."

The three opened their car doors simultaneously and set them back quietly against the car without engaging them. The bulb of the dome light had been removed, and Clive was careful not to bump the brake pedal and flash the brake lights as he got out.

According to plan, they each took a separate path. Clive circled the left end of the building to set up a rear perimeter and Kimmy veered right, up on the sidewalk and close to the window of a sub shop two bays down from Cassidy's.

Zeke took a direct route, crossed the street and stepped up on the sidewalk. He was at the front door in two steps and pulled the glass door open, ringing the attached bells.

A plain looking woman, probably in her sixties, looked up

at him from behind a counter. "Hello. Can I help ya?" she asked without enthusiasm. She was plump and obviously tired. Her gray hair was greasy and somewhat stringy, and her fingers were dirty. She was the only person in the room.

Zeke said, "I'm looking for Bart Conrad."

The woman looked away, started to glance toward the back of the shop, then looked back at Zeke. "He's not here," she said in her flat voice. Dismissive, disinterested.

The interior of the shop was set up with glass counters along both walls and the rear. An open space for customers occupied the middle area. The walls were covered with pawned equipment of all kinds, and there were stacks of merchandise for sale everywhere. Zeke looked around a moment, then back at the woman. With a smile he said, "Sure he is."

The woman shrugged and turned slightly to assure that Zeke could see the silver pistol in a holster on her large hip. The part that was visible looked like a Colt .45 Peacemaker.

Zeke tried again. "He knows I'm coming. We have an appointment."

Just then, the doorbells rang again as Kimmy entered the pawnshop. She looked around quickly, then walked past Zeke to the counter in front of the woman.

"I don't think so," the woman said, ignoring Kimmy and looking intently at Zeke. "I think you're a cop."

"He's in the back?" Zeke asked.

Kimmy leaned up on the counter on her stomach, far enough to slide the Colt out of the woman's holster. Then, in a quick movement, she bounced back, her feet planted on the floor, and reversed the pistol. When she was done, it was in her right hand, pointing at the woman. She held her Jericho 941 in her left.

"Are you Cassidy? Or Mrs. Conrad?" Kimmy asked with what sounded like a giggle.

The woman said, "Oh, honey, you don't want to do that…"

"Well, then, just keep your hands where I can see them," Kimmy said.

* * *

Zeke stepped to the rear of the building, effectively trapping Bart Conrad between himself and Clive, who would be waiting out back by now. He ducked into the back room, which was filled with shelving holding more musical instruments, rifles, boxes of electronics of various kinds, and in one corner, a dusty drum set. Across the concrete floor was the exposed wood skeleton of an office built of two-by-fours and plywood and closed off from the rest of the space.

Zeke opened the wooden door and stepped into the makeshift office. Inside, there was a small metal desk with a computer monitor on it, a chair, and a two-drawer file cabinet. In the chair was Bart Conrad, his head down on the desk as if he were sleeping. But he wasn't sleeping; he was dead.

CHAPTER 2

Despite seeing the gunshot wound to his right temple, Zeke quickly checked Bart Conrad's neck for a pulse. There was none.

A small gun was visible on the floor beside Conrad's chair. It was a .22 pistol fitted with a suppressor, and the room smelled as if the gun had been fired recently.

Zeke stepped out of the office and opened the metal door that led to the back alley. Clive Greene nodded to him and stepped in through the rear door of the pawnshop.

"Under control?" he asked.

Zeke said, "Well, sort of. Conrad's dead, a bullet in his head."

Clive mumbled something to himself and then said, "Bloody bad business."

* * *

The police spent what seemed to be an inordinate amount of time on the crime scene. In addition to the uniforms who were first dispatched, four detectives and a crime scene team showed up to look at the results of the suicide. The first set of detectives examined Clive's I.D., called in, and were promptly told that Clive Greene and company weren't to be detained.

"We checked with the FBI, and this guy's security clearance is through the roof," Zeke heard coming over the police radio. "He's good. Just take his statement and let him go."

When the cops arrived, Kimmy released the woman, who turned out to indeed be Mrs. Cassidy Conrad. But she was the dead man's mother, not his wife. Kimmy kept the Colt, hidden discretely, until the detectives had arrived. Then she returned the gun, sans bullets, over the protests of the crying Cassidy Conrad.

* * *

Zeke spent the next morning preparing for North Dakota before catching up with Clive for lunch.

"The Elephant and Castle?" asked Zeke. "Again?"

"You know you love it, old boy," said Clive. "Just what the doctor ordered."

Zeke smiled to himself and stepped into the establishment, following Clive through the door. A young server behind her podium said, "Just two?"

"Yes, two for lunch," said Clive, and he gave her a wink. "How are you, Amelia?"

"Just fine, Mr. Clive," said the girl in a faintly Scottish accent. "It's good to see you again." She was wearing a short black skirt and a white shirt with a red tartan tie. The colors matched the restaurant's decor.

Zeke noticed some energy between the two and took a harder look at Amelia. She was a tall, thin girl with clear skin and slight hips. He noticed the slightly exaggerated roll of those hips along with her almost military bearing as she led them to their table. It was obvious she knew she was being watched, and further that she liked it.

"A close friend?" he asked Clive after they were seated and the girl left to get their drinks.

Clive smiled. "You could say that, I suppose."

"She's a wee bit young for ye," said Zeke in a thick Scottish accent. "She's bound to wear ye out, ye know."

Clive nodded away the comment and said, "What do you think happened with Bart Conrad?"

"The police said suicide," said Zeke.

"They did, indeed," said Clive. "But…"

"But, it wasn't. A suicide."

"How do you know?" asked Clive.

"It's not just one thing," said Zeke. "It's several."

"Do tell," said Clive, rather dryly.

"OK. First thing, when I opened the office door, Conrad was lying on the desk with the left side of his face down. He'd been shot in the right temple."

"And we confirmed that he was right handed, so that makes sense," said Clive.

"Maybe," said Zeke. "Also, his head wasn't touching anything on the desk. So he hadn't been working on anything specifically before he was shot. Although he had papers stacked there, it doesn't appear that he was looking through any of them when he decided to kill himself."

"You think he should have been reading something?" asked Clive.

"It would be natural. If you felt trapped enough to kill yourself, you'd probably be re-reading whatever caused that feeling, looking for a last way out."

"He may have decided to keep it hidden, maybe to protect someone else," said Clive.

"It's possible," said Zeke. "But then there's the whole 'state of mind' thing. Here's a guy who has a local franchise on money laundering. He's got to be clearing $20,000 to $30,000 a month, and he has no idea that the FBI is closing in on him."

"Yes?"

"Why would he kill himself?" asked Zeke.

"Same reason as always," said Clive. "Love or money or disease."

"As in, he was terminal?" asked Zeke.

"In one of the three, yes, I'd say."

* * *

"What else did you see that made you think Conrad didn't commit suicide?" Clive persisted.

"Well, for one thing, wouldn't a right-handed shot to the temple tend to twist the head? The temple's about two-thirds of the way forward on the skull. I think he'd be much more likely to end up lying on the right side of his face than the left," said Zeke. "Think about the torque, the twist."

"Hmm," said Clive.

Just then, Amelia brought their drinks, a Sipsmith and tonic for Clive and a glass of Pinot Grigio for Zeke. She set the drinks down with a flourish.

"Your fav," she said, looking at Clive. "Anything to eat?"

"Not just yet," said Clive.

"Then I'll come back and check on ya in a bit," she said.

The girl hesitated. She looked at Zeke, then back at Clive and said, "Didja lose my number, then?"

Clive looked sheepish for a moment, but then he rallied. "No, Amelia, certainly not. This is our busy season, you know."

"Hmm," she said, feigning disbelief.

"But I was just telling Zeke, here, that I'll need to make it up to you..."

"Indeed you will," said Amelia. She wrote something on her servers pad, ripped it off and handed it to Clive. "Just in case," she said, and she walked away.

"More than you can handle," said Zeke, under his breath.

Clive ignored him. "I see what you mean about the suicide," said Clive, retreating to a safer topic.

"Let's chat about the bigger picture," said Zeke.

"Certainly," said Clive, taking a sip of his drink.

"The FBI asked for your assistance. They're investigating a huge money laundering operation across the northeastern United States," said Zeke. "How long have they been working on this operation?"

"Several years, from what I can tell," said Clive. "They've been playing it close to the vest, but once they realized the magnitude of the operation and how spread out it is, they asked us to assist. Their ultimate plan is to take down as many of the retail operations as possible, and all at the same time. What we were to do by serving the warrant for Conrad's arrest was a way for the FBI to access that data without showing their cards. This was supposed to look like a local law enforcement arrest."

"Where did Conrad fit into the picture?" asked Zeke.

"Small cog," said Clive. "They thought they might flip him and benefit from the information. And they thought that a peek at his financial records might give them specific direction when they ask for warrants for the rest of the franchisees. But they didn't want to tip their hand about the bigger effort yet."

"To the other franchisees, you mean?" said Zeke.

Clive nodded. "And the franchisor. So they sent us to arrest Conrad on a false charge, 'receiving stolen goods', and they were going to use that arrest to review his books."

"To justify the rest of the arrests, to get the warrants they'll need," said Zeke. "Makes sense."

"You're off to the Dakotas tomorrow, then?" Clive asked.

"I am. I'm hooking up with an FBI agent in North Dakota to take a look at the Jenny Lakota killing. A guy named Tillman Cord," said Zeke.

Clive shook his head. "Don't know him."

Just then, Amelia stopped by the table again. "Need anything?" she asked, looking at Clive.

"I do," said Clive. He looked her full in the face. "I need to see you again."

"I know," said the girl.

"Tonight, then? What time are you done here?" he asked.

* * *

Zeke walked briskly across the tarmac from the regional jet to the Williston, North Dakota airport terminal. The light wind was cool. He carried a backpack and pulled a small roller bag behind him. His weapon had been checked thru from D.C.

Inside, Zeke glanced around the terminal and headed for baggage to retrieve his handgun. Waiting for the luggage, he set his backpack on an empty seat and texted Sally. 'Arrived.'

"You must be Zeke," said a tall man with a sports coat and a bolo tie. He looked to be about fifty, and his cowboy hat matched the gray of his moustache.

"Guilty," said Zeke. "You're Tillman Cord?" Zeke had seen a picture of the FBI agent earlier.

"Yessir," said the agent. "Of the East Texas Cords. Here in the Great Plains via Denver. Seems like my career is heading in the wrong direction."

Zeke smiled. "Well, with the discovery of oil here, this has the potential to become a hot spot." Then, glancing at the incoming luggage, he said, "Here, I need to retrieve my weapon." They walked toward the luggage carrousel.

"Yessir," said Cord, nodding his head. "Mix up money and alcohol and drugs and semi-literate people, and watch out."

"Actually, North Dakota has one of the highest literacy rates in the country," said Zeke. "Tied with New Hampshire and Minnesota at 93%."

Cord looked at Zeke sideways as they walked. "You don't say."

Waiting for the baggage carrousel to start, Zeke said, "You have anything on the girl's death? Jenny Lakota?"

"Well, I don't have anything firsthand. The tribal officers were on it long before I arrived in New Town. I'm headquartered in Bismarck, about a three and a half hour drive from here. But, yes, I'm up to speed on what happened."

"Williston's big, with a population that's grown over 65% in the past five years. Almost like a gold rush town. Doesn't the FBI have an office here?" asked Zeke.

"We do, but it's understaffed. They called in for my support in New Town. We share like that when we need to."

"Has the M.E.'s preliminary report been completed?" asked Zeke. The luggage carrousel groaned as it continued to make its circuit.

"Only just. I looked at it before I came to get you. This whole thing is only four days old," said Cord. "They're being very careful."

Zeke spotted his locked gun case and scooped it up from the conveyor belt. "All set," he said.

"We don't have a base office in this area," said Cord, "but we can use space at the Fort Berthold Police Department facilities. In New Town."

Zeke nodded and followed Cord out to the unmarked car,

which was parked at the curb in a "No Parking" zone. It had a cardboard sign in the windshield that read "FBI" in familiar yellow letters on a navy background. Zeke smiled and shook his head.

* * *

The ride to New Town was uneventful, even boring. It seemed to Zeke that there were a disproportionate number of trucks on the roads, and most of them drove aggressively.

"So this is why they call it the 'Great Plains,'" said Zeke, looking across vast fields covered with browned grasses. They extended for miles in every direction.

"Until you get closer to the Missouri River," said Cord. "Then the view changes some."

"How so?" asked Zeke.

"Well, basically you can see the river, too."

Zeke asked, "Where did they find the oil?"

"Everywhere," said Cord. "We're sitting on a reserve large enough to supply all the oil needed in this country for six months. The Bakken Formation, it's called."

"I read that they estimate it at over four billion barrels," said Zeke. "And possibly as many as 11 billion. Maybe 200 billion in the entire region."

"Yeah. And a lot of it is on the reservation."

As they drove, Zeke asked Cord about the local politics.

"There's a lot of resentment in this part of the state," said Cord. "The population has grown up quick."

"Right. The county went from 7,500 people to almost 11,000 people over the last seven years. About 450 people a year," said Zeke.

"That sounds about right."

"Because of the oil," Zeke said. "So, is it the old guard versus the new residents?"

"Well, yeah, sure, you've always got that. But also the Native Americans versus the whites. And the oil workers versus the welfare recipients. Big oil just came in and took over."

The scenery hadn't changed much. And then Zeke noticed the steel blue water of the Missouri River in the distance.

"But there're a lot of people getting rich from the oil," said Zeke. "That should make for some forgiveness."

"Some," said Cord. "But the way I understand it, a lot of people sold off their mineral rights back during the depression. Sold them for a few dollars to feed their families. Now suddenly, with today's technology, it's feasible to get the oil out. But mostly the money stays with the oil companies."

"That'll cause some resentment," said Zeke.

"Which manifests itself mostly in thefts and assaults. Not to mention prostitution and drugs."

They both paused for a second, thinking.

"New Town's right up here," said Cord. "We're about ten miles out."

* * *

"Here's the police station," said Cord, pulling into a parking space and shutting the engine off. They'd driven for about 75 minutes and were now sitting outside a red building.

"This building?" asked Zeke.

"Actually, this is a Tribal Court," said Cord. "The police station is next door. That's where we're heading."

Inside, the precinct station house looked like any other, a long counter manned by a law officer directly in front of them, a sitting area off to one side, and several metal doors, all closed and presumably locked. Each had a keypad associated with it.

"Hello, Tom," said Cord. "You have that space ready for us?"

Tom, apparently of Native American lineage, looked at Cord for a minute and then said, "I'll check, Tillman." He picked up a phone and dialed three digits. He asked a question, listened, and hung up. He looked at Tillman and said, "Yeah."

Zeke signed in, then Tillman flipped his badge to the outside of his pocket and led Zeke through one of the locked doors into an office area, then to one of the offices along the outside wall. Cord signaled, and he and Zeke entered the office and closed the door.

"This is what we've got," said Cord, briskly. "We can spread out here, look at the files and reports. The M.E.'s preliminary report is especially gruesome."

"I heard," said Zeke.

"The girl was skinned alive," said Tillman, pushing the topic at Zeke, looking for a reaction.

Zeke nodded. "How closely are you working with the Tribal Officers?" he asked.

Cord shook his head. "Not very. That doesn't really work. We've got this case, and we'll prosecute after we find the bastard. The tribal officers, the tribal court…well, they don't really have any teeth. And everyone knows it."

Zeke nodded again. "OK, where's the FBI with the investigation? Have you guys finished interviewing the possible suspects?"

Cord made a snorting sound. "Closest FBI field office is in Minneapolis, about eight and a half hours from here. That office covers Minnesota, and North and South Dakota. The agents haven't even arrived here yet. The crime scene guys beat them by a couple of days."

"You have FBI satellite offices, though," said Zeke.

"Sure, in Fargo, Grand Forks, Minot, Bismarck, and Williston. But they're not staffed for this kind of a crime. The Minot office is responsible for Mountrail County and New Town, but they don't have the expertise to handle something like this.

* * *

"Let's start by talking with the witnesses," Zeke said, after they'd reviewed the police files and the ME's preliminary report.

"Alright," said Cord. "But there's not much there. Most of those folks were drunk or they just didn't see anything."

"You've talked with them?" asked Zeke.

"No, I read the interview transcripts for the most promising of the possible witnesses. Nada."

"OK, let's break it down," said Zeke. "Earlier in the evening, the victim was, what, in the bar, drinking?"

"Yes, the Salty Dog," said Cord.

Zeke looked at him. "We're eleven hundred miles from the nearest salt water..." he started.

Cord shrugged. "Don't ask me where the name came from," he said. "Maybe there used to be a mine around here..."

"What time was Jenny Lakota at the bar?" asked Zeke.

"A couple of the witnesses say she got there around 7:30 or 8:00 that evening. There was some axe competition going on and apparently Jenny's boyfriend was one of the players."

"Axe competition?" asked Zeke.

"It's the latest in bar games," said Cord. "They toss hand axes instead of darts."

Zeke paused. "And the tribal police were called to break up the fight...when?" he asked.

"Their report says they got the call at 10:37 that night," said Cord.

"Do we know what the fight was about?" asked Zeke.

"No one seems to know for sure. But Jenny's boyfriend, Sam Bearcat, was pretty drunk. A couple of guys said he might have started the fight," said Cord.

"So we think Jenny left the bar around the time of the fight, before the cops arrived. Where did she go from there?" asked Zeke.

"To Lakeside Trailer Park, we think."

Zeke looked up again. "Lakeside? Really? Is it near a lake?"

"Uh, that would be a big 'No'," said Cord, smiling.

Zeke shook his head. "And that's the place we think she was raped?"

"It was, according to the tribal police. They were first on the scene of the murder, also."

"Same officers?" asked Zeke.

"Yep, one was," said Cord. "That's how they connected the murder with the disturbance at the Salty Dog the night before. And they were smart enough to leave the body alone, to not touch anything."

"You said the body was found near the railroad tracks next to some silos," Zeke said. "How do we know about the trailer? How do we know Jenny Lakota went to Lakeside?" asked Zeke.

Cord shook his head. "The bartender heard her mention it earlier, when she was flirting with a guy. And one of the bar patrons confirmed it, said he'd heard it, too. Seems that it's a local…well, like a brothel," said Cord. "'A place to party,' is what he said."

Zeke nodded.

"Jenny Lakota was gone when the cops arrived. Sam was bent over, sleeping on a table, they said. The tribal police told Sam to go home when they showed up to break up the fight. Bartender says he did. At least he left the Salty Dog."

"And went looking for Jenny?" asked Zeke.

"That is possible," said Cord.

"Alright, let's go talk with the tribal officers," said Zeke.

"Suits me," said Cord. "They're next door."

CHAPTER 3

"Actually, we report to the BIA," said Lieutenant Mankato in a slow, heavy voice. "Bureau of Indian Affairs. They oversee our police force here on the reservation."

Zeke had the impression that very little would cause the man to change his pace.

"Are most of the tribal officers Native American?" asked Zeke.

"Mostly, yes," said Mankato. "The tribe has some input on our hiring, and for many it's been a pretty good job. Pays pretty well."

"Until the oil was discovered," said Cord.

Mankato nodded slowly.

Cord had made a phone call and arranged for them to meet with the tribal officers who had responded to the police call at the bar, and also the tribal officers who later found the dead body of Jenny Lakota. They were sitting at a conference table in the tribal police offices in New Town, waiting for the officers to return. Lieutenant Mankato had called them in from patrol.

The station was a part of the new Tribal Court building and next to the Fort Berthold Police Department. The monument sign at the entrance said, *MHA Nation Public Safety and Judicial Center.*

"Who are we chatting with?" asked Zeke.

"Well, actually, there are three tribal officers you'll want to talk with. Officer Tom Running Bear and Officer Bruce Doekiller responded to the bar fight at the Salty Dog…"

"Does that happen often?" asked Zeke.

"Bar fights? Yeah, sure," said the stoic Mankato in his slow voice. "More since the oil."

Zeke nodded.

"Officer George Redmoon is the third officer. He and Officer Doekiller responded to the call about the dead girl."

"Don't your officers partner up?" asked Zeke.

"Yes, they tend to stay with one partner. Doekiller was working a double shift, though. He worked four to midnight, then he went back out from midnight to eight in the morning."

Mind if I record the interviews?" asked Cord.

Mankato nodded his approval.

Just then the conference room door opened and three Native American men wearing police uniforms stepped into the room. Each nodded to Lieutenant Mankato; he nodded back and then at the chairs. They eased themselves into chairs across from Zeke and Cord and waited.

"These men, Tillman Cord and Zeke Traynor, are from the FBI. They're here investigating Jenny Lakota's death," Mankato said.

"How can we help?" asked the youngest of the three, looking over at Zeke. He was thick with black hair that touched his collar and Zeke guessed he'd played college ball at some point. His nametag read "Redmoon."

Zeke smiled at the officers.

"I know you've been through this a hundred times," he started, "but it will help us a lot to hear what happened that night directly from you."

The officers became sober, apparently thinking back on their experience of finding the girl's body that morning.

"I've read your reports. What I'm interested in is anything that may have happened, anything you noticed that might not have been important enough to include in the report. Feelings, an observation, something someone said..." Zeke added.

The three officers looked at each other.

"For example, when and how did you find out that Jenny Lakota had gone to the mobile home where she was raped?"

"That was later," said Bruce Doekiller. "We didn't find that out until we were interviewing witnesses who had been at the bar that night. The Salty Dog."

"You found them from their credit card receipts?" asked Zeke.

"Sure, and the bartender remembered most of who was there. It's a small town," said Redmoon.

Tom Running Bear spoke for the first time. "Actually, everyone knows about the mobile home. It belongs to the old man who owns the park. Sometimes they use it to turn tricks, the girls who came up here following the oilmen. Rest of the time it's pretty much vacant, unless someone's in there sleeping it off."

Zeke nodded encouragingly. Cord slipped his jacket off and, still seated, folded it over the back of a chair.

"Let's step through it, then," said Mankato. "Tom and Bruce were called out for the bar fight. You guys go first."

"Sure," said Running Bear. "We were patrolling when we got a call from dispatch. She said that she'd received a 911 call from the Salty Dog, a report of a fight."

Cord, in shirtsleeves and bolo tie was making notes on a legal pad. His recorder, on the table, blinked a small red light.

"That was at 10:37 according to the report."

"That's correct. We were going off at midnight, except on Saturday nights we tend to stay out on the streets a little later, in case of trouble. Like this," said Running Bear, holding his hand palm up, indicating the present situation.

"Sure," said Zeke. "What did you find when you got to the bar?"

"It was pretty much over when we arrived," said Running Bear. "The bartender, Sandy Henderson, said that there'd been a fight. Well, she said it was a scrum, really, between a few guys that were throwing axes and a few guys that were at the bar. But the guys were gone and no one else would admit they saw anything."

"Throwing axes," repeated Cord. "That's not dangerous?"

"The latest competitive sport," said Running Bear, sarcastically.

"How did you know who was involved? The police report names names," said Cord.

"The bartender knew several of them. They frequent the Salty Dog."

"And Jenny Lakota wasn't there when you arrived?"

"No," said Doekiller, "but apparently the men were fighting about her. She's a recurring problem. Drunk and obnoxious. Does drugs. We're pretty sure that sometimes she turns tricks..."

"She was drunk and coming on to some of the oil guys, trying to get a rise out of her boyfriend, I guess," said Running Bear. "When we got there, he'd fallen asleep on a table. Sam Bearcat is his name. Oh, sorry, you saw that in the file. The bartender said Jenny left without him."

* * *

"The fight was pretty routine, you know?" said George Redmoon. "We get called out to the bars about four nights a week."

Zeke nodded encouragingly.

"But the thing in the morning was way different," he continued. "Finding the body."

"That was a 911 call also?" asked Zeke.

Redmoon nodded. "A citizen was driving home from work and saw her sitting on the railroad tracks. Sort of slumped over and naked. He called it in."

"Where did he work?" asked Cord.

"At the casino, late shift," said Redmoon. "He's a dealer. A card dealer."

"The Four Bears Casino?" asked Zeke.

"Yeah, across the river. The guy's name is Randy Cunningham."

"His shift was over at seven AM, right before sunrise," said Doekiller. "He's lived in New Town his whole life. Lives alone, he's divorced. He's about forty-five and doesn't have a record."

Zeke nodded. "Then what happened?"

"Well, we were out on patrol when the call came in. We headed for the silos and found the body on the tracks. Cunningham was standing not far away and he'd vomited all over the ground," said Redmoon.

Doekiller added, "From a distance it looked like the girl was painted off-colors of red and gray, but as we got closer we saw that, well, she didn't have any skin." He blanched a bit at the thought.

"It was the worst thing I've ever seen. I can't get it out of my head," said Redmoon.

"I did a tour in Afghanistan, but I've never seen anything like this," said Doekiller, shaking his head.

"I went to the trunk of the patrol car and got a tarp and covered her up. It was obvious she was dead, but we confirmed it. No pulse." Redmoon wiped his right hand on his pant leg absently, as if wiping off the girl's blood again.

"Was there anyone else around?" asked Zeke.

"No, it was 7:48 when we got there and the railroad workers hadn't gotten in yet. The shift changed at 8:00, and the whole thing became a circus."

Cord made another note on his pad. "You stayed with the body until the M.E. arrived?"

Both men nodded. "We don't have a medical examiner in Mountrail County," said Doekiller. "So we have to wait for Dr. Adams to come down from Stanley."

"The body was on the reservation when it was found," said Zeke.

"Yes. But the closest M.E. is up in Stanley. We all cooperate out here. Tribal officers, Fort Berthold police, state police. And we share the resources," Doekiller added.

"Let's go back to Sam Bearcat for a minute," said Zeke. "The bartender, Sandy, said that he was in the middle of the fight?"

"Yeah, she said the fight was between Sam and some other guy. Said Jenny had been egging Sam on, flirting and such. Said Sam was drunk and out of control."

"It was over when you arrived?" asked Cord.

"Yep. But we didn't have anyone to arrest. They'd all pretty much cleared out after Sandy called it in," said Redmoon. "Sam was there, but he'd passed out by then. We sent him home."

"And the mobile home was specified by one of the witnesses?" asked Zeke.

"Right, a guy by the name of Chip Wellers. He was in the bar when we showed up that night. About the fight. He said he heard Jenny tell someone to meet her there later on," said Doekiller, taking over the conversation. "At the mobile home. She gave the guy directions to get there."

"Who was she talking to?" asked Zeke.

"Chip said he didn't know the guy's name," Doekiller continued. "Said he was sitting next to him at the bar and overheard the conversation between this guy and Jenny. The guy said he'd just got to town, and that he drives a big rig for the oil company. Chip said that all he could think about was how Sam better not find out or there'd be hell to pay."

* * *

"Tell me more about Sam Bearcat," said Zeke.

"Not much to tell. He's a local, was born and raised on the reservation here," said Doekiller. "He's a drunk and he likes to fight."

"Does he have a record?" asked Cord.

"Just misdemeanors, fighting and such. D and D," said Mankato.

"Does he work for big oil?" asked Zeke.

"No. I think he's on disability or something. Lives in one of those subsidized apartments over past the casino. Like I said, he likes to fight," said Mankato.

"Anything else?" asked Zeke.

Mankato said, "Now you know what we know."

"I think I'd like to visit the scenes," said Zeke. "Then Agent Cord and I will talk with the M.E."

"Head to the railroad tracks, then?" asked Cord.

"The bar. The trailer. The tracks. Sure, all of it."

"You want one of my guys to go with you?" asked Mankato.

"Sure. Could we borrow Officer Doekiller?" asked Zeke.

"Because he was military?" asked Mankato.

"Because he was at both scenes," said Zeke.

Mankato nodded slowly.

* * *

They climbed into a well-worn Ford Crown Victoria with black-wall tires and dirty windows. Bruce Doekiller got behind the wheel. "Where to first?" he asked.

"Let's follow the time line," said Zeke. "It's late afternoon. The bar's probably open by now."

"It is," said Doekiller. "They do a lunch business and stay open from there." He slowed and at the third street took a right turn. The Salty Dog was directly in front of them, a long block away.

"Looks like some of the boys are starting early," said Cord. There were four Harleys parked outside the bar in the street, backed into the curb, their front tires pointing out. The gravel parking lot across the side street from the bar was a quarter full.

Doekiller pulled up to one of several empty spots at the curb and parked. The three men stepped out of the car and into the bar.

Inside it was darker than Zeke expected, and the place was chopped up into three large rooms. One held a battered pool table, presently being used by two large white men with piggish faces and ponytails. They stopped and looked when the men entered the bar.

Doekiller looked at them, waved and said, "It's just the law, boys."

They went back to their game.

Zeke noticed an axe-throwing target mounted on the far wall.

The second room was the bar proper, a cozy sort of thing that was finished to a dull shine. The top of the bar was handmade wood, and had so many nicks and scars and cigarette burns that they looked like a pattern. Three men sat on wooden stools in front of it.

Behind it was a thin brunette woman with a long face. Zeke judged her to be in her forties. She looked up as they entered and nodded toward Officer Doekiller. "Sit anywhere you like, Bruce," she said. The third room was equipped with round wooden tables and captains chairs. Several of these were occupied by small groups of men.

Zeke and Cord followed Doekiller to a table and each pulled out a chair. Before they could sit, the woman appeared and asked them for their drink orders.

"We're on duty, Sandy," said Doekiller. "How about coffee all around?" He looked at the two men, who nodded. She left and everyone sat.

"This is pretty much it," said Doekiller. "The action took place in the billiards room, and Jenny Lakota, we were told, was talking with a guy by the bar.

No one said anything for a minute. Then Zeke said, "Where's the back exit?"

"Right through there, on the other side of the pool table. By the axe target."

Cord said, "So what happened when you guys got here. On the 911 call?"

"Not much," said Doekiller. "Like I said, the fight was over, and there was no one here to arrest. So we checked in with the bartender and hung around to be sure they weren't coming back." He hesitated. "This happens all the time, you know."

Cord said, "Roughnecks. Day after payday. Small town. Yessir, I can see that."

"You said that Jenny left when Sam Bearcat started fighting," said Zeke. "And a truck driver for the oil company met up with her soon after that."

"That's what we think probably happened," said Doekiller. "At Lakeside."

"The trailer park," said Cord. They sipped their coffee.

"Let's head over there next," said Zeke.

* * *

The Lakeside Trailer Park was half a square block of a wet mud track around what looked like the owner's house. The house was surrounded on all sides by single-wide trailers. The dirt road circling the house provided all the trailers access to East Avenue. The other half of the block was packed with more single-wides.

"It's over there," said Doekiller, pointing through the windshield as he drove. "The green trailer. It's sort of a flop house."

"Who owns it?" asked Cord.

"An old guy. The guy who owns the trailer park," he said. "He rents it out to a pothead who's in and out of jail. He lets a couple of girls use it when he's away. They're prostitutes. We call it 'single-wide heaven'." He shook his head.

"And Jenny Lakota was here the night she was killed?" asked Zeke. He was sitting in the front passenger seat. "How sure are we of that?"

"That's what the witnesses said."

"Do we know whether she met up with the truck driver?" asked Zeke.

"Not for sure. We know she was here, and we know she was with a guy. But we're not sure it was the same guy from the bar," said the officer.

"You said she left Sam Bearcat at the bar. Could he have come here, too?" Zeke continued.

"Didn't seem likely. He was quiet when we woke him up and made him leave the bar. He is the jealous type when he's drinking. Normally, he would've been out of control, boiling mad," said Doekiller.

"Mad enough to skin her alive?" asked Zeke.

* * *

The trailer had yellow crime scene tape across the door and around the steps, and a large padlock on the door. Doekiller unlocked it and handed out latex gloves and blue paper shoe covers, which the three men put on before they stepped inside.

"Wow. Talk about the nineteen seventies," said Cord. "Orange shag carpet and avocado green appliances. Ugh."

Inside, the living area had been converted with an open pullout couch and blackout shades for window covering. The small kitchen looked unused, and beyond it there was a door made of cheap wood paneling that most likely led to a bathroom and a bedroom. Cord opened the door and went through.

"Where were the witnesses that saw Jenny?" asked Zeke.

"Apparently, they were, eh, involved in a threesome in the living room when Jenny came through with a guy," said Doekiller. "Her presence didn't seem to stop them."

"But they positively identified her?" asked Zeke.

"They did. We had a pretty good DMV photo and a picture from her mother," said the officer. "Both girls said they thought it was her. Said she came by with the guy at about 11:45."

"Where did she work?" Zeke asked.

"She had a job at the Family Dollar in New Town. She'd worked there for a few months."

"This place is a dump," said Cord, coming back into the living room from the interior door. "Piles of towels on the bathroom floor, probably soaked in body fluids. Some sort of blackout curtains on the back windows. An Elvis picture on black velvet on the wall. The bed in the back's a mess."

"The only way in or out is through the living room?" asked Zeke.

Cord shook his head. "There's a second door that leads onto a small porch in the back. From the bedroom."

"Did your forensic people find anything here?" asked Zeke. "It doesn't look like anything's been touched."

"It hasn't," said Doekiller. They've got it on their schedule. They're sending a CS unit out this week, I think."

"A Crime Scene unit?" asked Zeke.

"Yep. This isn't technically a crime scene. We put the tape up and locked it to keep the lowlifes out while we're investigating. The real crime scene is over at the tracks. That's our next stop."

* * *

They drove quietly to the railroad tracks, next to the grain silos. It was only about five blocks from the trailer. Doekiller pulled the car over to the side of the road, put it in park and looked left across 2nd Street.

"Right there," he said. "The second set of tracks in."

There was yellow crime scene tape attached to wooden posts that had been pounded into the ground, running parallel with the street.

Cord said, "Won't the trains disturb the crime scene?"

"We had the railroad reroute everything onto the far track while the forensic team was here. But they're pretty much done with this area now," said Doekiller.

Zeke said, "She was sitting on the second track when you arrived?"

"She was. And Randy Cunningham, the guy who found her, was standing over there, closer to the road. Her skin was piled up close to her, just off the track. It was in small pieces, like it came off a little bit at a time," said Doekiller. He closed his eyes and shivered slightly at the thought.

Zeke opened his car door and crossed the road. The other two men followed him. There was a low layer of clouds and even though it was daylight, the place seemed overcast, cold and dirty.

"These silos hold grain," said Doekiller. "Ready for transport."

Zeke said, "Could someone come or go through the silos? Between them? Is it fenced off on the other side?"

"No, no fence. There's not much room between the silos, but someone could go around one end or the other, and head south from there, away from us."

Zeke nodded. He counted fourteen round silos, side by side. Each was fifty feet high and maybe thirty-five feet across. The area was industrial, and the sky was a steely blue-gray. *This is a horrible place to die,* he thought.

Doekiller held the tape up as the men stepped through, then he led them over to the place where the body was found. "Right here," he said. "Looked like she'd passed out, or was sleeping. Except she was naked. Never seen anything like it, and I'm a pretty big hunter."

"Was she tied up?" asked Zeke. "This seems like a crime of passion. Was there more?"

Doekiller hesitated. "Yeah, that was odd, too. She wasn't restrained that we could tell. The Crime Scene guys said there were no ligature marks on her, so she wasn't tied up. She was just sitting there, next to a pile of skin."

"Her skin," said Cord.

"According to the lab tests, yes," said Doekiller.

"Could they tell if it was done here, or if the body was brought in after she died?" asked Zeke.

"Definitely done here," said Doekiller. "The investigators said there was a lot of body fluid on the ground. Said the ground was soaked with blood and oils and vomit."

Cord nodded.

"But," Doekiller continued, "think about the noise. She probably screamed her head off. Out here, it's likely someone would have heard her. We're pretty close to the middle of town..."

"Did they notice anything else about the body?" asked Zeke.

Doekiller looked at him and shook his head. "This was a horrible crime," he said.

Zeke nodded. Then he said to Cord, "Let's see what the M.E. has to say."

"Drop me at the station," said Doekiller. "You can take this car."

CHAPTER 4

The two men took the dirty Crown Victoria for exactly thirty-two miles, first east then north on State Road 8 until they reached Stanley, the Mountrail County seat. Tillman Cord drove and Zeke sat next to him. The land was flat and agricultural the entire way, with an occasional swell, and sometimes a house or a church on the side of the road.

"Have you worked with Dr. Adams before?" asked Zeke.

"No," said Cord. "We haven't had a lot of deaths in this county. At least not deaths the FBI's been involved with."

Zeke nodded.

The scenery didn't change much as Cord pushed the Ford along the two-lane road.

In Stanley, the terrain didn't change either. Mostly flat and cold with wide open spaces. *You can see the enemy approaching from a mile away,* thought Zeke.

The M.E.'s office was a one-story brick building that reeked of 1930s institutional.

"Looks as if it was built under the WPA program during

the Great Depression," said Zeke under his breath.

Cord nodded. They opened the glass door and stepped into a small lobby area with some plastic chairs and a low table covered by used magazines. No one was in the room. Zeke approached a translucent glass partition and tapped on the glass.

Nothing happened.

"You called ahead?" asked Zeke.

"I did. Told the girl we'd be coming to talk with Dr. Adams. We're expected."

Zeke tapped on the glass again, with the same result.

Cord tried a solid, wooden door that looked like it led into the building and found it unlocked. The men stepped into an administrative area with desks and file cabinets and a large copy machine. There was no one in the room.

Zeke shrugged and they worked their way deeper into the building, stepping around furniture in the bullpen and into a narrow hallway that bisected the building, front to back.

"Exam rooms are probably back here," said Zeke, nodding toward the rear of the building. They moved in that direction.

Just then a young girl with an even tan and brown hair pulled into a bun stepped into the hallway and started in their direction. She was wearing a white lab coat, and when she saw them she looked surprised.

"How did you get back here?" she asked, concerned.

"There was no one out front to help us," said Cord. "I'm the FBI." He opened his wallet and showed his badge and I.D.

"Oh, sure, I was expecting you," said the girl. "I guess everyone went to lunch."

"You're...?" Cord said.

"I'm Dr. Dale Adams," said the girl. She smiled at his confused expression.

"You're the M.E.?" asked Cord.

"And the G.P. And the pediatrician. And sometimes the vet." She grinned.

Cord and Zeke introduced themselves.

Zeke said, "You're not from here, Dr. Adams."

"No," she said. "I'm from California. I went to medical school here on a government scholarship. My part is, after graduation, I get to work for the state for a while, wherever they need me."

Zeke shook his head. "How long have you been out of school?"

"Uh-uh. Never ask a woman her age." She looked at him with twinkling blue eyes and then giggled.

"Consider it rhetorical," said Zeke. "You handled the murder down in New Town? The body?"

"The body on the tracks. Yep, that was me."

"We're here to see the body. But before we do, did anything strike you as odd about the killing?" asked Cord.

"Just about everything," said Dr. Adams. "It's the strangest thing I've seen since I started here..."

"...last year?" asked Zeke.

"Nice try. No, we get a lot of accidental deaths. You know, car accidents, drug overdoses, occasionally someone freezes to death. But only seventeen homicides in the entire state in 2016. It's a pretty safe place to live."

"What was your take on the body?" asked Zeke.

"Pretty gruesome," said Dr. Adams. "The worst I've seen. And I can't help thinking about it, that it doesn't make any sense." She was serious now. Thoughtful.

"What bothered you about it?" asked Cord.

"Besides the obvious," added Zeke.

Dr. Adams said, "Let's sit. Follow me."

She led them to an empty office on one side of the hallway and they sat around a gray steel desk.

"The way she was killed was, well, horrible. I don't know what she could have done to deserve that," said Dr. Adams.

Zeke and Cord nodded at her encouragingly.

"She had a lot of drugs in her system. Something to tranquilize her, I guess."

"Which would keep her quiet," said Zeke.

"Quiet and compliant," said Dr. Adams.

"What did they use to, ah, remove her skin?" asked Cord.

"I'm not sure what the weapon was. But it was very sharp. We're trying to match the skin to whatever they used to cut her," Dr. Adams continued.

"You said 'they,'" said Zeke. "Do we know there was more than one assailant?"

"We don't, but she wasn't a tiny girl. It would take a very strong person, or more likely a couple of people, to carry her to the railroad tracks," said Dr. Adams. "We're running tests on all of that. We should have better information when the final lab results come in."

* * *

For most of the trip, the ride back to New Town was quiet, both men lost in their thoughts.

"You heading out tomorrow?" asked Tillman Cord.

Zeke nodded. "I have a late afternoon flight out of Williston. Heading to Florida and then to D.C. in a few days."

"I'll drop you," said Cord. "Then I'm heading back to Bismarck."

"I'll take another look at the police reports and the autopsy report when it comes available, and will do some research. You keep close to the Tribal Officers, stay in touch with them and see what else comes up. Maybe they'll remember something, or maybe something else will happen. And the killer could tip his hand."

Cord nodded.

"But before we go, I'd like to talk with Sam Bearcat," said Zeke. "Think we can arrange that? Maybe this afternoon?"

"Should be able to," said Cord. "After all, I'm the FBI."

* * *

"There are several things that don't add up," said Zeke.

Clive Greene, sitting in a club chair in his D.C. Office, waited. Zeke Traynor, still in North Dakota, was on the speakerphone with him.

"The girl's skin was flayed from her body. Who does that?" Zeke continued.

"And she died as a result?" asked Clive.

"The M.E. said she probably died of shock," Zeke continued. "But it doesn't look like her body had been moved after she was killed. That would have left a trail of fluids and blood."

"Hmm." Clive sipped his tea. "What about noise? She was found in a pretty public place there by the railroad tracks. Certainly she would have screamed, even shrieked with the pain. At the top of her lungs, I'd guess."

"The M.E. thinks she was drugged," said Zeke. "Probably a tranquilizer."

"Plus, think about the amount of time it would take to actually skin someone. A person. That's got to be difficult at best," Zeke continued.

"These aren't really images I care to retain," said Clive distastefully.

"It could have been anger," Zeke continued as if Clive hadn't spoken. "But that's a lot of anger."

"So drugs were involved?" asked Clive, diverting the conversation.

"More than likely," said Zeke. "You know the odds of that are high..."

Clive was silent, thinking.

"The officers I interviewed were first responders. To the bar fight, as well as when the body was discovered. They said she was found in the train yard."

"Is that queer?" asked Clive.

"Well, it was quite a distance away from the trailer park. Lakeside Park."

"Yes?" asked Clive. "Trailer park?"

"It looked like it was being used as some kind of a brothel," said Zeke. "A few blocks from the bar. Jenny Lakota was there earlier that night."

"Where is Lakeside?" asked Clive.

"Beyond the Salty Dog. So she had to leave the trailer, walk or get a ride back past the bar, and end up on the railroad tracks with the killer," said Zeke. "Seems like if she was with someone, it would have to be someone she knew."

"Yes, for her to end up there, unless she left alone and made her way..." started Clive.

"But there's nothing else there. I visited the site. Some old, abandoned industrial buildings, abandoned work-office trailers, and junkyards. And the rails," he said. "No reason to be there."

"Indeed," said Clive, thinking.

"Another thing," said Zeke. "She was most likely killed at the spot where she was found."

"How do we know?" asked Clive.

"The, ah, evidence of the crime was all around the body," said Zeke, delicately.

"My God, man," said Clive. "You mean her skin?"

Zeke nodded.

Clive seemed to withdraw in thought. "I'm thinking, 'Who would have done something like that?'"

"It certainly feels like a very personal attack. And not very practical," said Zeke.

"Indeed," said Clive. "So we should assume that it was done by someone she knew. Someone who was mad at her?"

"It could have been rage," said Zeke. "But it also seemed, in a sense, well, ritualistic...yet incomplete."

"How do you mean?" asked Clive.

"Around the year 1400, the Aztec's used to sacrifice their prisoners of war to Xipe Totec," said Zeke. "His name means 'Flayed One'. But back then they expanded the ritual by removing the prisoner's heart, then flaying him and wearing the skin, and dabbing his blood on statues."

"Grisly," said Clive. "Like stuff from the *Silence of the Lambs*."

"And it went on for twenty days or so, after the prisoner was dead," said Zeke.

"Well, this was more...immediate," said Clive.

"Yes," said Zeke. "Before that, the Assyrians did it. And the Chinese Ming Dynasty started and ended with a flaying."

Tongue in cheek, Clive asked, "Did you see any Chinese while you were up there?"

"No, but there are a lot of Native Americans in this part of the country. Native Americans used flaying, too."

"Ritual?" asked Clive.

"Not so much that, but as an excruciating punishment," said Zeke. "You might say they did it for revenge."

Clive was silent for a moment. Then Zeke could feel him shake himself.

"What's next, then?" Clive asked.

"I need to talk with Jenny Lakota's boyfriend. A fellow named Sam Bearcat. Seems that he was involved in a bar skirmish with Jenny just before she disappeared."

* * *

Zeke crossed the threshold of the small interrogation room and was immediately accosted by the odor of bad breath and stale beer. Officer Bruce Doekiller and Officer Tom Running Bear sat at a table on either side of a thick, bearded man with an ugly scar on his left cheek, who wore chrome handcuffs on his wide wrists. The handcuffs were attached to a D-ring that was welded to the metal tabletop. The man's face was a permanent scowl.

"Sam Bearcat?" asked Zeke with a disarming smile. "Hi, I'm Zeke Traynor."

The man glanced at Zeke with red anger in his eyes. He said nothing.

"Just need to talk with you for a few minutes," Zeke continued. "It's about Jenny Lakota."

Sam Bearcat looked away, as if he'd been slapped. He said, "You had to roust me for that? You could've come to my apartment if you wanted to talk."

Zeke offered a half-smile and sat across from the large man. His hair was unkempt, as if he'd just gotten out of bed, and he was dressed in a brown flannel shirt with the sleeves cut off. Zeke judged him to be a size XXL. Maybe an XXXL, all shoulders and neck and meaty biceps.

"That probably wouldn't have been the best environment for a constructive conversation," Zeke said. "This is better."

Bearcat said, "I didn't have anything to do with Jenny's

death." His voice was deep and he spoke slowly. "I told the cops that before."

"Tell us about the night she died," said Zeke.

"What do you want to know?"

"Well, start with the bar fight. What caused it?"

"It was a couple of those oil guys. We threw axes. They lost, but they didn't want to pay up."

"Why not?" asked Zeke.

"Said they weren't going to pay anything to Indian-scum. Said I cheated."

"Did you?" asked Zeke.

"What does that have to do with Jenny?" said Bearcat.

"She was in the bar when the fight started, right?" asked Zeke. "She was your girl?"

"Yeah. We were on and off. She was mad right then because I wasn't paying attention to her. And 'cuz I didn't get that money from the oil guys. She got drunk and was flirting with some guy at the bar."

"Someone you know?" asked Zeke.

"Yeah, I've seen him around, last few months. Don't know his name or anything. Hey, can you take these bracelets off?"

Zeke nodded to Running Bear, who stood up. Then he reached in his breast pocket, took out a small key and unlocked the handcuffs. Bruce Doekiller then backed away from the big man and stood against the wall.

"We're trying to find Jenny's killer," said Zeke. "You have any thoughts about that?"

"You mean about who killed her? I don't know. Could have

been the guy at the bar she was talking to. Or it could have been someone she ran into after she left the bar."

"She left the bar when?" asked Zeke.

Bearcat looked away and rubbed his eye. "I think she left when Sandy called the cops. She went out the back."

"Alone?" asked Zeke.

"Alone and drunk," said Bearcat.

"You stayed around?"

"I was going to leave before the cops got there, too. They can't arrest you if you're not there," Bearcat said as if he was sharing a street savvy secret. "But I fell asleep on the table."

"Uh-huh," said Zeke. "These next questions may make you angry, Sam, but that's not my intention. I want to find the killer."

"OK," said Bearcat.

"So what do you know about the Lakeside Trailer Park? That was Jenny's next stop."

* * *

Sam Bearcat abruptly stood behind the table, his eyes suddenly flashing anger.

"I don't need to hear any more of that talk," he said. "Shut up."

He was six foot five, Zeke judged, and was a mountain of a man. His fists clenched and his face contorted as he looked at Zeke, then at Doekiller and then at Running Bear.

"No disrespect intended," said Zeke, quietly. Calmly. "Just

asking. The forensics and two witnesses confirm that Jenny was there that night."

"I don't care," said the big man. "I don't know anything about that. I don't want to." He was almost shouting.

"I understand," said Zeke, still calm. "But we have to find out who killed her. I know it's painful, Sam."

"It's disrespectful. Just because she's a Native American doesn't mean she's a whore!"

"No, it doesn't," said Zeke.

The two men looked at each other, sizing each other up.

"I'll kill the son of a bitch that did this," Sam said finally. Then he sat down.

"What do you know about Lakeside in general?" asked Zeke, using another tack.

Sam snorted. "Those trailers, some of them're where the whores turn tricks. We don't go up there."

Zeke asked, "We?"

"Me. My guys. That place is for sex and drugs. The oilmen like it, though. They probably killed her." He held a hand to his eyes and squeezed, sobbed.

"Who runs Lakeside?"

"Ask these guys," Sam said, gesturing toward the officers. "They're up that way every week."

"But who's behind it, Sam?" asked Zeke again.

"I don't know. It could be a white man." He hesitated. "Nathan Douglas owns those trailers. Or it could be Charlie Whitefoot; he's Indian. Whoever it is, he lets the girls run the business for him, stays behind the scenes."

Doekiller nodded a confirmation to Zeke.

"Whitefoot's the guy who rents the trailer? Word is he's a pothead, in and out of jail," said Zeke.

"Yeah, like I said, Indians don't usually go up there a lot. But it sounds like you've been talking to people," Bearcat said, distracted. "Jenny wouldn't go up there. Especially not alone. She knows better."

"This, eh, this guy, he lets the girls run the business? That's really unusual," Zeke mused.

"I don't know, I never paid much attention to it."

"Any idea why Jenny would decide to go there?" asked Zeke.

Sam Bearcat shook his head.

CHAPTER 5

"You're heading back to the Keys," said Tracy Johnson. "You grew up there, didn't you?"

"I did," said Zeke with a small smile. "Marathon."

"As in Vaca Key? Mile marker 50? Seven Mile Bridge?" she asked.

"You've been doing your homework," he said.

"I pay attention," she joked lightly.

"That just adds to your charm."

Tracy was a Secret Service agent in the Atlanta office who Zeke had met while protecting a counterfeiter. They'd become an item over the past couple of years.

Now, they were sipping wine on the rooftop veranda of Tracy's midtown Atlanta condominium, watching the city light up as the sun set. The sunlight reflected off the high-rise windows all around them in bright, unpredictable patterns.

Zeke had flown in from Williston, North Dakota, and Tracy planned to join him on the last leg of his journey south. The Key West flight left in the morning.

Zeke had a habit of moving north in the springtime, finding a place to rent with an ocean nearby, and using it as a base of operations until just past Indian Summer. Then each year, as the inevitable winter approached, he'd pack up and head for a warmer climate. His present home was in Hyannis Port, but he was set to transition to the middle Keys.

"Did you ever wonder about your parents' deaths?" asked Tracy. "Was the explosion on your boat, the *West Wind*, really an accident?"

"Wow, where did that come from?" asked Zeke.

"I guess I just made the connection," she said. "You know, the Keys and your folks, growing up there. Just made me wonder…"

"I did wonder, actually. A few years later, after I'd grieved about the unfairness of it. After I'd moved away for college and the Olympics…"

They were sitting on a couch in front of a stone firepit, their wine glasses on the low table before them. The flames glowed yellow and red and licked at the cool air, and the piped music system played "Stuck Like Glue" by Sugarland. Tracy pulled her sweater closed against the cooling September evening.

"But?" she asked.

"I didn't have the resources or the skills to pursue it," said Zeke.

"But now you do."

"I do. And I probably will, once I'm down there."

"It was a fuel explosion, right?" asked Tracy, sort of carefully. "We don't have to talk about it if you don't want…"

Zeke shook his head. "No, it's OK. But I can't figure why someone would do that. It doesn't make sense that it was intentional."

Tracy sat quietly.

"I guess I'll poke around while I'm there, though."

She nodded. "I'm glad to help," she said.

He looked at her for a moment. "Yes. Thank you. But now, let's get inside where it's warm and find something to eat."

* * *

"First class travel suits you," said Zeke. He and Tracy were heading south out of Atlanta together on a flight to Key West.

"It does," said Tracy, tongue in cheek. "Is this a house hunting trip?"

"I've got a place picked out," said Zeke. "Up in Marathon. I think you'll like it."

"Can't wait," she said. "It has views of the ocean?"

"From almost every window," said Zeke.

Tracy was quiet for a minute.

"Where did you live in the Keys?" she asked.

He smiled at the memory. "We lived aboard the boat, the *West Wind*. Kept it at Boot Key Marina when we weren't sailing. After that, I stayed with some of my parents' friends there."

Tracy knew that he meant after his parents died. The boat, he'd told her, had been destroyed in a fiery explosion that he'd barely escaped.

Zeke was quiet. Then he looked at his watch and said, "Thirty minutes to wheels down."

* * *

The house was more than adequate, stilted with a large deck, a tin roof and a short pier leading to a boat dock. The exterior of the structure was painted a pastel color and was located on the ocean side of a road developed with similar style homes. There was gated access to the neighborhood and an alarm system, and beneath the house there was a single car garage and an open area for storage, or for parking a second car.

"Can we get inside?" asked Tracy, after they walked around the exterior of the place.

"Sure," said Zeke. He got their luggage out of the back of the rental car and climbed the concrete stairs. There was a keypad lock on the door, and Zeke tapped in some numbers and the door swung open.

"Oh my," said Tracy.

"Hard to beat the views," said Zeke.

Inside was furniture that Zeke found reminiscent of a surf shack, including a longboard attached to the wall over the couch. The rest of the walls were made up mostly of tinted windows and French doors that led to the open deck. The floor was hardwood and the kitchen looked as if it had been recently renovated, with a gas stove and subzero fridge.

"I like it," said Tracy, simply.

"And it's clothing optional," said Zeke, grinning.

"Even better."

"Then we'll stay here," said Zeke. "At least for a while."

* * *

"You choose the best spots to take a girl," said Tracy.

Zeke and Tracy were sitting on the wooden pier behind the house, their feet just touching the salty blue water. The sun was working its way down toward the horizon.

"Maybe you should stay for a few more days," he offered.

"I'd love to," she said. A small school of good-sized snapper swam by their feet and disappeared beneath the pier.

"A long weekend just isn't long enough," said Zeke.

"I know," she agreed.

Tracy was wearing a beach coverup over her red bikini. Zeke had on a pair of blue and yellow board shorts. They were sipping a couple cold Corona Extras. "I'll be heading to D.C. tomorrow," said Zeke. "Clive set up a meeting with the FBI about the money laundering ring."

"And alas, I need to go back to Atlanta tomorrow," she said.

Tracy looked around at the water for a moment, then leaned close to Zeke and whispered, "I'm feeling frisky."

Zeke said, "You're always feeling frisky."

She ignored him and kissed his ear lightly. Then she licked his neck.

"Do you always get what you want?" asked Zeke.

"Pretty much," she said and kissed him again.

Zeke straightened up and finished his beer. "I guess it's time for a shower, then," he said.

"Ooo, good idea," she said. "Can I get you to wash my back?"

"For starters," he said, and stood up. He slipped on his flip-flops, leaned over and helped Tracy up. She stood, stretched and whispered into his ear. Then she grabbed his hand and they walked toward the cottage.

"Be careful what you wish for," Zeke said.

* * *

"I hate that we have to go," Tracy said.

"Me, too. Seems a shame to be anywhere else." Zeke was packing a small carry-on while glancing out the bedroom window every few seconds. Tracy was lying across the bed.

"I'll meet you back here in a couple weeks," said Zeke. "In the meantime, see if you can find some extra days off."

"You said you're heading to D.C.?" she asked. "To meet with Clive?"

"About a money laundering situation," said Zeke. "A chain of pawnshops the Feds have targeted."

"We know about counterfeiting in the Secret Service," said Tracy, "but not so much about money laundries."

"I'm not an expert," said Zeke, "but logically, the whole thing is counterintuitive."

"How so?" she asked, lazily.

"Well, essentially the plan is to overpay for something, which allows dirty money to enter the cash flow stream of a business, and it gets mixed in with clean funds. Can't tell them apart," said Zeke.

"Like with the pawnshops?" she asked.

"Sure, that's an example," said Zeke. "A money launderer has a pawnshop full of pawned items for sale. Guitars and drums and guns and jewelry, or even stereo systems that people have hocked. He offers them at, say, 30% over their real value. The guys with the dirty money, maybe stolen money or money from drugs or from illegal gambling, those guys buy the item for list price. They pay with cash and the dirty money finds its way into the pawnshop owner's bank account."

"And voila, it's clean!" said Tracy.

"I didn't know you spoke French," Zeke teased.

"*Mais oui.* I do," said Tracy.

"Now multiply that now-clean money by a hundred pawnshops in multiple cities," said Zeke.

"That's big business."

Zeke nodded and set a pair of chinos in his carry-on. "The only bigger laundry I can think of would be Las Vegas."

"And you raided one of the pawnshops?" she asked.

"We did. The FBI wanted the owner arrested on a trumped up charge, so they could look at his financials. They hired us because they didn't want to tip their hand and reveal their interest in the entire pawnshop chain. It's a franchise operation, actually."

"So the FBI didn't want the franchisors to know that they were looking at them?" asked Tracy.

"Yes. They hired us to serve a local warrant and arrest the owner. But it didn't go as planned."

"What happened?" asked Tracy.

"We found the owner, but he was dead. It looked like a self-inflicted gunshot wound."

"That sounds like a pretty big coincidence," said Tracy.

"I agree," Zeke said.

CHAPTER 6

FBI Special Agent Robert Small sat uncomfortably in an overstuffed leather chair in Clive Greene's office. He obviously preferred straight-backed chairs with more support. As he squirmed, looking for an authoritative position while still seated, he said, "Thank you for inviting me to visit with you about this matter."

Zeke smiled to himself at the man's effort to retain control of the situation.

Clive said, "Certainly."

"As you know," Small continued, "I'm in white-collar crime. I'm one of the Bureau's experts on organized money laundering, as it were." He wiggled, still trying to find a comfortable spot.

Clive said, "Quite so."

"This pawnshop thing isn't unusual at all," Small continued. "Anywhere items of unknown value are purchased, you'll find some level of laundering going on."

Small finally slid forward in his chair and planted his feet on the floor. He was a thin man with a blond buzz cut and black rimmed glasses, dressed in a blue suit appointed with cufflinks and a tie clip. His shoes looked as if they'd just been shined.

Clive nodded encouragingly, and Small continued. "If it can be purchased at a premium without evidence of such, then resold, usually at a loss, the launderers walk away with what we call 'clean money'. They take a loss on every transaction, but that's the cost of doing business," Small continued.

"That's got to be a huge operation," said Zeke. "With a lot of coordination."

"It's an enterprise," said Small, sounding smug. "Not everyone can grasp it."

"How do you mean?" asked Clive.

"Well, there's a lot of momentum here. It's not an occasional thing. These guys are constantly feeding the pipeline. They jam dirty money in, and clean money comes out the other end. But it's taken years to build up to it. It got easier for them a few years ago when the pawnshops started franchising."

"I could see that," said Zeke. "And I'll bet the launderers helped finance the expansion of franchises."

"They did," said Small. "Tough to prove, but the short answer is 'yes, they did.'"

"And Conrad was involved in this?" Clive asked Small.

"He was. But we don't know why he'd commit suicide," said Small. "He had a good thing going."

* * *

"But now we're dealing with cryptocurrency," Small continued. "A new way to launder cash."

They'd discussed the situation at Conrad's pawnshop, and Small had reviewed the company books with them, showing them where the money laundering was occurring. They were taking a break from the accounting.

"How does that work?" asked Clive, sipping some Earl Grey tea.

"It's all credits and debits," said Small. "You don't actually take possession of Bitcoins. What makes it doubly hard is the new software; it makes the Bitcoin buyer virtually anonymous."

"How's it being used to launder money, then?" asked Clive.

"Several ways," said Small, warming to the topic. "Criminals can load up gift cards with illegal gains, such as drug money, money from human traffic, terrorist money, and use the cards to buy Bitcoins online. Then they can easily move that money around the world on the dark web. It's like it disappears."

"There's no central regulation for that?" asked Zeke.

"They're working on it. But, no, not like a bank would have. And there's no requirement for detailed transaction records."

"Hmm." Clive sipped his tea.

"Then there're the ATMs." Small plucked at something on the knee of his suit pants.

"ATMs?" asked Clive.

"Right, but not a traditional ATM. Take your currency to the machine and put it in. In return, you receive cryptocurrency, which you keep in your 'wallet' on the web."

"I don't think I've seen such an ATM," said Clive.

"There are about a hundred of them in and around London," said Small with a slight smile. "And over two thousand in the United States."

"Where?" asked Clive.

"They're in most states. They charge up to 7% to buy cryptocurrency and around 4% to sell it."

"That gets a lot of use by drug dealers and criminal organizations, I'd guess," said Clive.

"It really does. The arrests that the FBI has made were mostly based on a sting operation, not through detection of the cryptocurrency. FBI guys approach the bad guys to buy drugs or kiddy porn, and find the Bitcoins after they've arrested the guy."

"Interesting. Are there other ways to launder money using cryptocurrency?" asked Clive.

"There are many," said Small. "It seems as if there's no end to the creativity of the criminal mind."

"Next step?" asked Zeke.

"Francis Donovan will be calling to set up a meeting," said Small. "She's in charge of our Multiple Apprehension Task Force."

* * *

"So essentially, this money laundering is going on all around us, all the time," said Zeke. "And it runs contrary to logic."

"I knew it was a big operation, but I had no idea. What did agent Small say? Between 800 billion and 2 trillion dollars laundered worldwide each year?"

Zeke nodded. "And they're losing money on every dollar."

"So on the low end, they give up what, about fifteen percent?" asked Clive.

"And up. The lower the fee, the riskier the laundry, I'd say," said Zeke.

"How high does it go?"

"Maybe 30 or 35%."

"That's a lot more than a cottage industry," said Clive thoughtfully.

"Sure. But if it's originally drug money or money from illegal activities, it can probably be traced back to the crime. Once it's laundered, there's almost no chance of anyone proving its source," said Zeke.

"So, going back to the pawnshops. They'd need to be running, what, a couple hundred thousand dollars a month through a shop?"

Zeke said, "They've got to be careful that their gross revenue looks realistic. At the high end of realistic, I'd think."

"Hmm," said Clive.

"So they run an extra hundred thousand a month through the pawnshop, and the owner gets, what, up to thirty thousand of that? Each month?" said Zeke.

"Then the bad guys get an untraceable $70,000 and they stay out of jail. And there's no way to find the source of those funds."

"How many pawnshops in this franchise?" asked Zeke.

"There are 134 between here and New York."

"So D.C., Baltimore, Philly and New York?" asked Zeke.

"For this franchise, yes," said Clive. "But you can expand the operation pretty quickly with a guaranteed $30,000 a month. You can't open the doors fast enough."

* * *

"Electronic money laundering?" asked Kimmy. She and Zeke were sitting in Clive's D.C. Office, waiting to meet with him.

Zeke said, "That's where the bulk of the money cleaning happens. Online."

"Like in the 'Dark Web'?" Kimmy smiled. She stood up and went to the window, looking out on Pennsylvania Avenue. Foot traffic was brisk.

"No, actually it's simpler than that," Zeke said. "There're several ways to do it, depending on who the parties to the laundering are."

"Do tell," said Kimmy, still watching pedestrians and bouncing slightly on the balls of her feet.

"Well, on a small level, let's say I'm selling something illegal. Maybe drugs," said Zeke. "And I'm selling them to you. So, I might use diversion. I set up an account on eBay and list something for sale. Say a music CD, something innocuous."

Kimmy was nodding.

"And I list it for, say, a minimum bid of $100. Whatever the cost of the drugs you want to buy."

"OK…"

"But the price tag is a lot more than the CD is worth. So no one else actually bids on my listing. I send a link to the listing to you, or I tell you about it, and you get online and buy the CD. You pay the $100 for it," Zeke continued.

"The $100 goes through PayPal, then, when I buy it," said Kimmy, thinking ahead.

"Right, and eBay and PayPal take their cuts. Small percentages."

"And it looks like a legitimate transaction," she said, looking at Zeke.

"Sure, except the price is too high. The art of the deal is to set the price high, but not high enough to alert anyone."

"OK, and the drugs?"

"Well, to keep it looking good to anyone watching, after I receive the payment, I'd send you the CD through the mail. Then we'd meet up somewhere and exchange the drugs," he continued.

"Who'd be watching?" asked Kimmy.

"Law enforcement," said Zeke. "Local and state, primarily, because this type of an operation would generally take place at the local level. It's much tougher to get your drugs to you if you're across the country. Plus consider the time it takes to set something like this up, if you're dealing with a thousand buyers. That wouldn't be practical either."

Just then, Clive opened the door and stepped into the room.

"Bloody bureaucrats," he muttered. "Sorry for the delay. I was on with the FBI Training Facility in Quantico. They want us to run background checks on their latest class of recruits. They think they may have a dirty agent. But no one wants to risk being wrong."

Clive hung his suit jacket on a wooden hanger, shot his sleeves and sat in a leather wingback chair across from Zeke. "What did I miss, then?"

"We were discussing money laundering," said Kimmy. She came back to the grouped chairs and sat in one, pulling her legs up under her.

"Yes, well," said Clive, "it used to be pretty straight forward. Open a restaurant and deposit some of the dirty cash with the daily receipts at the bank. Well, you could do that with just about any cash business, I suppose."

Kimmy nodded.

"Not so much anymore," said Clive.

"Seems that there are two kinds of launderers," said Zeke. "The legitimate cash businesses that mix dirty money in with the clean, and then the pros who handle large volumes of dirty money for a fee. Nationally and internationally."

"The Pawn 4 All thing is the former, I'd guess," said Kimmy.

"But on steroids. The FBI says the pros, the high-volume guys, are international; and they move the money around the world using cryptocurrency and electronic transfers. Plus, don't forget the offshore banks in Switzerland and Grand Cayman and a few other places. Total privacy on transactions."

"So you somehow change your cash into electronic money, then deposit it offshore or spend it to clean it," said Clive.

"But the volume they need to move demands professionals," said Zeke. "It's a full-time job for a small organization."

"Can't it be intercepted? Like if it's converted to Bitcoins?" she asked.

"No, they use Blockchain technology to protect it. Very safe. It's there, and you can see it, but only the owner can do anything with it," Zeke continued. "And you never take possession."

Clive nodded.

"So what's the plan?" asked Kimmy. "What did the FBI say?"

"They're looking to do a coordinated takedown of most of the Pawn 4 All stores and shut down the entire operation."

"When are we meeting with them?" asked Zeke. "I mean 'her.' Francis Donovan of the FBI, right?"

Clive looked at his watch. "Yes, Francis will be calling us pretty soon, I imagine. Later today."

* * *

"How do you propose that we do this?" asked Clive.

The four men and a woman sitting around the table were from the FBI Multiple Apprehension Task Force tactical command and were experienced in wide-scale coordination of simultaneous apprehensions. They were a self-contained unit, called upon to run multiple arrests with no intelligence leaks, which resulted in the maximum return on the FBI's manpower and financial investments.

"Three rules," said the woman, who'd introduced herself as Francis Donovan. She looked to be in her late forties and had pockmarks along her jawline. Her hair was pulled back tight, her skin was coarse and she wore what looked like a man's double-breasted suit jacket with a white shirt. She looked around now to be certain she had everyone's attention.

"Three," she repeated. "First, we organize it all here, in house."

"OK," said Clive. He and Zeke were at FBI headquarters in Washington, D.C., at the invitation of Francis Donovan and the Assistant Director. The A.D. was not in the room.

"Then we pull in law enforcement without letting them know they're part of a larger operation. We want them to focus on their task at hand, not the bigger picture." She paused, probably for effect.

"And third?"

"We move quickly to take them down, cut off their communications and isolate them in local jails or detention facilities. If we do it right, we'll get the best intel."

"You've done this before," said Zeke.

"We have. We employed the same strategy and tactics closing down everything from a group staging dog fights to one selling snuff films on the dark web. The bad guys are becoming more and more decentralized, so our tactics have morphed as well."

Zeke nodded.

"In this case, we've identified most of the likely culprits. Low budget pawnshops that are outperforming their competition. Both their geographical competition and the industry averages for their business," she continued.

"You pull their income and sales tax filings and their bank records? And you compare them with other businesses in the immediate area, as well as other pawnshop norms, to look for anomalies?" asked Zeke. "Businesses making too much money for their demographic and their industry?"

"Exactly. Then we develop targets and look at them more deeply for common factors," she said.

One of the agents, a tall, thin man of about forty named Addison, added, "The franchise thing actually makes it easier. In this case, we found anomalies in pawnshops and tracked them back through their franchise arrangement with Pawn 4 All. Almost every Pawn 4 All franchisee in this area is tracking with the pattern. Which means they're all laundries."

"Possibly owned by someone who needs to launder their money," added Clive.

"Possibly so," said Francis Donovan.

"You want us to work from the top?" asked Clive. "Get close to the people in charge at Pawn 4 All in preparation for the FBI action?"

"We do," said Donovan.

"I'm not certain they're looking to franchise to people they don't know," said Zeke.

"It might give you a chance to see what's going on, to get a sense of who the players are," said Donovan. "Whether they accept you will depend, in part, on how much pressure they're under to expand the operation."

"That's true. We can approach as an interested potential franchisee. Maybe meet the people who are orchestrating all this," Zeke said. "See where we can take it."

"Good," said Donovan. "Everything helps."

"You're playing the long game with this," said Zeke. "But the longer you stretch this out, the higher the odds of a leak."

"Typically true," said Donovan. "But in this case, we'll take our time. The only ones in the loop are the five of us at this table. And now you two."

* * *

"What do you think happened to Bart Conrad?" Clive asked Zeke after they'd left FBI headquarters. "Why would someone kill him?"

"Not sure," said Zeke. "He was a franchisee, and we're assuming that he was making an extra, what, thirty thousand a month running money through his operation. Very local and very small, actually. Bad neighborhood, bars on the windows, mostly walk-in traffic…"

"Druggies and blaggers, I'd think," added Clive.

"…but the business wasn't of the size and scope to make Conrad dangerous to anyone. Just a sleaze being paid more than he was worth to clean some cash. Probably for the mob."

"Well, he got on the wrong side of someone," said Clive.

"It wasn't random," said Zeke. "The FBI said money was transferred in and recorded as if sales had been paid for in cash, at prices too high. And the money was deposited in Conrad's bank."

"Directly to the bank, then?" asked Clive.

"Directly to the bank by the mob or the drug guys. The guys with the criminal enterprise. Less chance of someone getting greedy that way," added Zeke.

"And Conrad distributed it?" asked Clive.

"Paid falsified invoices and faked property redemptions to receive the cash," said Zeke. "According to the FBI guys."

"Property redemptions? You mean pawned items?" asked Clive.

"Yes, they kept a record of nonexistent items that were pawned and then supposedly redeemed."

"And for that, Conrad netted an extra thirty thousand."

"Each month," said Zeke. "Like an annuity."

"So what do we do next?" asked Clive.

CHAPTER 7

"The Bart Conrad thing is a bad omen," said Chester Knowles.

He was a tiny man with small features and a rigid bearing that made one think 'Napoleon Complex.'

"And they made it look like a suicide, no less," he continued.

Jack Thurmond, his CFO, sat across the desk and nodded at Knowles. "Ugly business."

"Skimming," Knowles continued as if Thurmond hadn't spoken. "He was doing as well as he ever had, and then he goes and skims the money." The small man shook his head, lost in thought.

Gently, Thurmond said, "The numbers, boss..."

With a small shutter, ending one thought and starting another, Knowles refocused. "Yes. What do we have, Jack?"

Thurmond cleared his throat and looked at his notes.

"We're moving about twelve million a month, with twenty-five to thirty percent costs," he said. "A net of a little more than a hundred million a year, roughly."

"Just the East Coast operation?" asked Knowles.

"Yes, from D.C. up to New York City. Over 130 locations," said Thurmond. "But not Miami or Atlanta or Charlotte or Jacksonville or Richmond. We have more opportunities in those cities."

Knowles was nodding. "The franchise thing was smart."

"Like printing money," said Thurmond with a slight smile that disappeared almost immediately. "We just need to keep expanding that part."

"Indeed we do," said Knowles. "How quickly can we get more franchises set up?"

"Our team is setting up locations as quickly as is feasible," said Thurmond. "We're also looking at some buyouts of existing shops to turn them into franchisees."

"Can we accelerate the growth?" repeated Knowles. "There's pressure to do so."

"I'd suggest slow and steady," said the accountant. "We need to build this carefully."

Knowles nodded and thought, *I'm not sure we have time for that.*

* * *

"Where will we start?" asked Tracy.

Zeke shook his head. "It's been thirty years and several hurricanes since my parents died," he said. "Everything's changed in the Keys."

"Talk about a cold case!" said Tracy. "But it's important, Zeke. I think we need to do this."

They were chatting on the phone, Zeke in his hotel room at the Harrington, a D.C. hotel located a block from Clive Greene's Agency offices, and Tracy sitting on the couch in her Midtown Atlanta condominium. It was Sunday afternoon and both cities seemed to be resting up for the week ahead.

"I worked cold cases for a while when I first joined the Secret Service," said Tracy. "They were actually old counterfeiting cases, but there's some similarity, I'd think."

"In the process, you mean?" asked Zeke.

"Yes. Typically no real forensic evidence. And usually you can't find the witnesses. They've moved or died or just disappeared. When you do find someone who was there when it happened, their memory of the event is usually fuzzy. Or else they've thought about it for so long that they've built a scenario that may not be accurate. Mind tricks, you know."

"Well, we have no evidence in this case," said Zeke.

"Was there an investigation into the explosion?" asked Tracy.

"I'd think so," said Zeke. "I remember the Sheriff's Deputies coming around for days after the explosion, interviewing people at the marina and the staff. And I know the firemen went over what was left of the *West Wind* very carefully before they allowed it to be towed off."

"Tell me what happened again," said Tracy. "Can you, or does it hurt too much?"

"It hurts. But, yes, we need to revisit it."

"Take your time," said Tracy. "Let me put you on the speaker." She had a pad and pen in front of her on the table.

"We lived aboard the *West Wind.* It was a 52-foot Mandarin motorsailer that accommodated our family easily. Dad docked it at Boot Key Marina in Marathon when we weren't at sail."

"What happened the day of the explosion?" Tracy asked. "I know you've told me some of it, but let's start over, at the beginning."

"Sure," said Zeke. "We'd just returned from a cruise of Florida Bay. We actually did that a lot back then. Took several days and cruised along, stopping to fish and swim."

"Nice," said Tracy.

"It was. We had just come back into the marina and I jumped off the boat and ran to the dock store to buy a soda. That was a big treat for me back then."

"What year was this?"

"Late 1980s," said Zeke. "Actually, it was May 12, 1989 when all of this happened."

"And while you were in the store…"

"I was buying the soda when there was a noise like a thunderclap and the windows of the little store blew out from the pressure of the explosion. It was horrible. The top half of the boat just disappeared. It burned for hours."

"Had anything happened on your way back into the marina that day?" asked Tracy. "From Florida Bay, I mean."

Zeke thought for a minute. "Not really. We did stop to help a fisherman who was stuck. He'd been fishing in the shallows and ran aground when the tide went out."

"Really?"

"We were always doing things like that," said Zeke. "My

folks were practical, but they had big hearts."

"There's got to be a police report about the explosion," said Tracy. "And something from the Fire Inspector. Maybe an arson report?"

"It's possible," said Zeke. "I'm heading back to Marathon tomorrow. The FBI's running the money laundry project at their own pace, and I'm waiting for the forensics team to finalize their report in North Dakota. It'll probably be another few days before their analysis is completed."

"On the dead girl," said Tracy. "That's just horrible."

"I know," said Zeke.

Tracy was quiet for a moment, and then she mentally shook it off. "I'll meet you in the Keys then. Day after tomorrow. I can get away for a long weekend."

"That would be great!" said Zeke. "Bring your flip-flops and your sunglasses..."

"Will do. Anything else?"

"Nope. That's all you'll need."

* * *

"You're kidding, right?" asked the uniformed man.

"No, we're serious," said Tracy, and she smiled a dazzling smile at him from across the counter.

He noticed.

"You want to see records from thirty years ago? Sheriff's files and the Fire Inspector's records?" he continued, his ample belly lapping his belt and jiggling when he talked.

Zeke and Tracy were in the Monroe County Sheriff's Department building, a one-story concrete block building on High Point Road in Tavernier. They were looking for any records or files from the explosion that had killed Zeke's parents.

"Was there a crime committed?" the officer continued. "Blazen" was stitched over his left breast pocket.

"It was ruled to be an accident," said Zeke. "But I remember several Deputies interviewing people at the marina. And the Fire Inspector was around, looking for signs of arson or a bomb, I guess. He interviewed me several times."

"Back then, Billy Forester was the Sheriff," said Deputy Blazen. "We had computers, but it wasn't anything like it is today. I'm not sure those records survived."

"If they had," said Zeke, "where would they be?"

"In storage, no doubt," said Blazen, thinking. "But they could have been thrown out. Especially if they determined that there was no crime committed."

"And storage is…?" asked Tracy.

"Off site, for that far back," the cop said. He paused. "Wait, though, we went through a transition in the '90s. A lot got scanned into electronic storage. What you're looking for might be in the computers now."

"That's good news," said Tracy. "How can we take a look?"

"Can I see your badge again?" asked Blazen, picking up the business card Tracy had given him. "Secret Service, huh?"

She showed him her credentials, her badge and I.D. He took the wallet in his hand and held it at arm's length, squinting. He read her badge number, moving his lips, and handed it back to her and jotted the number on a scrap of paper.

"Let me see what I can do," he said. "Professional courtesy."

* * *

A short phone call later, Deputy Blazen stepped from behind the counter and said, "Follow me."

Zeke and Tracy followed the large man through long, narrow halls with vinyl tile flooring and walls painted a shade of sea foam green. After several turns, they entered a large room with eight-foot tables supporting multiple workstations. The sign on the door read, "Information Management".

"Susie, this is Zeke Traynor and Tracy Johnson. They have permission to check our files for a 1980s cold case. Can you help?"

A short blonde woman with long frizzy hair wearing jean shorts and a Margaritaville t-shirt said, "Sure, Pete."

"I'll leave you with Susie," said the Deputy. "Susie Franklin. If it's in the system, she'll find it."

She flashed him a smile and said, "Thanks, Pete. You're sweet." She turned to Tracy, "What are we looking for?"

"It was in May 1989. There was an explosion at Boot Key Marina, down in Marathon. A boat, the *West Wind,* was destroyed," Tracy said. "Two adults, the Traynors, were killed."

"Faulty gas pump?" asked Susie.

"They thought so. Or possibly a leak in the fuel line. But we'd like to double-check," said Tracy.

"Sure. Let's see what we've got in here," Susie said, shifting focus to her computer screen.

* * *

"Well, that was worth the visit," said Tracy as she and Zeke left the building. The sun was intense on the asphalt pavement and its heat radiated through the soles of Tracy's sandals. She stepped quickly to Zeke's BMW.

The car was a blue vintage M3 convertible, a 2006 model with a 338 hp engine and a six-speed manual transmission. He'd had it delivered from Boston via train, picking it up in Miami and driving it the last 100 plus miles to Marathon.

Parked in a shady spot beneath a gumbo limbo tree, the upholstery was warm but not hot as Tracy slipped into the passenger's seat. Zeke started the car and headed south.

"The accident seems suspicious," said Tracy, looking at her notes as they drove. "They were pumping fuel; they'd just started, apparently, and then there was the huge explosion." She paused.

"How long were you off the boat before the explosion?" she asked Zeke.

"I jumped off the boat at the dock and secured the lines. I got the stern lines, and the dockhand got the bow lines. Then as soon as the lines were secure, I ran down to the dock store. That's maybe a hundred yards away, so maybe forty-five seconds? Maybe a minute, tops, including the time at the cash register," said Zeke. "I was thirsty."

"And then it just blew up?" asked Tracy.

"Yes," said Zeke. "It was horrific. The explosion was devastating."

"Was there enough time for fuel fumes to accumulate?" asked Tracy. "Inside the hull?"

"I don't know," said Zeke. "Good question. What did the Fire Inspector say?"

Tracy looked through the papers in her lap, while Zeke pulled the car into a parking lot. Susie had found the fire department file on the *West Wind* explosion and had printed out a copy for Zeke and Tracy.

"Says here that the cause of the fire was determined to be a faulty valve in the gas pump. It says a spark must have ignited the fuel," Tracy said.

"Hmm," said Zeke. "A spark would ignite gas fumes, which could cause an explosion. But I doubt there was enough time for the fumes to collect. My dad had just started pumping after I ran to the store..."

"So the fumes had to already be in the boat, in the hull?" asked Tracy.

"Possibly, but I think we would have smelled them."

"Or it wasn't the gas fumes igniting at all. Maybe the explosion had another source," she continued.

"Could be. I guess I've just been too close to it. Never thought it was anything but an accident."

"Of course not. Plus the emotional trauma. That's too much for a child to wrap their head around."

"Let's go back home and read through this, and compare

notes," said Zeke. "Maybe the file notes will jog my memory."

"Your memory's just fine," said Tracy. "But we can spend some time on it together. Break it down, ask each other questions…"

"OK. I'll put it all out of my head, and we'll start from zero. You ask questions, and I'll try to put it together in my mind. Good."

Zeke pulled the BMW under the house he was renting and shut it off. Tracy, her right hand on the door latch, leaned over and gave Zeke a gentle kiss.

"This has got to be so difficult," she started.

"It is," he said. "And I could use some sympathy…" He kissed her back.

Tracy moved a bit, upright in the seat. "Sympathy. Yeah, lets call it that," she said with a broad smile.

Zeke nodded and said, "Bring the file in. We'll get to it in a little bit."

* * *

"It actually worked out better," said Zeke, hanging up the phone.

Tracy gave him a wide-eyed, questioning look. Her short, light robe was loose on her, showing off her long legs and even tan.

"It looks like I'll be heading to D.C. tomorrow. We have new information from the M.E. in North Dakota. Clive says it's surprising."

"Yes…?"

"So it's better that you can't stay this weekend."

"Oh, really?" asked Tracy. "Better for who?"

"Well, it wouldn't be fair if you were here, looking at the ocean and sitting in the sun, while I was working in D.C. or North Dakota or someplace equally un-sunny."

"No, it wouldn't be fair," she repeated. Then she sighed. "When do you have to leave?"

"Flying out of Miami tomorrow, late morning. Let's see if we can book the same flight to Atlanta, and I'll see you off there."

"Does this mean another night of wild, uncontrolled love and debauchery?"

"What do you think?" he asked.

"It better," she said.

Chapter 8

"It was extremely sharp," said Dr. Dale Adams. "I'd say surgically sharp."

She was on the speakerphone, talking with Zeke and Clive in their D.C. office. Dr. Adams was in Stanley, North Dakota, reporting the final results of the autopsy and the results of the forensic analysis of Jenny Lakota's body.

"What type of a tool was it?" asked Clive.

"It was small bladed. The cuts to her skin were round and symmetrical. Little round cuts, like if you were skinning an apple, but with a very small knife," she continued.

"Like a surgeon's knife," said Zeke. "That may be why the pieces of her skin were so small. Tiny cuts, resulting in skin pieces maybe an inch or two in diameter."

"Sounds like it must have taken a while to do all that," said Clive.

"Yes, to work over her entire body…that would take several hours, I'd guess."

"Like skinning an apple," repeated Clive.

"How about the lab results?" asked Zeke.

"She had alcohol in her system," said the doctor. "And barbiturates, enough to incapacitate her. Xylazine. Horse tranquilizers."

"Must have done," said Zeke. "That would have stopped her from screaming."

"The quantity we found would have disenabled her. But it wasn't enough to knock her out completely. I'm pretty sure she was awake for most of it. Just couldn't move or scream…until she died," said Dr. Adams.

"So this was probably personal," said Zeke, slowly. "Vindictive."

"It seems so," said Dr. Adams.

"Doctor, what did you find in her stomach?" asked Clive.

"Besides the Xylazine? Beer. Sperm. And what was probably her dinner, partially digested. It turns out that it was Chinese food. Probably from China Delight. The restaurant is located a couple doors down from the Salty Dog."

"I remember seeing it," said Zeke, absently. "Tell me more about the Xylazine."

"Sure. As well as being the M.E., I'm also the vet, remember?" said Dr. Adams.

Clive chuckled.

"Xylazine is a powerful drug. It's used to sedate horses and as an anesthesia for large animals. It's a muscle relaxer, a central nervous system depressant. An overdose, which our victim definitely had, would slow her heart rate until she died."

"Hmm," said Zeke. "Alcohol plus Xylazine. Probably a bad mix. Anything more about the, ah, skinning?"

"Very sharp knife. Very slow work. I don't know for sure how long she lived, but she was definitely dead before it was over."

* * *

Zeke's mobile phone rang. He looked at the screen. It was Agent Cord.

"Tillman Cord, hello," said Zeke.

"Hello to you," said Cord. "Thought you'd want to know. The FBI made an arrest in the Jenny Lakota case." Cord paused for effect.

"And..." asked Zeke.

"We arrested Sam Bearcat this afternoon."

* * *

Zeke stuck his head in Clive's office.

"Now that we have the forensics, we have better questions to ask. I think I'd better head back to North Dakota tomorrow," said Zeke. "I'll call ahead and ask the Tribal Officers to set up an interview with Randy Cunningham, the guy who found the body. And another session with Sam Bearcat."

"What about the man from the Salty Dog?" asked Clive. "The one Jenny Lakota was flirting with."

"The bartender, Sandy, may know who he is. And maybe the Tribal Officers will know by now. I'll follow up on that, too," said Zeke.

* * *

Zeke rented a jeep at Sloulin Field International Airport in Williston and drove the hour and a half southeast to New Town. As he approached he turned right, away from town, and crossed the Little Missouri River. At the end of the bridge he pulled off into the Four Bears Casino and Lodge.

The front desk clerk seemed genuinely happy to see him. She was a tall, thin woman with an eager face and quick movements that belied her age, which Zeke guessed to be about fifty-five.

"Welcome to Four Bears," she said. "Do you have a reservation?"

"I do," said Zeke, and he gave her the details. Ten minutes later, he was in a third floor King Suite with a middle-distance view of the steel-blue river.

Zeke's cellphone rang, and when he answered, Officer Bruce Doekiller said, "You get settled OK?"

"I'm in," said Zeke. "Do we still have time to interview Randy Cunningham this afternoon?"

"Sure," said Doekiller. "I'll come by and pick you up in ten minutes. Four Bears, right?"

* * *

Bruce Doekiller was driving the same maroon, black-walled Crown Vic as he had before, and spots of dirt still muddied the windows. He parked it and Zeke met him inside the casino entrance. A bus full of senior citizens was discharging its passengers.

"They're here for the slots and buffet," said Doekiller. "The bus runs every day, brings them in from the senior center down in Bismarck. They bring rolls of quarters with them."

Zeke nodded. "And I'm guessing the bus is full right after the first of the month," he said. "Social Security checks arrive."

"Like clockwork," said Doekiller. "Where's your partner?"

"Cord said the FBI won't pursue it any further. Now that they've arrested Sam Bearcat, I guess that's enough for them," said Zeke.

Doekiller nodded. "Then Cunningham first?"

"Yes," said Zeke. "He works at the casino. Is he around?"

"He typically works the night shift," said Doekiller. "But I called him and asked him to meet us here. He said he'd come in early."

"Where?" asked Zeke.

Doekiller signaled for Zeke to follow him as he walked into the casino and headed for a back-office door marked "Security." He knocked on the door. A moment later they heard it being unlocked, and the solid metal door swung open.

"Hey, Bruce," said an average sized man, obviously of Native American heritage. His face showed little expression, and his voice was a high monotone. He ignored Zeke and said to the Tribal Officer, "Come in."

Inside, the room was about four times larger than Zeke had anticipated, with one full wall supporting an array of large screen TV's, and numerous tables and desks arranged symmetrically. Three other people, two men and a woman, each wearing a red vest marked "Security" were in attendance. Each seemed preoccupied with the action on the TV screens.

"Did Mr. Cunningham make it in yet?" asked Doekiller.

"Yeah, we put him in the office over there," the man said, waving to the back of the room.

Doekiller glanced at Zeke, nodded, and walked to the closed office door. Inside was a desk and chair, occupied by a scarecrow of a man with long, loose limbs and what looked like a Dutch Boy haircut.

"Mr. Cunningham, hello," said Zeke, as he held out his hand.

Cunningham stood and shook Zeke's hand, then offered his hand to the Tribal Officer. Doekiller shook and sat down across the table from him.

Cunningham looked at them and shivered involuntarily. "It was just horrible."

"I know," said Doekiller. "I saw it, too."

Zeke nodded slowly and said, "That's a pretty ugly thing to come across."

"I can't make the images go away."

"We have a few more questions, Mr. Cunningham," said Zeke. "Mainly questions that came up because of the autopsy and the forensic analysis."

"OK," said Cunningham.

"When you came across the body, did you see anyone else? Anybody in the area, near the tracks or on the street?

"I didn't," said Cunningham. "But the light was pretty bad. Some of the streetlights were out, so it was tough to see anything."

"But you saw the figure on the tracks," said Zeke.

Cunningham nodded. "At first it looked like a big bag, maybe a gray or silver bag of debris. Like you use for yard work."

Zeke nodded.

"But then I thought, 'Maybe it's a drunk or a homeless person.' Whatever it was, it was on the tracks, which is part of the reason I stopped. To be sure the person was OK. The trains come through there..."

"You found the body and called the police?" asked Zeke.

Cunningham nodded, suddenly pale. He covered his mouth with his fist.

"Did the body move at all, or make any sound that you remember?" asked Zeke.

"No, nothing like that. It was all slumped over, no real shape."

"Did you touch it? Move the body at all?" asked Zeke.

"No, no way. As soon as I realized what it was, that it didn't have any skin, well, I got sick."

"How close did you get to the body?" asked Zeke.

"Oh," said Cunningham, thinking. "Maybe from here to over there," he said, signaling a distance of about five feet. "Remember, it was dark out there."

"Then you vomited," said Zeke, "What did you do next?"

"Well, I could see it was dead. I mean, you can't live without skin, right? And nothing moved, there was no movement, no sound. Everything was…well, it just felt so empty."

"Then?" asked Zeke.

"Well, as soon as I could talk, I dialed 911."

"As soon as you could talk?" asked Doekiller.

"As soon as I stopped upchucking. When I got my stomach under control."

"How long was that?" asked Zeke.

"I don't know, maybe thirty seconds," said Cunningham.

"Why were you there, Randy?" asked Zeke.

"What?" asked Cunningham.

"Why were you on Second Street by the railroad tracks?"

The man looked confused. "I was heading home from work."

"You live out east of town off Highway 23, don't you? If you were heading home, you would have stayed on Main Street, right? No reason for a detour into the industrial section of town…" said Zeke.

"No, well, I just…"

"Unless you were looking for something. Maybe trying to score some drugs?" asked Zeke.

Randy said, "No, no, it's not like that. OK, look, I had a couple of drinks before I left the casino. I saw lights flashing on Main Street, and I decided to avoid trouble."

"Trouble with the police?" Zeke asked.

Randy Cunningham nodded.

"Because you've got one DUI already?" asked Zeke.

Cunningham nodded again, glancing down at the table sheepishly.

* * *

"I don't think he knows anything more," said Zeke.

They had finished the interview with Randy Cunningham and were riding in Doekiller's Crown Vic on the Memorial Bridge, headed toward New Town.

"Yeah, he's like a lot of the guys up here," said the Tribal Officer. "Blue collar. High school education. They don't always make the wisest decisions."

Zeke nodded. "Well, I'm in favor of tracing the girl's movements the night she was killed. There seem to be some gaps in that time line."

"OK," said Doekiller. "Where do we start?"

"First, let's see if we can find the guy Jenny Lakota was talking with that night. The big guy in the Salty Dog."

"OK with me," said Doekiller. "The lieutenant said I should stay with you this afternoon."

"OK," said Zeke. "Then let's go talk with the bartender."

* * *

It was mid-afternoon when Zeke and Doekiller stepped through the wooden door into the Salty Dog bar. There was a small crowd of men sitting at a round table in the restaurant area, laughing and talking over each other. Three more men sat silently on bar stools, elbows on the pitted, wooden bar. The same bartender, Sandy, the thin brunette woman with the long face, was serving a draught beer to one of the men.

Zeke and Doekiller found an empty four-top table, off by themselves.

In a moment Sandy nodded to Doekiller and a minute later she walked over to their table.

"What can I get you boys?" she asked.

Doekiller said, "We've got a few more questions, Sandy. About the guy Jenny was talking to the night she was killed."

Sandy looked at Zeke, then back at Doekiller, and said, "Like I said, he wasn't a regular. Looked to me like an oil guy or a truck driver."

"Everybody looks like an oil guy to you, Sandy," said Doekiller. He said it lightly.

Sandy snorted. "I'll get you some coffee, then, and we can talk when I come back. Cream?"

The men nodded and Sandy quickly disappeared into the kitchen area.

* * *

"So, since the oil, everything's changed," said Sandy.

Doekiller nodded. Sandy stood facing Zeke, addressing him.

Zeke said nothing.

"This place used to be a local hangout, with guys from the Res and railroad guys and casino workers. It was a 'shot and a beer' kind of place. Guys'd come in for lunch and then come back for another shot or two after quitting time. You know, on their way home."

Zeke said, “You have a more diverse crowd, now.”

“Yeah, you could say that. After they started drilling more, around 2006 or 2007, things started changing. And quickly.” Sandy looked around, then sat in one of the empty chairs. “I’ve worked here since then.”

“The guy you saw with Jenny that night,” said Zeke. “Was he Native American?”

Sandy nodded. “He comes in every once in a while, spends a few hours drinking beer. Miller Lite,” she added. “I guess that’s why I thought he was a truck driver or something. He wasn’t a regular.”

Zeke nodded. “We’d like to talk with the truck driver. Any way to find him?”

Sandy shook her head slowly, thinking.

“What about a credit card slip? Did he use a card?”

“No, he pays cash. Three bucks a beer, plus a half dollar tip for each one.”

“Who was he sitting with?” Zeke asked.

“Well, he was talking with Henry Wellers before Jenny came over. Nickname’s Chip. Chip Wellers. They talked for a while.”

“Is Wellers a regular?” Zeke asked.

“Yes,” said Sandy. “Well, sort of. He comes in here after work most days. I think he does something with heavy equipment.”

Zeke nodded.

“It sounded like they were planning something, talking about money and business and such. But they got quiet whenever anyone would get close to them.”

"What time did the truck driver get here that evening?" asked Zeke, indicating the bar.

"Not until about eight thirty, I think. I remember Sam and Jenny started fighting before he arrived. He came in and got seated by Chip, and they talked for quite a while. But later on, she and Sam had another fight. Well, it was the same fight, just continued. After that, she went straight to the guy and started talking loud about him buying her a drink."

"Did he?" asked Zeke.

"Sure. Bought her a couple. All the while I was watching Sam Bearcat, who was just fuming."

"What time was that?" asked Zeke.

"Oh, I think it was a little after ten," said Sandy.

She looked at Zeke. "Do you need to write this down?"

"No," said Zeke. "Photographic memory."

Sandy nodded as if that were a normal occurrence.

"Did they leave together?" asked Zeke.

"Well, I'm not sure. See, Sam got madder and madder, and Jenny kept taunting him. And eventually he called out the truck driver guy."

"Called him out?" asked Doekiller.

"Yeah, he stumbled over to the bar and started threatening the guy. Said he was going to gut him with one of the axes that they throw, that sort of thing. They were yelling and screaming at each other. You know, 'I'll kill you!' threats."

"So you called the cops," said Zeke.

"Sure. I've been doing this a long time. Guys start with that stuff and I've got the Tribal Officers on speed dial."

Zeke looked at Doekiller, who said, "Not really. She called 911."

"And you guys arrived at, what, 10:37 PM?"

"Yep. Jenny was gone, and Sam was asleep. He ran out of gas after she left. There weren't many people here by the time we got here."

"Jenny left with the guy when you called the cops?" asked Zeke.

"No, she left first. Then the guy left," said Sandy. "They both left pretty quickly, but not together, and Sam was having trouble walking. After they'd gone, he sat down at a table and fell asleep."

"Let's circle back. Where can we find Chip Wellers?" asked Zeke.

"Well, he's not here yet, so he must be working. Shift change is at four o'clock, and then this place starts to fill up."

* * *

Sandy left to help a customer, and Zeke and Doekiller drank their coffee in silence.

"You want to hang around for this Wellers guy?"

"Yep," said Zeke. "It's 3:45 now. If shift change is at 4:00, he should be here by, what, 4:15?"

"Probably."

"Let's get some more coffee."

Doekiller waved at Sandy and pointed to his cup. She nodded and a few moments later she appeared with a fresh pot of coffee.

"Thanks so much, Sandy," said Zeke. "We're thinking that Chip Wellers should be here before 4:30…?"

Sandy nodded. "That's about right, if he comes in tonight." She turned back and walked to the bar and set the coffee pot down.

* * *

At 4:23, the front door to the Salty Dog opened and four men walked in. They all could have been equipment operators or mechanics. They wore overalls and work boots and crowded around the wooden bar.

Zeke saw Sandy talking to them, and one of the men looked over at Zeke and Doekiller and said something to her. She handed him a bottle of beer and he took a swig, then meandered over toward their table.

"Heard you want to talk with me," said the man.

"We do if you're Chip Wellers," said Zeke. "Have a seat."

Wellers narrowed his eyes, then he set the bottle on the table and pulled out a chair and sat. "You're cops. This is about that girl, isn't it? Jenny something."

"Jenny Lakota," said Zeke.

"Right. Yeah, I was in here the night before they found her body. But I didn't talk with her. Didn't even know her."

Zeke said, "You're not from around here."

"No. I moved here from Alaska a couple of years ago. Homer. Going back soon, too."

"Why's that?" asked Zeke.

"Best place I ever lived. There's an attitude of independence up there. Everyone's got it. It's empowering." He sipped his beer again.

"You came down here for the work?" Zeke asked.

"Yeah. Heard they were paying crazy salaries for mechanics. Guys to keep the heavy equipment running. So, yeah, I came down here for the work."

"Chip, can we ask you about the night before Jenny Lakota died?" asked Zeke.

Chip nodded slowly.

"I understand that you were talking with a guy in here for part of that evening," Zeke continued.

"Yeah, a big guy. An Indian. He's a truck driver. We were drinking and somehow we got onto us starting our own business. Like he would drive and recruit drivers, and I could keep the trucks in running condition. Short haul trucking. There's a need for that here right now. A shortage," said Wellers.

"There's a shortage of truck drivers nationally, isn't there?" asked Zeke.

"There is."

"Do you remember the truck driver's name?" asked Zeke. "Do you know him?"

"No, I've seen him in here a few times. Said his name was, uh, Will. Yeah, Will."

"Last name?"

"No idea."

"What happened when Jenny Lakota asked Will for a drink?" asked Zeke.

"Bad news," said Wellers. "She was with another guy, her

boyfriend, I think. They're always in here together. He was standing right over there, throwing axes, when she asked Will for the drink."

"Had she been drinking before that?" asked Zeke.

"Sure. Drinking and arguing. I thought she was trying to make her boyfriend mad."

"How do you know it was her boyfriend, not her husband?" Zeke asked.

"Well, when she came over and started flirting with Will, I looked to see if she was wearing any rings. You know, fourth finger, left hand. She wasn't."

"She was flirting?" asked Zeke.

"Sure, you know, rubbing his back and getting real close to him. I told him he may want to be careful," said Wellers.

"Do you know where he lives? Or where he works?" asked Zeke.

"Not where he lives. He said he stays in a motel when he's here in New Town. Company pays for it. But he works for Dean Stiller over at Stiller Trucking. They're pretty big, got operations all over this part of the state."

"Thanks for that," said Zeke. "We'll talk with Dean Stiller." Then, "Did he leave with the girl?"

"No, after that. He was working on his third or fourth beer when she came over. Had a couple of shots, too."

"How long after she left did Will leave?" asked Zeke.

"Not long. And he seemed distracted after that girl started flirting. Didn't say anything more about going into business. When he saw her leave he finished his beer and then took off."

CHAPTER 9

"I'm glad you were able to join me, Tillman," said Zeke.

"How could I resist?" asked Cord. "After what you found out at the bar, I figure I'd better come along, keep you outta trouble."

Zeke had called Tillman Cord and shared his conversation with Chip Wellers. It had piqued the FBI agent's interest.

"Besides, this is my day off," said Cord. "I'm on my own dime here."

Tillman turned onto a gravel driveway off the highway and slotted his car into a parking space.

The Stiller Trucking building was a red block structure that looked as if it had been built for some farm use, or maybe as a feed store. It was isolated in a flat field, surrounded with tanker trucks and dirt moving equipment.

Zeke and Cord crowded into a small lobby through the glass front door.

"Help you?" asked a gray-haired woman who looked like somebody's grandmother. She was sitting at a small desk. Her eyes twinkled.

"We're looking for Dean Stiller," said Zeke.

The woman looked confused.

"We're the FBI," said Cord. "Need to talk with him about one of his drivers."

"Oh, well sure, just a moment," she said.

She stood and walked through a door, and Zeke could hear voices in the next room. A moment later, she returned and said, "Go on back. He's in his office."

The office was a square, paneled room with an oversized desk, a large deer head mounted on an interior wall, and a credenza covered with photos of hunters in camouflage, holding their rifles and standing over dead animals. There was also a Rotary Club plaque hanging on his wall near the deer head.

Dean Stiller stood up and stepped around his desk. He shook hands with Cord and then with Zeke, saying, "Well, I'm not sure what the FBI wants with me, but I'm glad to help. Other than that Indian girl getting killed, we don't have much trouble around here."

Stiller was about sixty, a round man who wore his thinning hair in a combover. *He's big on personality,* thought Zeke.

"No, sir," said Cord. "Actually, we're here about the girl."

"Thought you might be. Sit, please," said Stiller, pointing at two chairs.

"The girl, Jenny Lakota," started Zeke, "was last seen with a driver named Will. We heard he works for you."

Stiller thought for a moment, then said, "Well sure. Will Carter. He's been on our payroll for about four years, I think. Mostly drives the circuit between here and Bismarck. He lives there. Sometimes he makes the run over to Minneapolis, too."

Cord nodded. "Have you heard from him lately?" he asked.

"Sure," said Stiller. "He's kind of independent. He checks in when he wants, mostly with Molly, the receptionist out there." He pointed toward the office door. "He's somewhere between here and Bismarck right now."

"How many rigs do you run?" asked Cord.

"We have sixty-one trucks. And it's a challenge to keep them all moving, let me tell you."

"When will Will be back in New Town?" Zeke asked.

Stiller frowned and stood up. "Just a second." He walked to the door, opened it, stuck his head out and asked Molly something unintelligible. He was back in half a minute.

"He'll be back here again tomorrow around noon."

"Is he staying in Bismarck overnight?" asked Zeke.

"Yep. He gets an overnight at home whenever we can arrange it. He's got an attitude problem, but he's a good worker. Don't want to lose him."

"Attitude problem?" asked Zeke.

"Yeah. He doesn't 'play well with others,' if you know what I mean. He's a big guy, and he grew up pushing people around. A bit of a bully. He's what you'd call 'surly'."

"So truck driving is a good fit for Will," said Cord.

"It sort of is," said Stiller, nodding.

Cord said, "Can we get his home address and his phone number, please?"

Stiller pulled a pad over and copied some information from his computer. He tore off the sheet and handed it to the FBI agent.

"We'll drive down and visit with Will Carter today," said Zeke.

Cord nodded. "It's a two and a half hour drive. We can catch up with him late this afternoon."

Stiller said, "This might help." He turned his computer screen and showed them a DMV picture of Carter. The photo was the headshot of a man with long black hair, large features and a ruddy, reddish complexion.

Cord dialed his phone, trying to catch Carter driving.

"Not answering," said Cord after a half minute. "It went to voice mail. We'll just meet him at his house."

"Before we go, we need to talk with Sam Bearcat," said Zeke.

* * *

"That's right," said Lieutenant Mankato. "We've got Sam Bearcat in detention here." Zeke and Cord were back in the Tribal Court building in New Town, working through the bureaucracy necessary to interview an accused killer.

"It's probably the safest place for him, anyway," said the Lieutenant in his deep, slow-paced voice.

"What do you mean?" asked Cord.

"Look, Agent Cord, I know Sam Bearcat just looks like a killer to you. But I grew up with him. I went to school with him. I knew him before he became a drunk. And his family lived on the same street as my folks."

"But you arrested him?" asked Cord.

"Had to. We got a warrant on Sam, and if we didn't arrest

him, someone else would have. With all this publicity, it could have been some of your boys."

Zeke nodded. "He's safer here?"

Mankato nodded.

"Who issued the warrant?" asked Zeke.

"There's lots of publicity about this," said the Lieutenant. "My boss was anticipating a Federal warrant, so he asked the Tribal Court to issue a, what would you say, a preemptive warrant."

Zeke nodded. "Can we see him?"

"Yeah, we got that request from the FBI office. We've got it set up in one of the interview rooms. I'll need Bruce Doekiller to sit in on it with you."

"That's fine," said Cord.

"He's been interviewed already," said Zeke. "How many times?"

"We've talked to him four times. He admits to being drunk and angry at Jenny, but he denies being involved with her death. Or that mess at the trailer park."

"Can we take a shot at him?" asked Cord.

"Yep, he's waiting," said the Lieutenant. "Come with me."

* * *

"Why should I talk to you?" asked Sam Bearcat. He was sitting at a wooden table in a gray prison jumpsuit with wide red stripes down the arms and legs. Handcuff chains had worn grooves in the edge of the wooden tabletop where destructive prisoners had sawed at it with their restraints.

"Sam, look, we may be your best chance. We're the only ones investigating. Most everyone else, including the Tribal Court and the FBI, is sure you did it," said Zeke.

"What're you, the good cop?" sneered Bearcat.

"Sure," said Zeke. "So we need you to walk us through what happened that night."

Bearcat was sullen, sitting with his back to the concrete block wall while Zeke, Cord and Doekiller sat across the table from him.

"Frankly, Sam, they looked at your record and decided that you're guilty. The FBI was anxious to wrap this one up. Your history made it easy for us," said Cord.

"And you're the bad cop," said Sam.

"I'm the bad FBI agent. I was anxious to wrap it up, too."

Sam scowled. "Sure, just lock up the Indian," he said.

"So, what happened, Sam? What do you remember?" asked Zeke.

"We were drinking and throwing axes. Jenny and I had a fight and I'd left her at home. Then she shows up at the bar. She was trying to make me mad," said Sam.

"What was the fight about?" asked Zeke.

Sam smiled a crooked smile. "The usual, you know? Sex and money."

"Do you have a job?" asked Zeke.

"I did, but I got laid off," said Sam.

"For…?" asked Cord.

"I was working security for one of the oil fields. But I failed the drug test," said Sam. He looked away as he said it.

"How about Jenny, was she working?" asked Zeke.

"Yeah, she was working at the Family Dollar."

"How long ago did you fail the drug test, Sam?" asked Zeke.

Sam looked away again. "Uh, it's been a while."

"Did you stop by the Salty Dog most nights?

"Yeah, I guess. I'd go by for a beer and to win some money throwing the axes."

"You did pretty well with that?" asked Zeke.

"Yeah, I usually came out ahead."

Zeke nodded. "Did you and Jenny live together?" he asked.

"We rented a place over on 4th Street. It's OK, not too bad."

"Been there long?" asked Zeke, keeping a rhythm.

"Yeah, a couple of months."

"So who would have wanted Jenny dead?" Zeke asked, avoiding accusation.

"Not me, that's for sure," said Sam Bearcat.

"They say you were pretty mad at her. Maybe it was an accident," said Zeke.

"Man, they said she was skinned. That's sick."

"Are you a hunter, Sam?" asked Cord.

"Yeah, sure, most everybody's a hunter up here. Bighorn sheep, elk, pronghorn…"

"Pronghorn?" asked Cord.

"Yeah. You're not from around here, are you?" asked Sam.

"It's sort of a cross between a deer and an antelope," said Doekiller. "About a hundred pounds and they run like the wind."

"How fast?" asked Cord.

"Up to fifty-five miles an hour," said Zeke. "Only faster mammal is a cheetah."

Doekiller nodded an affirmation, and Cord whistled between his teeth.

"Are they good for eating?" asked Cord.

"Pretty good. Some people like them better than venison."

"Thing about pronghorn," said Zeke, "is you need to skin them fast because their hair's hollow, and it holds the heat."

"That's right," said Bearcat, looking at Zeke oddly.

"So, you and Jenny fought about sex and money," said Zeke. "Sam, was alcohol involved when you fought? Or drugs?"

"No, I try not to get high if I know I'll be throwing axes," said Bearcat. "At least until I get up to the Salty Dog."

"Witnesses say you were pretty wasted that night, Sam," Zeke continued.

"Yeah, I was pretty pissed at Jenny. When I got to the bar, I had a couple shots to calm down."

"A couple?" asked Cord. "Bartender said four."

"Yeah, coulda been. I guess they were double shots."

"So you were drinking and throwing axes," Zeke paused and looked at Sam, "and Jenny showed up at the Salty Dog a little bit later. She was still mad at you?"

"That's an understatement. When I left the apartment, she was threatening to move out..."

"What did she do when she got to the bar?" asked Zeke.

"I don't know, I didn't pay much attention at first. But after a while, she got louder, started flirting with guys, talking about stupid crap."

"Like…?" asked Zeke.

"Like how she wanted to be with a real man. Like she was more woman than most men could handle. She was toasted, too."

"She was flirting?" asked Zeke.

"Started out she was just loud talking and putting me down. Like I said, I was throwing axes so I wasn't really paying attention. I think she started flirting when she saw I wasn't taking the bait," said Bearcat. "Probably made her mad."

"Did you see her with anybody?" asked Zeke.

"Yeah, she was talking to some Indian guy. He was a pretty big guy. At a table over by the bar. It looked like he was buying her drinks," said Bearcat.

"What did you do?" asked Cord.

"I finished the match, and then I confronted him. Told him to stay away from Jenny," said Bearcat.

"Some patrons said it was a screaming match," said Cord.

Sam Bearcat looked at him. "Yeah, I guess it was," he said.

"Then what?" asked Zeke.

"The bartender dialed the police. She yelled, 'I'm calling the police, now.' And then Jenny left. So, I sat down at a table. I guess I fell asleep," said Bearcat.

"Jenny left alone?" asked Zeke.

"I don't know. No, wait, I do remember. I assumed that she left because she didn't want to deal with the cops. Tossed her drink down real quick and walked out, alone," said Bearcat.

* * *

When she sat like this and listened to the storm, she felt the ebb and flow of the universe with every breath. The energy was palpable. This was the closest she had been to it in a long while, and the raw power of its presence invigorated her.

The woman sat cross-legged on the floor of a small room. She felt old. The carpeting was filthy and threadbare from years of use. It looked like it had never seen a vacuum cleaner. Her eyes were closed. She could hear the rain pelting hard outside.

The walls in the room were full of holes the size of a fist, a few from the fists of unremembered men, evidently angry to the point of violence. Others were from her careful application of a Sawzall blade to the drywall. These latter holes were more uniform and square. She called them "hidey-holes".

The blanket she'd wrapped around her shoulders was from the Apache, a man who had lived with her here for the better part of a year, before moving on suddenly. It was red and blue and cream and white with squared off patterns that repeated across the length of it. She'd cut holes in the blanket for her arms with the Sawzall, and now she wore it like a poncho.

But the energy was pure. It was from the spirits of her ancestors who had lived in this same place and hunted these same lands. Now, she was one of the only ones left, one of the few hunters.

Thunder cracked outside and the small house shook from the impact of the sound. The rain accelerated suddenly, drowning out other noises. It smelled damp.

She thought of the small creatures in the forest. The squirrels and the birds and the chipmunks. They must be soaked by now, hiding in a nest or under a rock to stay dry.

In front of the woman, on the floor, was a skinner's knife. It was her only knife. It had a short, wide blade and a strong edge. There were two metal rivets binding the wooden handle to the blade. They looked back at the woman like dead eyes. A short lanyard hung from a hole in the handle. This was more of a tool than a weapon. She closed her eyes for a moment, then opened them again and picked it up. The silver blade and the wooden handle looked back at her silently, judgmentally, she thought. She whispered, "You don't have to understand. You just do your job."

She set the tool down and closed her eyes again. Felt the energy.

The rain continued to pour down, but the wind had stopped. In her mind, the woman visualized the powerful drumming of the heavy raindrops on the ground, the kinetic energy dissipating as each drop plummeted the fertile topsoil, then bounced and fell again finally to be absorbed in the dirt. This was a part of the energy she felt. It was her energy.

The hidey-holes were dark places in an already dark room. Some were just openings, while others were cut just above the wood framing and had a support below to keep things from falling inside the wall. Those were where she hid her things.

The rain beat down, relentlessly. The woman got up and picked up the knife. She looked at it with some disdain, then walked to the wall and set it back in its place in the hidey-hole.

* * *

"Gramm, are you alright?" asked the girl.

The woman looked at her with a vacant expression, and then her eyes seemed to focus on the girl. She nodded.

"Yes, dear," she said.

The girl stood very still, uncertain. The small room with the barren carpet and holes in the walls was dark with the dusk of the evening and cold with the brisk wind. The storm had passed through. The woman pulled the blanket tighter around her.

The animals must be shivering, the woman thought. Then she said, "Are you hungry, dear?"

The girl, fourteen and still pudgy with baby fat, nodded.

"I'll get you something. Would you like macaroni and cheese?"

The girl thought for a minute and said, "No, do we have any soup left?"

The woman nodded and said, "Come on, I'll get you some."

In the kitchen, the woman took a container from the refrigerator and set it on the counter. The wahonpi soup inside gave off the strong scent of bison meat, prairie turnips and wild potatoes, and the woman felt the edge of hunger approaching her. She spooned some soup into two bowls and put them in the portable microwave by the stove to warm up.

She turned back to the girl. "What have you been doing today, Mika?"

"I've been drawing," said the girl. "It's too cold and windy to play outside, Gramm."

"What are you drawing?" asked the woman.

The bell on the microwave dinged and the woman removed the hot soups. She set one bowl in front of the girl and the other in front of herself.

The girl picked up her spoon and started eating.

"Did you say your meditation today?" asked the woman.

The girl spooned some soup into her mouth, swallowed and said, "Not yet."

"Well, don't forget," said the woman. "'Whatever you do in life, do the very best you can with both your heart and mind…'"

"I know how it goes, Gramm. I'll say it after we eat."

"Everyday. You must repeat it every day, child. It is your heritage."

The girl didn't respond. When they had finished their soup, the woman went back into the small living room and sat in her place on the floor, legs crossed. She thought about the tribe and the larger nation. She thought about white men getting rich from their oil, and how years ago her father had sold the mineral rights on their land in return for a pittance. She thought about the shame of the Sioux, once a proud people, now reduced to second class citizenship and relegated to unwanted lands.

They were a laughingstock, and many were drunks that gambled away their paychecks every weekend. They were predictable and impotent. And they had lost their way.

CHAPTER 10

Tillman Cord pulled his Crown Vic up in front of a small brick bungalow with a long, triple-wide driveway. There was a Peterbilt eighteen-wheeler in the driveway attached to a trailer that read, "Stiller Transport." A large garage dominated the front of the house with three overhead doors. The sod looked like it had been laid recently.

Zeke, in the passenger seat, said, "Looks like the right place."

Both men exited the car and walked up the driveway to the door. The house was one of a few completed in a partially filled subdivision not far from the Bismarck airport. It looked new.

Zeke rang the doorbell and a moment later a tall man with heavy jowls opened the door. He was dark complected, ruddy like his picture, and his hair was jet black.

Cord said, "Will Carter? FBI. We tried to call earlier."

The man nodded and said, "I saw your call. Just didn't want to answer it. What do you want?"

"It's about the dead girl up in New Town," said Cord, staring at the man. "You were one of the last people to see her alive."

"Oh, that. I guess you may as well come in and talk about it." He pushed the screen door open for them, unconcerned. He was chewing something. "Just eating dinner." He wore a red windbreaker with 'Stiller Trucking' stenciled on the front.

He led them through a living room to a separate dining room with mismatched maple wood furniture. On the table was a plate half-filled with meatloaf and potatoes, and a tall glass of milk. Will Carter sat in the chair in front of the plate. Then he took another bite of his meatloaf.

"Mr. Carter, like I said, we're here about Jenny Lakota's murder," Cord started. "I'm with the FBI and we need to ask you a few questions."

Carter looked at him, shook his head and said, coolly, indifferently, "That was a horrible thing." His flippant attitude belied his words.

"It was," said Cord.

"I guess someone at the bar told you about me, right?" he asked.

"Yes, sir. They said the girl was flirting with you, and that you'd gotten into it with her boyfriend," said Cord.

"Now wait a minute," said Carter. "Yeah, I was there, and yeah, I bought the girl a drink, but if you think I'd hurt her… No way. She was just, well, friendly, and she asked for a drink, so I said, 'Sure'."

"Had you seen her before? Did you know her?" asked Zeke.

"Well, sure, I'd seen her there in the bar before. But this time she was tipsy, and like I said, friendly. So I played along.

She was sort of cute, ya know."

"What about the boyfriend?" asked Zeke. "Had you seen him before?"

"Maybe a couple times," said Carter. "Mostly he threw the axes. Sometimes he looked like he was high on something. Anymore I just mind my own business, drink my beer."

"Did you follow the girl to the trailer park? Have sex with her there?" asked Cord.

"Trailer park? No, nothing like that, man. I mean I finished my beer and left after she did. I heard the bartender call the cops, and it didn't sound like someplace I wanted to stay, so I drank up and left."

"Did you see her outside?" asked Zeke.

"No. I admit, I looked around for her when I went out, but I didn't see her. So I went back to the motel room."

"Can anyone verify that?" asked Cord.

"What, that I went back and watched TV alone? I doubt it," said Carter. "I fell asleep around 11:30, I think."

"Are you a hunter, Mr. Carter?" asked Zeke.

"Sure. I'm an Indian. I grew up hunting. Just about everyone up here is a hunter."

"What do you hunt, mostly?"

"Big Horn Sheep. Sometimes pronghorn. But those suckers are quick," said Carter.

"Have you skinned animals?" asked Cord, pushing a bit with a pointed question.

"Once or twice," said Carter. "It's not something I favor. I usually take the animal to be processed and let them do it all."

"But you do know how to skin, then," said Cord.

Carter swallowed his food and leveled his eyes at Cord and said, suddenly serious, "I don't like your questions. I didn't kill that girl."

"Folks in the bar said that you and her boyfriend had a confrontation," said Cord. "A fight."

"Wasn't a fight, really," said Carter, back to his meatloaf. "Just a lot of jawing and some threats. He was gesturing around with an axe, but his friends got hold of him before he did anything crazy. He coulda gotten hurt."

"And you stayed there, in the bar?" asked Zeke.

"Yeah, I'm not really one to run from a fight," said Carter. "I just stayed in my chair by the bar. Let the two of them talk it out."

"The man and the girl who was killed, Jenny Lakota?" asked Zeke.

"Yeah, they were both pretty drunk. Soon as she left, he sat down at a table, all unsteady. And then he put his head down and fell asleep."

"He fell asleep?" asked Cord.

"Yeah. Here, I took a picture." Carter started scrolling through his smartphone. "In case he made any trouble for me. You know, got his friends together and caught me outside or something."

He showed them a picture of Sam Bearcat, head on his arms, sprawled across the top of a table. The interior of the Salty Dog was obvious in the background.

"We're gonna need a DNA sample," said Cord. "To eliminate you from the list of suspects."

Carter set his fork down and looked at Cord. "Uh-uh. No way," he said.

Cord shrugged. "Then you stay on the list. We'll get a subpoena and compel the test. And we won't be quite so polite."

"I know what you're doing," said Carter, suddenly aggressive. "You're trying to set me up. No way."

Cord looked at him and remained quiet.

"You're trying to frame me for killing the girl. No way. Get outta my house. Git out!"

"Actually," said Cord, "we have a Federal warrant to bring you in. You're a person of interest in the death of..."

Zeke sensed it before the man moved. His rage was palpable, suddenly emitting from Carter with a force that made Tillman Cord flinch. The sudden hot anger in Carter's presence had a physical impact. Carter reached under the table and lifted it, sending it over on its side and spilling everything on it. Carter reached to the small of his back.

Zeke stepped into the violence, closer to the big man. He said, "You'll want to keep your hands where I can see them."

Cord stepped in also, evidently noticing the man's movement.

"Like hell," said Carter. His right hand came clear of his windbreaker. He was brandishing a Ruger American Pistol, a .45 caliber semi-automatic. It looked small in his large hand. He waved the gun at Cord, who was already twisting away from the big man.

Zeke wrapped his left hand around the barrel of the Colt and twisted the gun upward. Then he pulled the gun toward himself and, with both hands on the barrel, he wrenched it farther, up and back, pointing it upside down toward Carter's head.

Will Carter, his index finger caught in the trigger guard, screamed in pain and tried to push Zeke away with his left hand. But he had no leverage. Zeke stepped in and stayed close to the large man, keeping Carter's gun and right arm between them so that Carter couldn't reach him.

There was a loud, sickening crack as Carter's forefinger dislocated. He released the gun and cradled his right hand in his left, swearing to himself in pain.

"Bet that hurts," said Zeke.

* * *

"Alright, look," said Carter, now sitting at the uprighted table, his hand swelling and misshapen. He was wearing a pair of Cord's handcuffs. "I may have gone with the girl after I left the bar. Ran into her. She was, like, waiting for me outside. DNA's gonna tell you that."

Zeke nodded encouragingly.

Carter said, "But I didn't kill her. Why would I? Just had some fun, consenting adults and all."

"Why was she waiting for you?" asked Cord. "Does she like ugly?"

Carter flushed red. Then he said, "Apparently she likes 'big'."

"Really?" asked Cord.

Zeke said, "You go, what, two-eighty? Six seven?"

"About," said Carter, still staring at Cord.

"And she was tipsy," Zeke continued.

"It was nothing but a fun time. No harm in that."

"You accompanied her to the trailer?" asked Zeke, confirming.

"Yeah, I did. She invited me. I hadn't been there before."

"To Lakeside Trailer Park?"

"Yeah."

"And you went inside?"

"Yeah. There were people on the couch, so she took me back in the bedroom," said Carter. "We weren't there that long, ya know."

"Who was on the couch?" asked Cord. He was holding a pen and a small notebook.

"I don't know them. A couple of girls and a man. I'd seen one of the girls at the bar. And the man, I think."

"Names?"

"Naw. I don't know."

While Cord was interviewing Carter, Zeke walked to the kitchen, found a zip lock bag and filled it with ice. He gave it to the big man who immediately pressed it against his index finger.

"Then what happened?" asked Cord.

"Then we went in the bedroom."

"What happened in there?" asked Cord.

"Whatdaya think?" said Carter.

"Pretty cramped in the trailer for someone as big as you, Will," said Zeke.

"It was, yeah."

"So..."

"So when we were done, I left. The girl stayed there."

"How'd you get out?" asked Zeke.

"There was a backdoor off the bedroom," he said. "Led to a small porch around back, and steps down."

"What time was that?"

"I left about 11:45," said Carter.

"How much did you pay her?" asked Cord.

"She wouldn't take any money. I tried, but she just giggled and said she was happy to do it."

* * *

After a couple of phone calls and a bit of coordinating, they dropped Carter off at the Bismarck FBI Field Office.

"Can you drop me near the Bismarck airport?" asked Zeke. "I need to catch a red-eye back to D.C. My partner texted that they've moved the timetable up on something I'm working on. Another FBI thing."

"Sure. Anything interesting?" asked Cord.

"Has to do with a chain of pawnshops."

Cord nodded. "You got somewhere to stay tonight?"

"Booked an airport hotel," said Zeke.

"No problem. I'll drop you there and head back to New Town."

"Any chance you can stay on the Jenny Lakota killing? Now that we know Carter was involved with her that evening?" asked Zeke.

"I'm thinking I could do that," said Tillman Cord. "The Bureau doesn't know exactly what to do with me anyway."

* * *

Francis Donovan, FBI Agent in Charge of the Multiple Apprehension Task Force, arrived at The Agency, Clive Greene's consulting firm, with a small entourage of FBI agents. Each was carrying a briefcase, and each had his or her FBI I.D. displayed prominently.

They're proud to be the good guys, thought Zeke.

Clive had arranged for the meeting to be held in their primary conference room with windows looking south over Pennsylvania Avenue. The afternoon weather was mild, and the sun was bright.

The agents followed Francis Donovan into the conference room single file and moved around the table. Zeke thought there was probably some sort of order to the seating arrangement, but it wasn't clear what that was. Donovan sat at the head of the table and arranged her paperwork. Then she opened her laptop and connected to the Internet.

Kimmy followed Clive and Zeke into the room. They took the remaining seats.

"We're here to initiate an operation that will result in the seizure and closure of over one hundred businesses that are money laundering fronts," Donovan began.

A junior agent pushed a stapled list across the table to Clive and Zeke. It contained business names, addresses and some individual's names, probably the business owners or proprietors. Clive looked it over as Donovan continued.

"This sort of operation must be done quickly, quietly and with precise timing. There's no room for error. We'll coordinate local law enforcement to handle the raids and the arrests, and to cordon off the pawnshops after they've been raided."

Clive nodded to her.

"Before the raids, local law enforcement won't know that their efforts are part of a larger sweep. They'll be invited by their FBI offices to participate in a 'joint effort' to take down what they'll be told is a fencing operation, perpetrators receiving stolen goods."

"You'll coordinate this centrally?" asked Clive.

"I will," said Donovan. "We've done this type of thing before, all over the country."

"You're specialists, then?" asked Zeke.

"You could say that." Donovan eyed Zeke obviously and suspiciously.

Maybe it's my long hair, he thought.

"Do we know what happened to Bart Conrad?" asked Zeke. "Was there any new information about his death?"

"Suicide, most likely, but that's not part of our investigation," said Donovan. Then, quickly back on point, "You gentlemen are welcome to join us for this operation. We'd prefer you stay with us in the central coordination area. Washington Agent in Charge, Osborne, asked for you both by name."

Clive nodded.

If he had a hat on, he'd have tipped it, thought Zeke.

"There's still quite a bit of planning and coordination to accomplish. This is Agent Matthews and next to him, Agent Robbins. You'll be working with them," Donovan concluded. "Agent Matthews, please bring these good people up to speed on our operation."

* * *

Chester Knowles was dressed in a green Izod sports shirt, white slacks and a matching cap as he entered the 12th tee-box of the Spring Brook Country Club golf course outside of Morristown, New Jersey. The small man favored the private club for its rigid dress code and archaic rules.

"Alright, Chester, let her fly," said Cal Harmon, president of Union First Bank of New Jersey. Harmon was a tall thin man who deferred to Chester Knowles regularly. Knowles business, Pawn 4 All, was a major account for the bank, which was the lending source for the majority of its franchises.

Knowles was quiet, serious. He teed the ball and took a long look down the fairway. *A short par 4,* he thought. *Three-thirty five from the blue tees. Good opportunity for a birdie.*

Without a practice swing Chester Knowles addressed the ball and in a fluid motion drove it straight and true. It landed in the middle of the fairway to the polite applause of the rest of his foursome.

"Say, Chester," said Cal, after the smaller man had sheathed his club.

"Ride with me," said Knowles, looking around quickly.

They jumped into the golf cart and headed for the center of the fairway.

"What is it, Cal?"

"We were looking over your firm's proposal," Cal said. "I'm sure we can accommodate the new franchises with our Pawn 4 All lending program."

"Good," said Knowles. "We'd rather source our financing from one bank."

"But we noticed that none of the loans we've made—and there are over 120 of them—none of the loans have gone into default. None are even in arrears," said the taller man.

"Is that so?" asked Knowles. Cal pulled the cart around Knowles' ball and stopped it a respectable distance away. Knowles chose a club and walked to the ball.

"Can't understand it, Chester. I've never seen anything like it."

"Are you complaining?" asked Knowles with a wry smile. He addressed the ball and, with his four iron, advanced it onto the left side of the green.

"No, no," said Cal. "Just never seen anything like it. I hope the new franchisees are as creditworthy."

"We do screen our people well, Cal," said Knowles. "Can't just let anyone have a Pawn 4 All franchise. It's my reputation, you know."

"Yes, I see," said Cal.

The men rode in silence to the 12th green. Then Knowles said, "We have an aggressive expansion plan, you know. Can you fund it?"

"How much are we talking about?" asked Cal.

"I'd like to see another thirty to fifty franchises this year," said Knowles. He thought for a minute. "Actually, some of that will come in our acquisition of existing pawnshop chains. I have my eyes on a couple small chains that would do nicely."

"Well, we can handle it," said Cal. "We may have to offer participation, but we'll find a way to make it work."

Chapter 11

"Are you sure you can't visit next weekend?" asked Zeke. "I'm heading to North Dakota tomorrow, but I should be back there by then." He was in his D.C. office, chatting with Tracy on his mobile phone. Tracy was in her condo in Atlanta.

"I'm running low on Personal Days," she said. "For some reason, the Secret Service actually wants me to do some work up here."

"Can't imagine that," said Zeke. "I'd have sworn they hired you for your good looks."

"That's 'great looks' to you, mister. You wouldn't compromise on a thing like that."

"You're right."

Then, more softly, she said, "I'd come if I could."

Zeke smiled. "I was hoping. I could use some more help with our *West Wind* investigation. Hands-on help."

Tracy laughed.

"Last I checked, it's eighty-four and sunny, with a slight breeze," said Zeke. "Supposed to stay like that for a few more days, maybe a week."

"I don't want to hear it," said Tracy. "Have you read the file through?"

"I have. And I've thought about it a lot. It's not easy to relate what I'm reading to what I experienced. It's a whole different perspective."

"I could see that," said Tracy.

"When we were headed in to the marina on the *West Wind*, I remember it as being late afternoon, and sunny and bright. The file report said there was a storm brewing and the water was rough."

"I read that, too," said Tracy.

"You said it earlier. What if the explosion wasn't an accident? What if it was some sort of explosive device?" said Zeke.

"I know. We have to look at the possibility..."

"Yes. I agree," he said.

"What do you remember about the fisherman?" Tracy asked.

"The one we stopped to help? Not a lot. I think he was stuck on a reef or a shoal or something, and we stopped and rescued him, took him to shore. He was a big guy, kind of going to fat, with dirty skin and nails, and rough stubble," said Zeke. "But a lot of fishermen look like that."

"They do?" asked Tracy. "How do they ever get a date?"

"I'm not sure they care much about that," said Zeke.

"Their loss," said Tracy.

"I'll say."

* * *

Zeke hung up the phone and pulled the Monroe County file over in front of him. He'd read through its contents several times and had looked at the pictures again, disturbing as they were. Now he set a legal pad on top of the file and started making notes.

Let's start with the time line, he thought.

A few minutes later, he'd completed the sequence of events that he remembered from that fateful day. Sailing. The stranded fisherman. Boot Key Marina. Running up the dock for a soda. The explosion blowing the windows out of the small store. And then everything had changed.

He remembered the *West Wind*, and how they'd made that marina stop so many times. He thought about the dockhand who had been helping, and his dad, who'd been pumping fuel when it all went up in flames. He remembered how different the motorsailer looked, with its masts lying across the docks and the top half of it burnt out, a flaming, charred mess.

The fisherman. He dialed the phone again.

"I guess you miss me," said Tracy.

"I was just trying to catch you getting naked," said Zeke from 630 miles away in downtown D.C. "How'd I do?"

Tracy chuckled. "Not bad, actually. I was just getting into the shower."

"Hmm. You'll have to tell me more about that," said Zeke. "But I called because there was one thing that was different, out of place."

"With your folks?" asked Tracy, her voice becoming serious.

"Yes. The fisherman. The guy we picked up and took in to the marina. The one with his boat stuck on the reef."

"Sure," said Tracy. "I remember."

"I remember thinking at the time, 'How could he hit a reef? He's gotta be fishing these waters every day.' At least he said he did when we rescued him."

"Was he drinking?" asked Tracy.

"No, I don't think so. He didn't drink on board. And he seemed spry, even agile for a big man. And happy. It didn't seem to bother him that he was stuck. He told us stories all the way back to the marina."

"Did he have anything with him?" asked Tracy.

"I think he did. I think he handed a white canvas bag up to me before he boarded the *West Wind*. It was heavy."

"You lifted it? Are you sure?" she asked.

"Yes, cuz my dad was at the wheel. I remember being surprised by its weight. And he said, 'Careful, boyo. This one's heavy.'"

"Had he caught any fish?"

"I didn't see any. I had the impression that he was heading out when he ran aground. But that can't be right, because it was too late in the day."

"Could he have been waiting for you? A setup of some sort?"

"I don't know," said Zeke. "I need to think about this."

"Did your parents know him? Is that why they stopped?"

"It didn't seem so at the time," said Zeke.

"What does the sheriff's file say about him?" asked Tracy.

"Nothing. It doesn't mention him at all."

* * *

"There're two things I want to do," said Zeke into the headset mic.

"What's that?" asked Cord. His voice sounded tinny and mechanical in Zeke's ears. The FBI agent was concentrating on his pre-flight checklist and looked up briefly, then back at the clipboard in his lap. The engine noise was engulfing them.

"I want to dig into Jenny Lakota's past," Zeke said. "And then I'm going back to Lakeside Trailer Park to talk with the neighbors there."

Cord nodded at the clipboard. "OK."

They were on the tarmac at Sloulin Field in Williston, North Dakota, this time in a twin-engine plane, a Beechcraft 76 Duchess. They were about to depart for the New Town municipal airport.

"This airport's busy," said Zeke.

"Yessir, they've been talking expansion, but nothing's happening yet," said Cord.

"Is this FBI issue?" asked Zeke.

"The plane? No, it's mine. I just got tired of the drive between here and New Town, so I flew it up from Bismarck."

"Well, thanks for picking me up," said Zeke. "We can talk on our way to New Town."

Cord, preoccupied with the readings on the instrument

panel, said nothing.

A few moments later he taxied the plane onto the tarmac and down to one end of the runway. He tested the brakes, revved the engines, and throttled back while he positioned the Duchess on the runway. Nose pointing to the southeast, he accelerated and, at about 160 knots, the plane slowly lifted into the air.

* * *

"Just to recap, we still don't know much about the victim," said Zeke. "She was Native American. She was living with and fighting with this Sam Bearcat guy. She had three kids, who were staying with her mother. And she worked at the Family Dollar store."

"Yessir," said Cord.

Zeke looked at him.

"Where did she live? She and Sam?" asked Cord.

"They had an apartment heading west out of New Town. Just past the river," said Zeke.

"That's the Chief Four Bears Apartments," said Cord.

"Low income?" asked Zeke.

"Yessir, government subsidy. And she was on food stamps. He claimed some sort of disability. Playing all the angles."

"Do we know where her people live?" asked Zeke.

"Her mom stays in New Town. She rents a small house on 6th Avenue. Works at the Cenex."

"Cenex?" asked Zeke.

"It's a convenience store. Next to the West Dakota Inn Motel."

"Have you got a car in New Town?" asked Zeke.

"Yessir, a Crown Vic."

"Let's head over there and talk with her mom. I want to get a feel for who Jenny was."

* * *

The Cenex was a gas station-convenience store located on the north side of Main Street, east on the way out of town. The adjoining parking lot was stacked with heavy equipment, work trucks with iron and steel attachments painted in primary colors. Cord pulled through the gas pump islands and found a parking spot in front of the building.

The front windows were covered in colorful signs advertising the North Dakota Lottery and a variety of different flavors of beer, including a new, orange pilsner.

Zeke opened the door for Cord, then followed him into the small space. An electronic bell signaled, and the woman behind the counter called out, "Hello!"

Cord said, "We're looking for Miriam Lakota."

Wearily and without much emotion, the woman said, "You're a cop."

"FBI," said Cord. He took his I.D. from his pocket and flashed it at her.

She nodded it away. "Yeah, I figured you'd be coming by. It's about Jenny, right?"

Cord nodded and said, "We're sorry for your loss, ma'am." He sounded subdued.

"They arrested Sam for it," said Miriam. "But I don't think he could've done it."

"No?" asked Zeke.

"No, he wouldn't take the time, you know? Whoever did this had a lot of time, and a lot of motivation. Otherwise, why bother?" She shook her head. "It's almost…what do they call it, a symbol?"

"A ritual," said Zeke.

"Yeah, that," said Jenny's mother, pointing at Zeke. "Or a religious thing."

"Have you ever heard of anything like this happening around here?" asked Zeke.

The woman stopped moving for a moment, thinking.

"You know, maybe," she said. "A few years ago a girl went missing. They said she was a wild one. Part Indian and pretty independent. She'd had a boyfriend, but he was killed in a drive-by shooting, I think. I remember something about that…"

"She was murdered?" asked Cord.

"She was found dead. They didn't say that she was skinned, exactly. At worship they said that the girl'd been laid open, clean before the Lord. Something like that."

"What else do you remember about it?" asked Cord.

"It was the talk for a few months. They didn't find the person who did it, best I know. That's been three or four years." Then she turned away from the men and called across the store, "I'm gonna take my break now, Alice."

From behind a tower of twelve-packs stacked floor to ceiling Zeke heard, "OK, honey."

* * *

"I thought you'd want some privacy for your questions," the woman said after they'd stepped out of the shop. "She don't need to know all my business anyway."

Cord nodded as if he agreed.

"The incident you just mentioned, the Indian girl who was killed a few years ago," Zeke started, "tell us what you know about her."

Miriam Lakota shrugged and looked away for a moment, organizing her thoughts.

"It's been a while," she said, shaking her head. "Lemme think." She took out a cigarette and lit it.

"Was she found in New Town?" asked Zeke, prompting.

"Well, yes, she was," said Miriam. "But not by the railroad. She was found up north near the Evans Site."

"The Evans Site?" asked Cord.

"Yeah, up north of town. They said it was some kind of an archeological campsite or something. It was a big deal when they found it."

"Not so much now?" asked Zeke.

"Well, we have a lot more people here now. And the oil is what everyone's interested in, one way or another," she said.

Zeke nodded. "Do you remember anything else about it? About the murder?" asked Zeke.

"Well, we don't get very many murders around here. Years ago, when I was a girl, there was some oil, but not like today. And no real money, so there was nothing worth fighting about. There were maybe half as many people living here as there are now, and most everyone was poor. Farmers, mostly."

"How old was the girl that was killed?" asked Zeke.

"Well, I remember that she was about my daughter's age. Maybe in her mid- to late-twenties."

"Did you know the girl's family?"

"Her older sister used to babysit Jenny sometimes," said Miriam Lakota. "When she was little. Sister's name was Cheryl, Cheryl Black."

"And the girl who died?"

"Casey Black."

"You said they didn't catch the killer?" asked Zeke.

"No, never did. It's a shame…"

"Did she have any other siblings?" asked Cord.

"Casey? She had a younger brother, too. He went away to college a few years after that. Kansas State. He never came back here."

"Is Cheryl still around?"

"She is. I see her at the Jason's grocery every once in a while. I think she got married and moved out to Van Hook."

"Van Hook?" asked Cord.

"By the lake."

"Mrs. Lakota, we need to ask you some, uh, sensitive questions now," said Cord.

"I know. Believe me, honey, I know. But people are just going to do what they want to do. You can't change their minds."

"No, ma'am," said Cord. "We've talked with a lot of people, but some of it will be better coming from you."

"So, ask…"

"Jenny was living with Sam Bearcat," said Cord, starting.

"They say he killed her. She couldn't say no, was her trouble. If a man gave her some attention she'd get all excited and dreamy and start thinking about marriage and such. She moved in with that Bearcat man a few months ago. But he wasn't no good."

"And her children?"

"She has three. I guess I should say she had three," she said.

"How old are they, Mrs. Lakota?" asked Cord. He was taking notes.

"Pretty young. They're all in elementary school."

"Boys? Girls?"

"A boy, seven. Then a girl, six, and another girl, five. All different daddies."

"We heard that they've been staying with you, ma'am," said Cord.

"Just for a while, until Jenny could get situated. It's tough for a single mother to get by."

"Yes, ma'am," said Zeke. "What was she like?"

"She was a good girl, really. But when she was on those drugs, well, you wouldn't recognize her. That girl had a mouth on her!"

"What drugs did she favor, ma'am?" asked Cord.

"I'm not for sure," said Miriam Lakota, "but from what I

heard, it was probably meth. There's a lot of it around here. And oxycodone, I'd guess." She frowned. "I had a bottle of pain pills from when I hurt my back, that was about a year ago or so, and Jenny came over to see the kids one day and when I looked in the bottle later, there was only one pill left. Out of ten, and I hadn't used but one of them."

"You're sure Jenny took them?" asked Cord.

"Oh, yes, sir. I asked her about it, and she started swearing at me, cussing me for accusing her. Oh, the mouth on that girl! And when she wasn't stealing drugs, she was stealing money. You couldn't leave anything sitting out when Jenny was coming by."

"Were you able to get help for her?" asked Zeke.

"She didn't want it. She was too hard core. Got to the point that, if you didn't have pills or money, she didn't have time for you," said Miriam Lakota. "She'd just drop off the kids and go back to her apartment with that Sam Bearcat."

"Sam's been arrested," Cord started.

"Don't I know it?" said Miriam Lakota. "Word travels fast around here. But like I said, I don't think he could have done it. He's just not that patient."

Chapter 12

The stick-built house in the middle of the Lakeside Trailer Park was a one-story affair, yellow with brown trim. It looked as if it had been built in the 1970s, although it was neat and fairly well maintained. There were three cars parked in front of the small garage.

Zeke and Cord approached the front door of the house and Cord knocked loudly. There was no doorbell. They heard, "Just a minute," from inside the house, and a few moments later the front door opened.

"Can I help you?" asked a man, maybe sixty and small, wiry. He was wearing formless blue jeans with a too-long belt pulled tight through the belt loops. The end of the belt was tied in a knot. His shirt was flannel, and his shoes were black, steel-toed work boots. His yellow and green ball cap read "John Deere".

"I'm the FBI," said Tillman Cord. "Are you the owner here?"

"I reckon I am," said the man. "I'm Nathan Douglas." He held out his large calloused hand and shook first Cord's and then Zeke's hand.

"How can I help you two?"

"We're here about the green trailer," said Cord. "Need to know more about who rented it from you."

The small man squinted a bit and then got a gleam in his eye. "This has to do with the dead girl, right? No other reason you'd be poking around up here."

"It does," said Zeke. "Did you know her?"

"The man who rented that trailer from me, he's in jail right now. So I'm not getting any revenue for it. And the Tribal Police told me I can't rent it to someone else being as it's associated with that girl who died."

"What's his name?" asked Cord.

"Charlie Whitefoot," said Douglas.

"What's he in jail for?" asked Cord.

"For drugs, I think."

"Know anything about the girls who hang out there on the weekends?" asked Zeke.

"I work nights, four to midnight, so no, I'm not here at that time. I wasn't aware that anyone was staying over there until the police told me."

* * *

The crime scene tape was tattered by the wind, but it still blocked the door to the green trailer. The white trim on the trailer had yellowed years ago, and tin foil was visible covering some of the windows from the inside. The large padlock still hung from the hasp that some police deputy had affixed to the outside door.

"This place looks even better the second time around," said Cord, shaking his head. "Hope we don't catch anything."

Zeke said, "Let's knock on some doors."

"We can, but we'll likely scare the bejesus out of anyone who's home," Cord said, laughing.

The rest of the trailer park was equally seedy, with third-hand cars parked on the small, concrete pads in front of several trailers. Most of the cars had some damage, one with a broken window partially repaired with duct tape, one with a flat tire, and one truck with a precise vertical crease on the back of its bed gate.

"Well, let's get to scaring," said Zeke.

The closest mobile home with a car parked out front was two down from the green trailer with the yellow tape. It was a single-wide, and as Zeke and Cord approached, they could hear the drone of a television turned up too loud. Cord knocked authoritatively.

There was no response. He waited a moment and knocked again.

The volume on the television dropped suddenly, and they heard a doorknob being unlocked and turning. Behind the door, a young teenage boy looked at them accusingly.

"Yeah?" he said.

"Is your mom home?" asked Cord.

"No," he said.

"Is she working?" Cord said.

"No, she's not working. Who're you?" asked the boy.

He was about five feet tall and ninety pounds, and his hair was matte black, obviously cut using a bowl of some kind as a guide. His right leg was in a cast.

"I'm the FBI," said Cord. "Who's home besides you?"

"You're the FBI?" asked the kid. "The whole FBI?"

Cord looked at Zeke and rolled his eyes.

Zeke said, "I think you may be able to help us solve a crime."

The boy said, "Why would I want to?"

"It's a murder. The murder of that Indian girl down by the railroad tracks."

The boy's eyes shifted slowly from suspicious to excited. "Yeah?"

"What's your name?" asked Zeke.

The boy hesitated a minute, obviously weighing the pros and cons of answering. Then he said, "Tyler. Why do you think I can help?"

"Well, Tyler," Zeke said, "I'll bet you've been laid up with that broken leg for a while, judging by the way the cast looks."

"Yeah, a couple weeks. Doctor says I've gotta wear it for at least another ten days. It itches like crazy sometimes in there."

"So you're bored sometimes, right?" asked Zeke.

"Sure."

"What do you do when you're bored?"

The boy looked at Zeke and then looked away. He rubbed his nose. "Nothing. I just hang out and watch TV."

That's a lie, thought Zeke.

"Tyler," Zeke said.

The boy looked up at him.

"What do you know about that green trailer over there?" He pointed to the trailer with the crime scene tape.

"Nothing. Sometimes people go there at night, but not since the police locked it up."

"What kind of people?" asked Zeke, gently. "Like us?"

"No, not like you. You look like a cop," he said to Cord. "And you look like a surfer."

Zeke nodded. "These people were…?"

"Like oil field guys. Like the guys who work with the derricks. Or do the fracking."

Zeke nodded again.

"They went there to get laid," said Tyler, suddenly worldly.

"How do you know?" asked Cord.

"They were always talking about it. Loud talking, as they went in the trailer."

"Whose trailer is it?" asked Zeke.

"The old guy who owns the park lives in the big house over there." Tyler pointed to the house in the middle of Lakeside Trailer Park, across from his front door. "He rents it out, but the guy he rented to is in jail. So two girls were using it."

"Girls?" asked Zeke.

"Yeah, they're about the same age as my teachers," he said. "They mostly come here on the weekends."

"Right after payday," said Cord.

"Guys stop by all the time. Sometimes other girls stop by, too," said Tyler.

"What do you think is going on there?" asked Zeke.

"I don't know. They like to party, I guess."

"But you've got a clear view of that trailer from your window," said Zeke, turning and eyeballing the space. "Do you ever see anything, uh, odd?"

Tyler looked away. "No, not really."

"But…"

"Well, sometimes they get drunk. And sometimes they fight."

"Out here?" asked Cord, looking at the space between the trailers.

"Sometimes, but mostly it's inside. I can hear them real good, hollering and cussin'," Tyler continued.

"When they come outside, what have you seen?"

"Mostly it's the guys. They yell at each other for a while, and then they usually leave."

* * *

"So, Tyler, what's your last name?"

"Simpson," said the boy.

"So, Tyler Simpson, where's your mom?"

"She said she went shopping."

"But…?"

"I don't know. She could be visiting Bob."

"Bob's her friend?" asked Cord.

"Yeah. He lives over by the casino. She works over there."

"At the casino?"

"Sure. She's a cocktail waitress at Four Bears," said the boy with some pride.

"How about your dad?" asked Cord.

"I don't have one."

"I'm sorry," said Cord, automatically.

"Well I'm not," said the boy. "He wasn't no good anyhow. He was a cop."

Zeke changed it up. "Were you home last Saturday night, Tyler? The night before that girl was killed on the railroad tracks?"

Tyler said, "Sure. The tribal cops asked me about that."

"Did you see anything strange happen that night?"

"Yeah, I told 'em. The two girls were here, like always…"

"You know that because…?" asked Cord.

"Their car was parked out front. It's a green car. And they had the music turned up loud."

"OK. And did you see the girls?" Cord continued.

"Sure. They had to unload the beer and stuff from the trunk. But that was before dark."

"OK. Then?"

"That's all. That's what I told the cops."

"But you don't really like cops, do you, Tyler?" asked Zeke. "You're not one for helping them much."

"So?"

"So this is very serious. This is about a murder. And if you don't tell us everything, you might end up in some serious trouble," said Cord. "Matter of fact, we might just need to take you in right now."

"OK, OK, after it got dark out, I was watching TV and I heard a girl laughing outside. She was with a really, really big guy with black hair. She sounded kinda drunk, you know loud and stuff, and laughing. Saying stuff and teasing the guy, I guess."

"Saying what kind of stuff?" asked Cord.

"You know, like women do sometimes. 'You know you want some of this,' things like that. Like I said, she was drunk and laughing and stuff."

* * *

At the next trailer, Cord knocked again, authoritatively. There was no answer, and no sounds coming from inside.

"Nobody there," said Tyler, looking out the window at them. "He said he was going to the bar."

"He told you?" asked Cord.

"Yeah. He said I should watch his place, make sure nobody tried to steal anything."

"Do you do that often?" asked Zeke.

"Yeah, sometimes," said Tyler. "But I think he feels bad about my leg. He gave me five bucks to keep watch."

"Who's 'he'?" asked Cord.

"His name's Jimmy. He's pretty cool."

Zeke said, "What makes him cool?"

Tyler thought for a minute. "Well, he rides a motorcycle, a Harley," the boy said. "And he's got a cool tattoo on his arm. He let me see it. It's an eagle."

* * *

The next trailer with a vehicle parked on the small slab was an old but neat single-wide with a wooden handicap ramp giving access to the front door. The trailer was a faded blue with white trim and plantings around the small front yard. Zeke and Cord walked up the ramp and rang the doorbell. A small dog started barking enthusiastically.

In a minute, the door cracked open a couple inches and an elderly woman peeked out. The screen door, still latched, kept a ferocious Pomeranian at bay.

"You two aren't Mormon missionaries, are you?" the woman asked. "You're not wearing white shirts and ties, or I wouldn't have opened the door. Didn't see your bikes, either."

"No, ma'am," said Cord in his polite voice. "We're the FBI. May we ask you some questions about that green trailer over there?"

"FBI? Like on *Criminal Minds*, that TV show? I watch that one."

"Good show, yes, ma'am," Cord continued.

Over her shoulder and through the door, Zeke could see a slice of the interior of the trailer. He saw a couch covered with an afghan blanket, low pile brown carpeting on the floor with tufts from the dog's nails, a window over the couch with red and white drapes that matched the colors of the afghan, and wood paneled walls. There were several pillows propped up on the couch.

"We're sorry to bother you, ma'am," said Zeke. "We're investigating the murder of..."

"Of that Indian girl. I thought so," said the woman.

"One of the things we're trying to understand has to do with the green trailer over there," Zeke continued. "Maybe you can help us."

The dog kept barking.

"I'll step out there with you," said the woman. "Hold on."

She closed the door for a moment, then opened it again and stepped out in front of the trailer. Zeke and Cord walked down the ramp, and, gripping her cane, she followed them to a grassy area, about four feet square.

"Be careful where you step there," she said to Cord, pointing at the ground. "Miss Tanya does her business in the yard."

"Yes, ma'am," said Cord, looking down and checking his shoes.

"I'm Mabel Olsen," said the woman. "I've lived here for ten years."

"So I'm sure you know what's going on around here," said Zeke casually.

"Well, sure," said Mabel. "I'm old but that doesn't make me dumb."

"No, ma'am," said Cord, politely.

Zeke said, "What do you know about the green trailer? Who lived there?"

"There were a couple of girls over there," said Mabel. "But they were there mostly at night. Until the cops put that lock on the door."

"Did you know them?" asked Cord.

"Sure, to wave to. But they were working girls, you know? Like hostesses. I was a hostess."

"Like USO Hostesses during World War II?" asked Zeke.

She thought back a moment, then said, "Yes, sort of like that."

"You weren't old enough to be a Hostess during the Great War," Zeke said.

Mabel Olsen flushed pink. "Well, I lied about my age, and they let me," she said. "Anyway, that's old news. You want to know about that trailer."

"Yes, ma'am," said Cord.

"Well, those girls had a lot of friends. Mostly men, but not all of them. And they liked to party. Sometimes their music was too loud. But they always turned it down when I asked."

"Was it always the same friends? The guys who came to visit?" asked Zeke.

"I don't think so. They seemed to have a variety of man friends. They were pretty popular, I guess," Mabel said, and she rolled her eyes.

"Did they have a car?" asked Zeke.

"Sure. They shared an old green thing."

"Do you know what kind of car it was?" asked Cord.

"Better. I've got a picture," said Mabel. "Just a second."

Mable stepped back up the ramp and opened the door to the still barking Pomeranian. She reached inside and a moment later she was back on the front lawn, scrolling through her phone for photos.

"Did you speak with the police?" asked Cord. "After the girl was killed?"

"Yes, I did. They asked me a few questions, but they didn't

say anything about those girls or their car. Here it is." She held out the smart phone and showed the men a picture of the front of a faded green Camry that had seen better days.

Zeke said, "May I see that for a moment, please?"

Mabel handed him the phone, and he pinched and unpinched the screen. Then he gave it back to her.

"Was there anything else about the girls or their friends that you can remember?" asked Zeke.

"Well, like I said, they didn't bother anybody. I think they just liked to have a party. They were always carrying beer and wine in from the car."

"Did you know their names?" asked Zeke.

The dog was still barking in the background and scratching on the inside of the door.

"Not really. One was Cindi, I think. Cindi something. The other one, Cindi called her 'Angel'. Listen, I'd better go before Miss Tanya hurts herself. It'll take the better part of an hour to calm her down…"

CHAPTER 13

"Cindi and Angel," said Cord. "Sound like stage names."

"Possible," said Zeke as they drove away from Lakeside Trailer Park. "Is there a strip club around here?"

"Used to be a famous one in Williston," said Cord. "Called it 'Heartbreakers'. Couple years ago, they turned it into a gay bar, the only one in North Dakota."

"That doesn't sound like it'll help us," said Zeke.

"No, it doesn't," said Cord. He thought for a moment.

"I guess we can check back with the bartender," said Cord. "Sandy might know."

"Maybe," said Zeke. "But there may be a better way."

"OK," said Cord.

"We know the license plate number of the green Camry."

"From the picture?" asked Cord.

Zeke nodded. "Let's see where that leads us."

* * *

The Tribal Police station was quiet, with just a skeleton crew in the precinct that afternoon. Cord asked for Lieutenant Mankato at the front desk, and both men waited on a low bench across from the Sergeant's counter. A minute later, the lieutenant opened a door and joined them in the lobby.

"We've got a license tag number for some possible witnesses to the murder," said Cord, exaggerating slightly. "Can you run it for us?"

"Sure."

"Plus, we wanted to report in, let you know what we're finding."

"Sure," said Mankato, skeptical. "Come on back."

He ushered them into the restricted area and toward his office. Once seated he said in his slow, gravelly voice, "Whatdya have?"

Cord took the lead. "We found the two women, the hookers, who were using the trailer the night Jenny Lakota was killed."

Mankato raised an eyebrow.

"We have a license tag number from their car, and we want to find them."

"For questioning?" asked the Lieutenant.

"We need to know what they know," said Zeke. "They must have seen Jenny Lakota enter the trailer while they were, eh, involved in there."

"OK," said Mankato. "What's the number?" He turned his chair around, facing the computer screen and keyboard behind his desk.

Zeke repeated the license plate number from memory. He noticed Cord jotting it down.

"Just a minute," said the Tribal Officer. "OK, here we go."

He read off the information. "That tag is registered to a Cindi Havant," he said. "It's a 2001 Toyota Camry, green. Says her address is over on 5th Street. That's not the address of Lakeside."

"OK," said Zeke. "Do you know her?"

"I don't, not personally. But I'll check with the patrol guys and let you know. Fifth Street is kind of a rough area." He gave them the address.

"I think we'll head over that way and talk with Cindi Havant," said Cord.

"She's probably sleeping," said Lieutenant Mankato.

* * *

The home was a one-story, duplex affair on a street of similar homes. Some of the houses were in partial disrepair, and most had several cars parked haphazardly in the front yard. Cord drove up to Cindi Havant's address and parked his Crown Vic in the street with two wheels on the front lawn.

"Let's go," he said.

The two men got out of the car and crossed the lawn to the front door. The house seemed quiet.

Cord knocked authoritatively on the door and stood back with his hand on the butt of his holstered gun. They waited thirty seconds and then Cord knocked again, a hard, rapid, aggressive knock. "FBI!" he called out. "Police!"

Twenty seconds later the door opened wide and a bleary-eyed girl in a blue and white kimono looked out. Her hair was in disarray.

Bed head, thought Zeke.

Cord said, "Cindi Havant? We're the FBI."

The girl put her hands in front of her, palms out, stopping them, and asked, "What do you want?"

Zeke noticed the tattoos on her wrists. A rose in blue ink wrapped around one wrist, and an oil derrick was etched on the other.

"Relax," Zeke said. "And…nice pumpjack."

The girl looked at her right wrist as if seeing it for the first time. Then she said, "Yeah, thanks."

"Can we come in?" asked Cord.

"Uh, sure," said Cindi. She held the door open for them and they followed her into the cluttered living room of the small home. She sat on an upholstered chair, picked up a pack of cigarettes from the side table and lit a Marlboro.

Zeke sat on the edge of a matching chair, and Cord remained standing.

"We're here to talk about the Lakeside Trailer Park. And Jenny Lakota. Specifically, number seven Lakeside, up there."

Cindi shook her head as if she were shaking off a bad memory.

"What happened to Jenny was awful. I still can't believe it." She shook her head again.

"Did you see her the night before she was found?" asked Zeke.

"Yeah, she came to the trailer, number seven. She came in

and went back in the bedroom."

"Where were you?" asked Cord.

"I was on the couch with a friend of mine." She looked down briefly and pulled on the short kimono to better cover her crossed leg. Then she looked up at Zeke.

"What time was that?"

"Oh, around eleven, I think. I didn't check."

"What happened when she came in? Did she say anything?"

"No, my friend and I were, uh, involved, so she just walked through the living room and the kitchen with her friend, to get to the bedroom. She closed the door."

"Who were you with?" asked Cord. He was using his hard voice.

"Like I said, my friend, Carl."

Cord looked at her.

"Carl Jensen."

"He's from around here?"

"Yeah, he works for one of the oil companies."

"What were you doing with Carl Jensen?" asked Zeke.

"You know. Partying..."

"Anybody else there?"

She looked away. "We were pretty drunk. But yeah, Angel was there, too."

"Angel?" asked Cord. "Last name?"

"Uh, it's Wilson. Angel Wilson. We went to the same high school five or six years ago. We're not in trouble, are we?"

"Depends. Did you have anything to do with Jenny's death?" said Cord.

"No, of course not..."

"And are you telling us everything you know about that night?" he continued.

"Yeah, I don't know anything about..."

"Who was Jenny with that night?" asked Cord, interrupting the girl.

"That guy. I've only seen him a couple times. He doesn't come in the bar very often..."

"The Salty Dog?" asked Zeke.

"Yeah, I've seen him there once or twice. He keeps to himself, mostly."

"What did he look like?" asked Zeke.

"You think he killed her? Oh, my."

"He was the last person seen with her. We'd like to find him and ask him about it," said Zeke. *And confirm that it was Will Carter,* he thought.

"Don't know much about him. But he was a pretty big guy. He made Jenny look small. And he was an Indian. Definitely an Indian." She looked at Cord and Zeke, then rubbed her eye and lit another cigarette.

* * *

"I've been crashing here since they put the lock on the trailer," said Angel Wilson. "So what?"

Cord looked at Zeke, and then back at the small woman. She had short dark brown hair parted in the middle and wide, chocolate brown eyes. Her jeans were skin tight, and she wore a flannel shirt with no bra. She was barefoot and slightly pudgy in her waist and thighs. She obviously had some Native American blood.

They were standing on the steps outside a small, brown house on the north side of New Town, an address that Cindi Havant had given them. It was raining lightly, and they huddled under a metal awning that covered the small front steps.

"This is your mom's house?" asked Zeke.

The girl looked at him but said nothing.

"We want to know about the night before Jenny Lakota died," said Cord. "What you saw in the trailer."

"I told the police what I saw," said the girl.

"It's a murder investigation," said Cord. "There's no limit on the number of times we can ask you questions."

The girl shook her head dismissively, but said, "OK. So…"

Cord said, "How well did you know Jenny?"

"I seen her around," said Angel. "At the bar sometimes. She hung out with Sam mostly."

"Sam Bearcat," said Cord.

"Yeah. Heard he got arrested for killing her."

"He did. We're looking at it from a different angle," said Cord.

"Shame. I like Sam," she said as if Cord hadn't spoken. "We hooked up once or twice."

"So Jenny probably wasn't very fond of you," said Cord.

"Wasn't me, it was her boyfriend that did it. She needed to put him in check."

Cord looked at Zeke, then back at Angel Wilson.

"How about you walk us through the evening before Jenny died. What happened in the trailer?"

"Yeah, OK. It was kind of a surprise," she said.

"What was?"

"We were partying, drank some shots and smoked some, and Cindi was with Carl. I was with Pete, my friend, but he had to leave," she said.

"What time?" asked Cord.

"What time did he leave? About ten. Just after ten."

"So you were resting?" said Cord.

"Carl talked me into partying with them. With him and Cindi. So I did."

"Did money change hands?" asked Cord.

"What do you think?" said Angel. "Geez." She shook her head.

"Then what?" asked Zeke, keeping her on track.

"Then, well, the front door opened and Jenny walked in. Didn't knock or nothin'. That's the rule, you always knock…"

"Was she alone?" asked Zeke.

"No, she was with this big guy. Really big. He looked Indian, too. You know, black hair and dark skin."

"And you and Cindi were naked on the couch with Carl?" Zeke ventured.

"Well, yeah."

"Was music playing?"

"Yeah, there was some Madonna playing, now that you mention it," the girl said after a moment.

"Could you see him? The Indian guy?" asked Zeke.

"I was turned around the other way on Carl's lap. I wasn't facing the door, so I only saw them for a moment when I looked over my shoulder. But he was big. And he was an Indian, no mistaking that."

"Then what?" asked Cord.

"Like I told the other cops, they went in the bedroom and she closed the door, and that's the last I saw of them."

Chapter 14

In part, she knew it could be blamed on the drugs. That drug, alcohol. The heroin. The opiates. And most of all the meth. So much meth was coming out of this area of the state it had earned the nickname, "Williston White." Brought here by the oil workers, the oil pipeline, the white men.

The woman sat on the floor of her small home, legs crossed, meditating and chanting quietly to herself. She had seen so much in her lifetime.

Her grandson, once a black haired imp with a crooked smile, had grown to become a man. And she had taught him about their history, about the great warriors from whom he had descended.

As a boy, he learned well. He understood the lessons and he understood his grandmother's wisdom, her insights into what she called 'The Nation,' which was actually several nations, now relegated to the barren lands of North Dakota.

"The Nation was driven here because of the Iroquois," she told him. "The Lakota Sioux were forced west by the Iroquois people many years ago. In the late 1600s. From Minnesota and Canada, the Nation ended up in North and South Dakota."

And she'd told her smiling grandson, "Your heritage is fierce. You are the son of many warriors."

"Otaktay" she had named him, a fierce name for a Lakota warrior. It meant, "Kills many." In English he was named Robert.

When he reached the right age, he'd attended Nueta Hidatsa Sahnish College, a college chartered by the Three Affiliated Tribes of Fort Berthold Reservation. He went there for a year and two months, but like many of his friends, he lost interest and quit.

He had been born on Standing Rock reservation, on the south border of North Dakota. When he was small, the family moved to New Town and the Fort Berthold Reservation to be near the Bakken Formation, the oil.

Now, in her trance-like state, his grandmother clearly remembered the many oppressions they had suffered as a people. *No more,* she thought.

Slowly, she stood and went to the wall. She found the hidey-hole and took out the skinner's knife. It was cold. There was little insulation in the walls of the small house, and the metal knife had absorbed the night cold from outside.

She said to the knife, "You are my Bakken Blade. We will call on you again soon."

* * *

It had started with the rumor of the pipeline, a few years ago. It wasn't enough that the white men were taking the oil from their ground, the Sioux' sacred soil. But they were doing it without regard for the ancestors buried there, or the clean water of the Missouri River.

It was all about the money, she thought.

The white men had pushed the Indian aside for centuries, whenever something that they desired was found on tribal land. And now, with oil worth billions, the Indians were once again being pushed aside, discarded. Their voices were being drowned out by the loud sound of the white man's greed.

Years ago, the great Missouri River flowed south and east toward the Mississippi, carrying hunting parties and trappers and pioneers. The Sioux had used the mighty river for fishing and hunting, and as a source of water for their tribe.

Then the whites had dammed the river, covering Sioux villages and burial grounds with a new lake. Ancient tribal settlements were destroyed, as were Indian villages and towns like Old Sanish. New Town was formed at that time, over sixty years ago.

And now, when oil was found on this "worthless land," the white men were once again pushing the Indian out of the way.

She shook her head in disgust. She said to the knife, "This must stop!"

* * *

"We use it for the horses," said Dr. Adams. "It's an anesthetic. I combine it with ketamine when we use it. It's pretty common out here."

"Out here being northwest North Dakota?" asked Zeke.

"Pretty much."

"You're the Medical Examiner," said Zeke. "Have you had many drug-related deaths from Xylazine?"

"Rompun is the brand name. Bayer manufacturers it," said the doctor absently.

Zeke waited.

"But not really, not so many. Deaths, I mean."

"It can be used to cut heroin, right?" Zeke asked, prompting.

"I didn't know that," said Dr. Adams. "We haven't seen that around here. Around here, it's mostly opioids. And meth. Meth is almost a staple."

They were again sitting in the M.E.'s small office, gathered around her desk. Cord was reviewing Jenny Lakota's final autopsy file, which he had open in front of him as they talked.

"Narcotics-related deaths more than doubled in 2016. But even so, there were only 43 in the entire state that year."

"Puerto Rico," said Zeke.

"What?" asked Cord, absently.

"In Puerto Rico, a lot of Xylazine has been stolen to cut heroin. It was stolen from equine vet suppliers," Zeke continued. "Nothing like that here?"

"Nope." Dr. Adams shook her head slowly. Then she flipped her light brown hair back over her shoulder and thought for a moment. "Nope."

"They call it the Zombie drug," said Zeke.

"What?" asked Cord.

"Xylazine. The Zombie drug."

"Anything like the 'date rape drug'?" asked Cord.

"Not so much that. I've read that addicts tend to walk bent over, forward, and slip in and out of consciousness," Zeke added.

"It's a killer on your body, though. Heart. Brain. Kidneys," said Dr. Adams.

"Doc, it says here that Jenny had it in her stomach," said Cord.

"That's right."

"But isn't it a drug taken by injection?"

"It is. She had it both in her stomach and in her blood stream. Here." She took the autopsy file and pointed halfway down a page full of chemical names.

"If she'd injected it, why would she have it in her stomach?" asked Cord.

"Good question," said Zeke.

* * *

"So this is Joyce's," said Zeke. He was sitting across the red, laminate-topped table from Dale Adams in the diner-type restaurant.

"It is. One of Stanley's hot spots."

They looked at their menus. The Nodak Burger caught Zeke's eye.

"Every small town needs a Joyce's," said Zeke. He looked around, noticing the cake displays on the counters. "Bet they have good desserts here."

"Best in three counties. They win ribbons at the State Fair every year," said Dr. Adams. She had an easy, California confidence.

"It doesn't look like you eat much cake," said Zeke.

Dr. Adams ignored the remark. "So Mr. Cord is coming back to join us?" she asked.

"He wanted to check in with the local police while we were up here," said Zeke. "And the staties. I think they were all getting on a conference call..."

The waitress, a thin woman with thin lips and a nametag that read "Gail" took their orders. She brought them two thick ceramic cups and splashed coffee into each.

"Cream and sugar are right there, honey," she said absently, and she walked away.

There were a dozen people in the diner, and it smelled of French fries and grilled onions. Zeke sipped his coffee and found it to be surprisingly good.

"The Xylazine you found in Jenny Lakota's system..." Zeke started.

"Yes, it was the Rompun. The dosage in her blood stream was huge, more than I'd prescribe for a typical horse. Some of it got there from her stomach—she'd obviously taken a pill or a capsule—but most of it was from an injection," said Dr. Adams.

"Where was the injection site?" asked Zeke.

"Good question. It was in the left thigh, actually. On the outside of the leg."

"That's a good spot."

"It is. Quick dispersion into the body."

"She would have gone into zombie mode pretty quickly after that, then," said Zeke.

Dr. Adams nodded. "Very quickly."

* * *

"I checked on that other murder," said Cord when he joined Zeke and Dr. Adams at Joyce's Diner. "The three year old one."

"While you were coordinating with the tribal police?" asked Zeke.

Cord nodded. He took out his small notebook and opened it. "It took place in early 2016. North of New Town, near the Evans Site, like the mother said."

"Miriam. The mother's name is Miriam Lakota," said Zeke.

"Yessir. The victim was Casey Black, and she was twenty-four. Died of knife inflicted wounds. But she wasn't skinned," said Cord.

"The Evans Site is an archeological dig," added Dr. Adams. "It's just north of New Town."

"What kind of wounds?" asked Zeke.

"The coroner's report said knife wounds," said Cord. He looked at Dr. Adams.

"I wasn't here then," she said.

"Good. We're narrowing down your age estimate," said

Zeke. His eyes twinkled.

"From what I could determine, it was a series of slashes and gouges. The report says she went into shock, then died of a loss of blood," Cord said. "So, similarities to the Jenny Lakota killing…"

"…but differences, too," said Zeke.

"Could have been the same killer," said Cord.

"But the differences. Not saying it's not possible, but…" said Cord.

"Or an accomplice. Or two killers," said Zeke. "Even with Jenny drugged, it would be hard for one person to transport her to the railroad tracks. Much easier for two."

Cord nodded and said, "Or one very large man."

Dr. Adams sipped her coffee.

"Motive?" asked Zeke.

"Just speculation," said Cord. "The location, the site where they found Casey Black's body, could have been symbolic. The Evans Site was discovered around 1980." He checked his notes. "They found a number of Avonlea projectile points up there."

Dr. Adams said, "Projectile points?"

"Arrowheads," said Zeke. "The murder could have been symbolic," he repeated.

"Might be," said Cord.

"Or possibly a statement. Or a ritual?" asked Zeke.

"No one could tell. There wasn't anything to confirm it. And no posing of the body or anything else to explain why she was killed. Or why she was killed right there," said Cord.

"Anything else in the report?" asked Zeke.

"No, not really. There wasn't a trail to follow, and the cops really didn't have a suspect. They interviewed Casey Black's family and friends, but nothing came of it. One day she was alive, and the next morning they found her dead."

* * *

"Dr. Adams," said Zeke, "Can we talk about the weapon for a minute?"

Cord looked up from his notebook, then set it down on the table, paying attention.

"Sure, anything we can do to help," said Dr. Adams.

"Jenny Lakota and the weapon they used on her. What was it?" asked Zeke.

"It was some sort of knife or blade…"

"Was it surgical?" he asked.

She shook her head. "I don't think so. I don't think it was that small. A lot of the skin was cut off in small, flat pieces."

"But very sharp…" he continued.

She was nodding, serious. "Yes, almost surgical in that way. The blade was extremely sharp. I could tell by the clean cuts. Whoever it was cut the parameter of a section, then sliced the skin out. Sort of peeled it out. Whatever they used had to be very sharp."

"Sharp like a surgical knife," repeated Cord to himself. "Are we looking for someone with a background in medicine?"

"Hmm. No, not exactly," she said. "Like I said, surgical knives are typically very small and very sharp. The blades are usually disposable, single-use blades. They're built for very precise use, and they allow for a lot of control by the surgeon. This, though, this must have been a wider, flat blade with a very sharp edge. Not really surgical…"

"A hunter's knife?" asked Zeke.

"Might be. Something used to skin an animal after its been killed? Yes, perhaps," she said.

* * *

"I need to talk with a trapper," said Zeke. "Quick." Dr. Adams had left for her M.E.'S office and Zeke and Cord were waiting for the check at Joyce's Diner. Gail, the waitress was nowhere to be seen.

"What're you thinking?" asked Cord.

"Well, there're a lot of hunters up this way," said Zeke. "And a fair number of folks who trap. Common thing is, they both need to know how to skin an animal."

"Or they know where to find someone to process their kill," said Cord.

"Or that," Zeke agreed. "Can you get me a contact?"

"I'll ask local law enforcement in New Town and see what we have between here and there. We can stop on our way back. Is that soon enough?"

Zeke nodded.

* * *

It turned out that the closest meat processor was in Ray, North Dakota, about thirty miles due west of Joyce's Diner. Cord called Lieutenant Mankato, who gave him the name and address.

Cord drove quickly, and they arrived outside Larson's Meats, a worn out one-story concrete block building with a red clapboard front and white trim in need of some serious paint. There was a hand painted cardboard sign in the window that read, "We accept debit & credit cards."

Inside the small space, Zeke and Cord saw no one. Cord rang the bell on the counter.

They heard a shout, and a couple minutes later, a tall, thick man wearing a metal butcher's apron and smelling of copper walked through the curtain dividing the front of the shop from the rear.

"Didn't expect anyone this late, ya know," he said.

"You're Ronald Larson?" asked Cord. He was looking at the man's metal mesh gloves, which were holding a bloody boning knife loosely.

"I am. You're not from around here, are you?" asked Larson as he set the knife down.

Cord smiled a sardonic smile. "More than I want to be, just now."

Larson nodded as if he were agreeing.

"Well, how can I help you?"

"We have some questions about meat processing tools," said Zeke. "And we thought we'd talk with an expert."

Ronald Larson looked blank for a minute, then he said, "Oh, that girl down in New Town. Thought you looked like a cop." This last he said to Cord.

"I'm the FBI," said Cord.

Larson nodded slowly, as if confirming his suspicions.

"Whattdaya got, then?"

"We want to talk about the process and the tools. Have you always been a meat processor?" asked Zeke.

"Yeah, since I moved here from Minnesota. And that was over twenty years ago."

"How do you know Lieutenant Mankato?" asked Cord.

"He's with the Tribal Police down in New Town," said Larson.

"It sounded like he knows you pretty well."

"Well, yeah, he's arrested me a couple times. Drunk and disorderly. But that was a while ago."

"How long?" asked Cord.

"Oh, maybe three weeks or so," said Larson sort of sheepishly.

"We're not here about that," said Zeke.

"But the Lieutenant's a hunter, and sometimes he brings his kills up here to me to process," Larson continued.

"Do you get work from many Native Americans?" asked Zeke.

"Some. Some do it themselves or take it to a relative on the reservation. They're not all licensed, but, well, it's the reservation."

"We're specifically interested in the tools you use," said Zeke.

Larson looked at him a moment. "You don't think I had anything to do with that down there, do you?"

"No reason to," said Zeke.

"OK. Well, most of the hard work is done with the meat and bone saw. You know what that is?"

"Sort of looks like a band saw?" asked Zeke.

"Sort of."

"What about skinning the animals?" asked Zeke.

"Just a skinning knife. I have a six-inch one that works fine. It's sort of bowed, you know, to let you get the blade to the skin easily. Gotta keep it sharpened, though."

"Would it work as well on human skin?" asked Zeke.

"Well, it probably wouldn't be the best tool for that." He made a face. "But to do what they did to that poor girl, yeah. A sharp one would take her skin off pretty easily."

* * *

Zeke drove his rental car down the street slowly, watching the addresses on the mailboxes and above the front doors. Van Hook was clearly a step up from New Town socioeconomically.

Although many of the homes were manufactured housing, they sat on landscaped lots, some with mature trees, just a couple of blocks from the Van Hook Arm of Lake Sakakawea, a large sporting lake. It looked like it was the result of a damming project.

Cord had dropped Zeke off in New Town where he'd rented the car and was now trying to find Cheryl Black. A tired Tillman Cord had said that he had no interest in a three year old murder.

Zeke found the address using his hotel's local phone book. He parked in the street and approached the one-story manufactured home with vinyl siding and bright blue shutters. There was a three-step staircase that led to the front door, and Zeke climbed the steps and knocked.

A large woman wearing a green summer dress covered by a gray sweatshirt opened the door.

"Cheryl Black?"

"I'm Cheryl," said the woman. "Are you the guy who called?"

"Yes, ma'am. Zeke Traynor. I'm working with the FBI."

"Unofficial, you said."

"Yes, ma'am. They've granted me no police powers. I'm just here to find out what happened to Jenny Lakota."

The woman stepped out on the porch and closed the door. Then she shook a cigarette out of a pack and lit it. "My folks are inside watching T.V. *The Price is Right*. Not sure what I can do to help, but, well, here I am."

* * *

"Did you know Jenny Lakota?" asked Zeke.

"Sure, I knew her to see her. I used to babysit her a little, quite a while back. But when she got older, Jenny ran in a whole different circle than I do."

"Your sister's death had some similarities to Jenny Lakota's murder."

She exhaled, a big smoky breath. "Casey. Yeah, from what I've heard, it sure did."

"How did she die?" asked Zeke.

"She was stabbed."

"Did they find the weapon?" asked Zeke.

Cheryl shook her head. "No. They said the wounds looked like she was stabbed with a flat bladed knife. When I heard about Jenny, well, you know…" she shivered.

"Your sister was found up north. The Evans Site?" Zeke prompted.

The woman was nodding. "Worst day of my life. One day we were working together, and the next she was gone. And up north, there's no reason she went up there."

"You worked together?" asked Zeke.

"Yeah, we both worked for the Town. She was in Administration and I have a job in Public Works. A desk job. She got it for me."

Zeke nodded and waited.

"Was anyone ever charged with the murder?" he asked.

"No. They never accused anyone." She took a long drag from the cigarette. "Said they were working on it, but after a while it just sort of fizzled out."

"What about trace evidence? DNA?"

"No, they said the body was soaked in bleach…no, it was Oxiclean. Said after that, they couldn't match the DNA."

"Sodium carbonate peroxyhydrate," said Zeke. "Destroys all the blood DNA. They used the same thing on Jenny's body."

Cheryl nodded blankly and took another puff.

"Did the police have suspects?" asked Zeke.

"They were looking at our family pretty hard. Said it looked like a crime of passion. Somebody had to be pretty emotional to go to all that trouble."

"She had a husband? Or boyfriend?" asked Zeke.

"Casey was, well, she was a free spirit. I used to call her a weekend hippy."

"Meaning?"

"She wasn't like other people. Sure, she worked for the government, but those are the best jobs. Benefits and paid vacation and insurance..."

"OK."

"But she loved to travel. She loved to go to yoga retreats. And she always went to Bike Week in Sturgis, every year."

"She rode a motorcycle?" asked Zeke.

"Sure. She'd ride it over to Interstate 85, just west of here, then it's a straight shot down to Sturgis. She'd ride with her friends. About a five-hour drive."

Cheryl paused. "And she had her causes."

Zeke said, "Causes?"

"Sure. She was always spoiling for a fight. A protest. Demonstrating about some unfair thing or another. Protesting. She said it was our duty."

"Who were her friends?" asked Zeke.

"Mostly people she grew up with from High School. She was pretty social, stayed in touch with her friends for years," Cheryl said. "But truth be told, everybody liked Casey. She always had a lot of friends."

"But no husband?"

"No, that wouldn't be Casey."

"Why do you think she was killed?" asked Zeke.

"I dunno. She was sweet to most everyone."

Zeke nodded.

"We've been thinking about it for a long time. I just don't know why someone would do that to her."

"We're looking into the Jenny Lakota murder," said Zeke. "We'll let you know if we find anything that might be connected to your sister's death."

"I know, it just seems too weird. Both of them killed almost the same way."

CHAPTER 15

"I'm back," said Zeke. He was standing in the doorway of the Monroe County Police Information Management room, talking to Susie again. Her blonde hair was still frizzy, and today she wore pink shorts and a t-shirt with "Changes in Latitudes" lettered across the back.

Susie turned in her seat and looked at Zeke. *Her lack of expression is a huge contrast with her sharp mind*, he thought.

"Pete Blazen let you come back here without him?" she asked. "He must like you."

With a dose of false modesty, Zeke joked, "What's not to like?"

"Well, it's OK with me," she said.

"Thank you. I flew back down this morning. We're chasing down a lead on that boat explosion," said Zeke.

"Your parents' boat."

"Yes."

"Where'd you fly in from?" asked Susie.

"You're not going to believe it," said Zeke.

"Try me."

"Williston, North Dakota," Zeke said.

"You're right. I don't believe you. So, how can I help with the explosion?" asked Susie.

"We picked up a man about an hour before the explosion, I think. He'd run aground and couldn't get his fishing boat off the reef. I think he threw an anchor out and rode back to the marina with us."

"You think?" asked Susie.

"I'm pretty sure. But that was a long time ago. I suppose I could be remembering it wrong…"

"Do you remember the name of the boat?" she asked.

"No, not really. It was a workboat, the kind you use for raising and lowering lobster traps, and for serious commercial fishing. Boxy and worn and professional. And it had the winches and pulleys and stuff attached."

"You're looking for a single boat in the Keys?" asked Susie. "There're over 930,000 boats registered in Florida alone."

"Yeah, I know it's crazy."

"Did anyone radio in the location of the boat? Where it had run aground?" she asked.

"That's something my dad would have done. He was pretty meticulous about that kind of thing," said Zeke.

"So what was the date of the explosion?" asked Susie. She turned her chair back to her computer terminal, fingers ready, waiting.

It was May 12, 1989," said Zeke.

"How old were you then?"

"I was eight, almost nine. We lived aboard the *West Wind*, sailed all around these waters."

Susie was nodding, but her attention was on the screen in front of her.

"You said it was called in that afternoon?" she asked.

"Yes, I'm pretty sure."

"We have access to the Coast Guard radio reports for vessels in our waters. Monroe County, that is. These radio logs would have been scanned into our system with a lot of others. After the Mariel Boat Lift in 1980, the Coast Guard got big on redundancy, and they used our computers and our files to keep duplicate copies of most everything in Monroe County. Let's see..."

Susie clicked some keys, read her screen and clicked some more.

"How about that," she said. "Here's a radio call from the *West Wind* to the Coast Guard on that day, reporting a fishing boat that ran aground on a sandbar next to the channel that runs under Seven Mile Bridge. That's not far from Boot Key, either."

"That sounds like it was us," said Zeke. "Can you get me a copy of that?"

"Sure, I'll print it for you," said Susie. "Says here that the name of the boat was the *Ellen Sue*. Fishermen are notorious for naming their workboats for women. Usually it's a wife or girlfriend. Sometimes it's their mom."

* * *

"How could I check its registration?" asked Zeke. "See who owned the Ellen Sue."

"Wow, that's a big ask," Susie said. "Thirty years ago."

"Sure," said Zeke.

"There's no guarantee that this boat was even registered in Monroe County, or even in Florida, for that matter."

Zeke waited.

Susie, still looking at the radio log, said, "There is a registration number here, though. We could run that."

"It was radioed in?" asked Zeke.

"Yes, when the boat was reported as stranded, the name and the number were reported."

"Good," said Zeke. "What's the number?"

Susie said, "FL-4533-ZW. Let me cross reference that with..." With her attention focused, she stopped talking as she typed quickly.

Then she said, "Monroe County. You're in luck."

Zeke said, "Happens sometimes..."

"It's a retired number. Inactive registration."

"Makes sense. The boat's probably about 50 years old by now. Maybe older," said Zeke. "Do you have the last owner's name and address?"

More rapid clacking of the keys. "It was registered to an Owen Parks," Susie said. "Want his address?"

* * *

Zeke pulled up to the rusty iron gate set in coral rock pillars on both sides of the driveway. The house beyond the gate was a conch house, built from Dade County Pine, a wood impervious to termites. There were many such cottages here. Zeke thought, *Most of these were built well over fifty years ago when the Keys were quite different.*

Through his windshield, Zeke saw a heavy steel chain covered with surface rust and locked with a large padlock. It, too, was covered with rust.

It appeared that the cottage was empty. There was an old blue F-150 truck in the small driveway but no sign of life in the yard or through the glass windows. The yard was overgrown, and beyond the house Zeke saw the ground fall off gradually about three feet to reach sea level. The ocean behind the house was bright blue and calm.

Zeke shut off the car, exited and tried the padlock. It was locked. There was a deep ditch on either side of the gate, probably dug to discourage intruders and door-to-door salesmen years ago.

He looked in the mailbox, a rusted old structure mounted on a fencepost. Nothing inside.

"No time like the present," he said to himself, and he stepped down into the overgrown ditch, quickly bounding up on the opposite side. His car was parked squarely in front of the gate, which should prevent an escape if someone was so inclined.

With no care in the world, Zeke strolled to the cottage, his Beretta tightly concealed at the small of his back under his Pier

House t-shirt. Nothing happened.

It was late afternoon, and the sun was low on the horizon. It cast stark shadows across the yard of the overgrown palm fronds and the gumbo limbo trees. The air smelled of stagnant heat. Zeke walked to the door and knocked.

Nothing.

After a minute, Zeke stepped down off the stairs and circled the house, watching the windows carefully as he went. He saw no lights, heard no air conditioning, and smelled nothing out of the ordinary. He continued, cautious as he approached the back wall of the house, moving in and tight against the side wall.

Suddenly, an orchestra of sounds lit up the area as the Giant Florida katydids, in unison, screamed their righteous song from the mangroves.

Zeke paused at the corner of the house, peeked around the corner, then stepped out into the back. The entire rear of the small cottage was a screened porch that overlooked the back yard, the bay and an old wooden boat dock, a few deck boards missing in several places.

Zeke looked at the house for a moment, feeling for any presence. The entire place seemed empty and abandoned.

Zeke walked to the dock and scanned the horizon. The clear, bright water, translucent in places, calmly covered the coral and rock that made up the shallow bottom.

There were signs of a boat. White plastic fenders, stained yellow by the sun, lined the dock. A fish table, strapped to a pylon, was rigged with a green garden hose feeding its rusty spigot. The top of the table was bone dry. Next to it sat a red gas can, the one-gallon size, with "Diesel" written on the side in marker. Zeke picked it up and sloshed its contents. Then he set it back down.

Tracing his steps back toward the house, Zeke let himself in through the screen door, then opened the back door. It was unlocked and he slipped inside.

The cottage was one open area comprised of a small kitchen, a living area that looked out at the water, a bedroom with a closet, and a small bathroom. The couch was folded out into a bed. A shower was out back.

Won't take long to see what's here, he thought. He checked the front door and found it unlocked. *There's my escape route.*

It was hot and muggy in the cottage, but he didn't turn on the small air conditioning unit. Within two minutes he felt the sweat forming on his skin and dampening his shirt. In five minutes he was sweating profusely. The hot air made breathing hard.

He tossed the place in less than fifteen minutes, one eye watching and both ears listening for the returning boat. In all, he found some bills piled on the kitchen shelf addressed to Owen Parks, a flour canister on a kitchen shelf with $765 in currency in it, a box half filled with nine millimeter cartridges, but no gun, and some men's clothing in a stinky pile on the floor of the closet. In the bedroom, the bed was used but unmade. There were two dirty coffee cups in the single sink. In the refrigerator, he found four beer cans still connected by their plastic holder, and some hot sauce. The freezer was filled with ice and wrapped white packages labeled "fish" with a dull sharpie.

Zeke found the sharpie and the white paper a minute later in one of the kitchen drawers.

The county records that Susie had accessed showed that this property was owned by Owen Parks and had been built in the mid-1960s. There had been no transfer of ownership since then, and the records showed that the real estate taxes were paid and current.

"If Owen Parks is the same fisherman we rescued," Zeke had told Susie, "he looked to be around forty back then. So he's got to be in his seventies. Or older."

Susie had clacked some more keys on her keyboard and said, "It looks like he's still alive. He's got a boat registered in his name, and a truck, an old F-150. Taxes are current on them, too. Let's see…he's seventy-three this year."

The rest of his search revealed nothing of interest. Zeke stepped out on the screened porch and listened for a minute. He heard the humming of an inboard motor becoming louder and stronger.

Time to vanish, he thought.

Zeke circled to the front of the house, crossed the ditch and slid into the front seat of his car. Air conditioning blasting, he pointed the BMW back toward U.S. Highway 1.

* * *

"I've found him," said Zeke. He'd returned to his cottage and called Kimmy in D.C. to share the news.

"That's great, Zeke," Kimmy said. "Did you talk with him?"

"Not yet," he admitted. "It was a sort of a B&E, and I didn't want to take a chance and lose the advantage. Plus, the guy, Owen Parks, it looks like he's seventy-three."

"You mean he could have lost his memory? Dementia?"

"Or he could pretend to have lost it. No, there's too much wiggle room. Plus, he might call the Sheriff's office, 911."

"You don't want to do this with the Sheriff?"

"No, I may have to do some things the Sheriff doesn't agree with..."

"Got it. What did you find out when you were there?" she asked.

Zeke hesitated. "I'll tell you, but it'll take a while. First, can you make time to come down here and help me with this?"

"Hmm. Funny, I was just thinking about a vacation..."

"Well, it is the Keys," said Zeke, innocently.

"It is that. Yeah, I can break away for a few days."

"Great," said Zeke.

"Tracy told me you've got a sweet setup down there," Kimmy continued.

"You talked to Tracy? About us?" asked Zeke.

"You know how I am with boundaries, Zeke."

He ignored the comment. "How soon can you be here?"

"Tomorrow. I can fly into Key West tomorrow noon, and drive up to Marathon..."

"I'll pick you up at the airport. We can talk on the way back to the cottage."

"OK. Will I need heavy equipment for this trip?" she asked.

"Just bring your Jericho," said Zeke, referring to Kimmy's favorite handgun. "It should be enough."

* * *

"So, what's the plan?" Kimmy asked after they'd cleared Stock Island and were heading north on another pristine day. The azure sky was cloudless, and the bright blue water glistened on both sides of the narrow highway.

"It looks to me as if the old man lives with someone else, possibly a relative. It's a small place. We need to visit with them and find out what he knows about the explosion."

"Do we have any leverage?" asked Kimmy. She was bouncing lightly in her seat, a tune obviously playing in her head. Her lime green shorts and white bikini top showed off her pale, fit body.

"We need some. I've been thinking about that," said Zeke.

"More than a gun to his head, I guess," Kimmy said with a laugh.

"Yeah, maybe."

"What's the setup?" she asked.

"It's a small house, private, with a boat dock behind it and a gated entrance. Oversized lot, and a lot of foliage blocking out the neighbors on both sides. It's old, and the house isn't more than 900 square feet at most," said Zeke.

"Private. Good. Once we're in, we won't be disturbed."

"Well, this isn't wet work," Zeke said, referring to Kimmy's experience in Mossad.

"Ah, but Owen Parks doesn't know that," she said.

* * *

They parked the rental car in the driveway of an empty house with an overgrown front yard hosting a tattered, blue and white "For Sale" sign, and walked a block to the gate embedded in the coral rock in front of Owen Parks' house. Kimmy had pulled a black hoodie over her bikini top and strapped her Jericho to her lower back. They both had traded their sandals for gum-soled shoes.

"Black's the hottest color, you know," said Kimmy.

"Actually, black isn't a color. It's the absence of all color," said Zeke.

Kimmy nodded to herself and hummed as they walked.

The leverage, they'd decided, would be a push/pull approach, an act with Kimmy trying to talk Zeke out of doing bodily damage to the fisherman. The script would be ad libbed.

"Here we go," said Kimmy, looking around. They skirted the gate and crossed the shallow ditch to the front yard. The truck was in the driveway, partially in the shade of a palm tree.

Zeke led the way, quickly and quietly around the side of the small house to the back porch after confirming the boat wasn't in residence at the dock. They entered the screened porch and then the small house.

"No air conditioning," he said.

"I can tell. But it's no worse than when I was on assignment in the Gaza Strip," she said.

Zeke stopped. "That's Palestinian territory. What were you doing there?"

Kimmy smiled but said nothing.

"The other day the boat pulled in the middle of the afternoon, about 3:30. Probably be in around the same time today."

"Creatures of habit?" she asked.

"Time and tides. And it has to do with when the fish are running."

Kimmy nodded to a beat only she could hear. She sat on the edge of the small couch and waited.

* * *

The engine of the fishing boat was a diesel, and the breeze pushed the hot smell of it along like a dump truck with a leaky exhaust.

"Whew," Kimmy sighed, reacting to the odor as she ducked down behind the couch to stay out of sight. Zeke had slipped into the bedroom.

"There're two of them," said Zeke. "Maybe father and son Parks. Let's take them when they get inside the house."

"I'll seal off the rear exit," said Kimmy, quietly.

The Parks took their time about it, unloading the boat, emptying the bait wells, offloading the cooler with the fish they'd caught, washing everything down and hosing it off. Owen Parks worked on the fish table, filleting their catch and saving the scraps in a bucket for tomorrow's bait and chum.

When he was done, the younger man, who looked to be about fifty, picked up the oversized cooler and carried it up to the cottage. He set the cooler in a shady spot outside the back door and entered the small home. His first action was to turn on the air conditioning. Then he walked to the kitchen and washed his hands.

Owen Parks, the elder, followed him into the cottage and used the small bathroom.

Zeke stepped out of the bedroom and stood blocking the bathroom door. He had his Beretta M9 out, safety off and pointed at the younger man when he turned around.

"What the hell…?" the younger man said, loud.

"We need to talk," said Zeke. Kimmy stepped up and covered the man. Zeke holstered his gun.

Suddenly Owen Parks stepped out of the bathroom, his fish knife in his hand, slicing blindly in a side-to-side motion. The leather knife holster hung empty on his belt.

Smart money would put him down quickly, thought Zeke. *But I need him to be able to talk. And I need him shaken up.*

Moving with practiced rhythm, Zeke followed the senior Parks' slash to the left, grabbed his wrist with both hands and, still standing, rolled into the man. The effect was to create substantial leverage on the man's elbow, hyperextending it. The knife fell to the floor with a metallic rattle.

Zeke released the man and immediately jabbed him twice, once in the solar plexus and once in the throat, then kicked the knife away and danced back a couple steps.

Owen Parks looked stunned. And then he sat hard on the

floor, holding his throat and coughing in a raspy voice, trying to catch his breath.

The younger man looked on, stunned.

Kimmy said, "Be careful, you don't want to kill them."

"Sure I do," said Zeke in an angry voice.

"Damn you! If I were thirty years younger..." started Parks, his voice starting to recover.

"That's exactly why we're here," said Zeke.

* * *

Both men sat on the small couch, their wrists duct taped together behind them, their ankles crossed and taped. Kimmy stood to the side of the couch, her Jericho 941 held loosely in her hand. Occasionally, she moved the barrel back and forth between the two men, pausing at each for effect. Their eyes watched her cautiously.

Zeke had checked their wallets. It turned out that the younger man was indeed Parks' son, Todd.

Zeke took a kitchen chair, reversed it and sat in it looking directly at the men, about two feet away. He held his handgun in his right hand, propped on the back of the chair, pointed at Owen Parks.

"Thirty years ago," he started, "you were stranded in your fishing boat near the Seven Mile Bridge. On a sandbar. Does any of this sound familiar?"

No one spoke.

"A motorsailer rescued you and gave you a lift to Boot Key

Marina."

Parks looked down and away. "I don't know what you're talking about."

He's lying, thought Zeke. The aversion of his eyes and the change in the tone of his voice were the clues Zeke was looking for.

"Look, you can't break in here and rob us like this. It's illegal. I have friends, you know," said the senior Parks. "Friends with the Sheriff's Department…"

Zeke reached over and swatted Owen Parks' temple with the barrel of his gun. Then he hit him again, hard, in the same place.

"Ow!" said Parks, drawing his head back in pain. His eyes were watering.

"Pay attention," said Zeke. "You were there. I remember you."

Owen Parks stopped. He narrowed his eyes and looked at Zeke, as if for the first time. "You remember me?"

Zeke nodded. "You caused the explosion that killed my parents. I'll never forget that."

"Sorry, kid, it wasn't me."

His son said, "What're you, crazy?"

Zeke decided to let the elder Parks think about it for a minute.

"You're his son," said Zeke. "You're Todd Parks. Said so on your driver's license."

Zeke had looked through both men's wallets while Kimmy secured them with the duct tape.

"So?"

"You're forty-seven. That means you were in your teens when it happened. I'd bet you were the one who picked your dad up at Boot Key Marina after the explosion. Helped him escape." Zeke was speculating now. But it made sense. Besides, accuracy didn't matter. This was about intimidation.

"What? What're you talking about?" asked Todd Parks.

At the same time his father said, "You're crazy!"

Zeke leaned forward and rapped Owen Parks smartly on the temple. "Shut up."

"What I want to know is who was behind it. Who paid you to leave the bomb on the *West Wind*?"

"What?" asked Todd. "A bomb?"

"Did you think it was an accident?" asked Zeke.

"Yeah, an explosion. They said gas pumps or something."

"Who said?" asked Zeke.

Todd looked at his dad, then looked away. "You know, the newspapers…"

Zeke shook his head. "This man," he pointed at Owen Parks with his gun barrel, "left a duffle bag on the *West Wind* after we'd rescued him. A few minutes later, it exploded and killed two people."

He paused.

"My parents."

The older Parks looked away, reacting to the intensity in Zeke's voice and eyes.

"Why would I do something like that?" he asked the floor.

"You tell me. Now. Or I start shooting your boy, here. I'll ruin his knees first."

"Man, you're crazy. I don't know what you're talking about!"

Zeke cocked the gun and pointed it at Todd's left knee. "I've got nothing to lose."

Kimmy intervened. "Wait, hold on. You didn't say anything about torture..."

"Doesn't matter," said Zeke, his voice intense with anger. "Step outside if you want. It's going to be knees, ankles, elbows and shoulders, to start."

"Then what?"

"Then I'll reload and..."

She turned to the Parks. "I'm afraid I can't help you. If it were me, I'd be inclined to tell him what he wants to know."

CHAPTER 16

"It wasn't supposed to be like that," said Owen Parks. "No one was supposed to get hurt."

Zeke was listening, his face turned to Todd Parks, who at that moment had the barrel of Zeke's handgun in his mouth.

"Let the boy go," Parks continued. "He wasn't a part of it."

Zeke said, "Keep talking."

"OK, look, I was just a fisherman. I fished these waters for years. My people were conchs. They came down to help build the overseas railroad and they stayed. I was born in the Keys ten years after the Labor Day Hurricane in 1935. Lived here all my life..."

"Not interested in history just now, Parks," said Zeke.

"I'd seen the *West Wind* plenty. Always goin' in or out of Boot Key. Didn't know it was your family, though."

"And the bomb?" asked Zeke, staying on point.

"I didn't know it was a bomb. You've gotta believe me," said Parks. He looked at his son, still obviously scared with the gun barrel in his mouth. He was shaking badly, and sweating, his eyes now closed.

"You're wasting my time. I think I'll just finish this," said Zeke. He tightened his hand on the pistol grip.

The older Parks saw the tension in his hand and said, "No, wait!" The younger Parks, hearing the tension in his father's voice, wet himself.

Zeke looked at him, then back to his father. He said, "You thought you were really something thirty years ago, didn't you?"

"I was part of the gang," said Parks. "They're mostly dead now, but it was something years ago. We had each other's backs. We protected each other. We kept commercial fishermen from fishing our waters."

"A gang of thugs," said Zeke. "Spin it any way you want."

"We joined together to keep the Keys for the conchs. They passed a law, wouldn't let us use gill nets to fish anymore. Between the tourists and the commercial fishermen from the mainland, we were all losing money. So we joined together."

"And, back to the bomb," said Zeke.

"It was supposed to be a warning, a dud. They told me it wouldn't detonate. It was supposed to give off smoke and make some noise. It was supposed to scare them, that's all."

* * *

"Why the *West Wind*?" asked Zeke.

"It was an opportunity, not personal. I ran my workboat, the *Ellen Sue*, aground under the bridge and waited for someone to come by and help." Owen Parks looked away.

"And the plan was?"

"To scare people, to create publicity. I don't know, to make them go away and stay away, I suppose." Parks was grasping now.

"You're saying that it was random? That whoever had stopped to help you would have been blown to bits?" asked Zeke. "You think I'll buy that?"

"Look, I was the soldier. I didn't plan it. I was told what to do, and I did it. I didn't know it was a real bomb! I didn't!"

"So who targeted the *West Wind* for you?" Zeke asked.

"You've gotta believe me, I didn't know," said the fisherman.

Zeke relaxed. "Who gave the order, Parks?"

The fisherman hesitated. His eyes flicked up and away from Zeke.

"The truth, Parks."

"Ah, hell," said Parks. "It was Billy."

* * *

"Billy Forester?" asked Zeke. "The Monroe County sheriff?"

"Back then, yeah."

"Also a conch?"

"Yeah. Billy was in charge. I mean, we didn't hold an election or anything, but somehow Billy emerged as the guy in charge."

"Let me be sure I get this," said Zeke. "You local guys, you conchs, decided that the best way to get the Keys back was to scare people off? Make them think twice about coming down here?"

Parks nodded slowly. "That's what they said. It sounded right..."

"Did it work?" asked Zeke.

"Not really," said Parks sourly.

"That wasn't long after the Keys seceded from the USA, was it? Five or six years?"

"Yeah," said Parks. "Hey, would you take your gun outta his mouth now?"

Zeke looked at the younger Parks, nodded and removed the gun barrel.

"Tell me more," said Zeke, quietly.

* * *

"It was a muck up, is what it was," said the elder Parks. "When the bomb exploded, I about had a heart attack."

"Where were you when it happened?" asked Zeke.

"Todd was driving me up US 1, heading back here. You were right that he picked me up at the marina. I hopped off the boat and got out of there fast. He'd just turned onto the highway when we heard the explosion."

Kimmy, standing behind Zeke in the living room of the small house, shook her head.

"Doesn't ring true," she said.

Parks said, "I'm not lying. I had orders to get off the boat fast and get outta there, so I wouldn't be associated with any of it."

* * *

"Why don't you tell me who all was involved in your gang," Zeke said, his voice flat and empty. He sounded dangerous.

Owen looked around the room, as if for help. He said, "Well, there weren't that many."

He's already minimizing, trying to control the situation, thought Zeke.

"It was Billy and me and a couple others."

Zeke reached across the back of the chair and smacked Parks on the temple. Same spot as before.

"Hey, ow, crap," said Parks.

"How about some names?" asked Zeke.

"Snyder. Darrell Snyder. Everybody called him Snyder," said Parks. "His family owned the Holiday Motel, and he ran his fishing boat out of the inlet behind it. He was a drunk."

"He's still here?" asked Zeke.

"Naw, died of lung cancer about ten years back," he said.

"Who else? And I'd prefer names of people who are still alive…"

"Well, Crabby Cabot was one," said Parks, grudgingly. His eyes were following the gun barrel on its erratic path.

"Crabby? What's his real name?"

"Jerry, I think it was Jerry. He fished. His people made their money fishing and building lobster traps and selling them to the fishermen. Made crab traps, too."

"Where is he now?"

"I think he's in a nursing home in Miami. He's got the memory loss."

"He's your age?" asked Zeke.

Parks nodded.

"Who else?" asked Zeke. He smacked Parks' temple again.

"OK, OK, geez," said Parks, ducking his head. "That hurts."

"It's supposed to," said Zeke.

"OK. There was Skinny Gonzalez. He was there, in the gang. He had an attitude, I'll tell you."

"First name?" asked Zeke.

"James, it was James Gonzalez."

"Where's Skinny now?"

"He lives on Little Torch Key. He had one of those conch houses, you know, concrete block, one-story thing on a canal with a lot of land. Maybe three acres. So when the developers came looking, he got rich."

"But that would be later, after 1989…" said Zeke.

"Yeah, Skinny sold it to some guys from Miami. Probably around 1997 or '98."

"Who else was involved?" Zeke looked at Todd Parks and said, "Open. Now. Or I break your teeth."

Todd opened his mouth, and Zeke shoved the gun barrel back in it.

"Well, the Sheriff, of course," said Owen.

"Where can I find the Sheriff?" asked Zeke. "Billy Forester?"

"Oh, he's around. Has a house on Marathon and a big fishing boat. Had to do something with all the money he took…"

"He took?" asked Kimmy.

"Sure. Everybody knew it. If you wanted to get something done, Billy Forester was the one to talk to. He was slick, made enough to buy that big boat with cash, and the house is oceanfront. Has to be worth a couple million dollars," said Parks.

"Anyone else I need to know about?" asked Zeke.

"Captain Brown," he said. "He's up in Key Largo, I think. Lives with his daughter up there. He was sorta half in and half out."

"Meaning?"

"He'd get worked up when he'd see the commercial fishing boats from up the coast coming in. Then he'd get cold feet when it was time to do something about it. Only reason they let him stay around was that his family are conchs, been here longer than mine."

"What's his first name?" asked Zeke.

"That is his first name. His folks named him Captain."

"Who else?" asked Zeke.

"Nobody, man. Most everyone else is dead," said Parks. His son, beside him, nodded carefully. A small nod around the gun barrel.

Zeke relaxed a bit. "I'll be heading out of town," he said. "But I'll be back soon."

He took the gun out of Todd Parks' mouth and slipped it in his pocket. "If you're lying to me, we'll visit again," he said. "Plan on it."

* * *

He remembered the moment as if it had just happened.

"We have much to do, Otaktay," his grandmother had said.

He'd been watching television and drinking a Coke. He'd nodded in her general direction.

"Are you listening?" she asked. The woman disliked television as much as she hated the drugs. They were distractions that interfered with important things.

"Yes, Gramm," said the young man.

He was sitting on the sofa in the living room of the small house, the Coke can on the coffee table in front of him, the local newspaper spread out on the table beside the Coke. He wore a vest over a white t-shirt, jeans and plastic shower sandals. His black hair was pulled back into a ponytail and held with a green rubber band.

"We must look forward," said the old woman. "There's not much time!"

"What would you have me do, Gramm?" he asked.

"They must pay for their weakness," she said. "We must stand strong together against the white man and his evil drugs."

The young man nodded, still distracted by the television screen.

"Do you know what we must do now?" she asked.

"We must eliminate the weakness," he said, speaking by rote. It was a mantra.

She nodded. "It is time now."

He got up slowly from the couch and shut the television off with the remote. He stretched his back and shrugged out of the red and tan vest, setting it carefully on the coffee table. Then he walked over to the woman.

"Who's next, Gramm?" he asked.

* * *

He could see it all from the shadows. He'd been there for hours, it seemed, ever since the sun went down.

He was a hunter, like his ancestors before him. *A silent, deadly hunter,* he thought.

The small bar was lit up with activity, cars parked askew in the lot and motorcycles on the street in front of it. The girl stepped out and for a moment he heard a Johnny Cash song wafting from the open door. It was "Ring of Fire". Then the door closed and the girl stood on the sidewalk, looking at the door, watching and waiting. She swayed, caught herself, and leaned against a wall, still facing the door.

Good, this will be easy, he thought.

Nothing happened for a long time. Then, the door opened and a large man stepped out under the streetlight. An Indian. He was dressed in a plaid work shirt, blue jeans and boots, and he looked to his left, squinting. Then he looked to his right and saw the girl. He walked over to her and said something.

The girl laughed, said something back and leaned against him. Then she hooked her arm through his and led him away, around the corner and up the street.

The hunter followed, distant and patient. They walked east a block, then two, and then turned up East Avenue. They didn't seem to be in any hurry.

The trailer park was like so many others in New Town. Beat up and worn out, from being there long before the oil, from being a place of hopelessness. The drugs did that, he knew. His Gramm had told him.

He watched as the big Indian and the girl walked to a green trailer. They stopped and the girl, still giggling, pulled him toward her by the shoulder until he was close enough to kiss. Then she kissed him lightly and laughed again.

He straightened and waited while she opened the front door to the trailer. Yellow light spilled out of the door onto the dirt driveway. Standing in the door, she looked back at him and made a motion, and he followed her inside.

* * *

It was about twenty minutes later that he emerged from the trailer, the large man with the dark hair. The man was big, but the hunter wasn't afraid. He looked around, and then he walked briskly away from the trailer.

The hunter waited.

The light of the harvest moon was calming, reassuring. It had always been the best light for hunting. Judging from its position, it was close to midnight.

Five minutes later, the girl emerged from the trailer. She exited a side door, not the door she'd entered with the man, and she closed it quietly. She stepped off the small porch and walked across the dirt drive, hesitating as she went, uncertain.

Then she decided something and started walking back in the direction of downtown and the bar.

The hunter stepped out in the darkness and felt the weight of the knife in his pocket. The Bakken Blade. It was in an outside pocket of his cargo pants. He unbuttoned the pocket flap as he followed her.

* * *

It had to be done. A message had to be sent. The pride of the Sioux Nation was at stake.

It was a retaliation for the many wrongs they had suffered. Their history was one of loss and abuse. And the latest abuse was the worst. The sacred grounds of their ancestors had been violated by ruthless men who valued money over truth.

It wasn't difficult. The girl had walked to the town, past the bar, and then she'd headed to her mother's home, her route along the railroad tracks. She walked slowly, but she had steadied herself and was no longer laughing.

The hunter had caught up with her, smiled at her. She'd seen him before, around town, in tribal meetings, at social events on the reservation. He was her neighbor.

He offered to walk with her. She said she wasn't afraid. Then she asked him if he had anything he could share to help her take the edge off. She'd fought with her boyfriend, she confided.

The hunter handed her a pint bottle filled with Smirnoff vodka, 90 proof. He was carrying it in another pocket of his cargo pants.

She thanked him and tipped the bottle up.

As she did, distracted, the hunter jabbed her thigh with the needle, injecting the Xylazine into her system. The needle hurt, and she lowered the bottle and said, "Ouch! Crap!"

He said, "What was that?"

As she looked at him, her eyes lost focus and she dropped the bottle, weaved for a moment and suddenly sat down in the middle of the road. She whimpered.

* * *

Then it was simple. The hunter moved her to the tracks, set her down and sat down beside her in the dark and emptied his pockets. He still held the needle. He snapped it off on a railroad tie and slipped both parts of the broken hypodermic into his shirt pocket.

First he pulled on the rubber gloves. They were yellow housecleaning gloves that reached almost to his elbows.

The girl sat next to him, head bowed. She snored lightly.

He took out the small plastic container with the Oxiclean and set it aside. He picked up the folded plastic bag, a thirty-gallon size, unfolded it and tore a hole in the bottom before wrapping it around his neck like a bib.

Her head lolled.

He took out the blade. It was razor sharp. He carefully cut her shirt from her body and then her bra. He did it by feel, for the most part. There was very little light in the rail yard. He'd broken the nearby streetlights earlier, and the grain silos cast long shadows over the two of them.

The night was cool and quiet. He worked quickly and quietly. Occasionally, the girl would make a noise, a whimper. After an hour, she was silent. The hunter finished up and removed the plastic bag and rolled it around the blade, inside out. The blood spatter stayed inside with the knife. He took off the gloves, left them inside out and shoved them back in his pocket. Then he stood and stretched. He spilled the Oxiclean all around and on the girl.

He said his mantra, slowly and quietly as his grandmother had taught him, and walked away.

Chapter 17

"Tribal Leadership offices," said the pert, blonde receptionist. "How can I direct your call?"

She appeared to be in her mid-twenties, with light blue eyes and a turned up nose.

Zeke watched her handle the phone calls efficiently and listened while she worked the bureaucratic triage, diverting callers to members of the Tribal Leader's staff.

Her teeth were even, white and capped, and she smiled into the phone each time she spoke. The smile was audible.

She's good at it, thought Zeke.

Clive Greene had agreed that the killings seemed to be random. The killings could have been the result of a sick mind, a serial killer preying on Native American girls. The victims had enemies. Or the killings could be politically motivated or committed by someone who was angry. Or they could have been personal, motivated by jealousy or rage. Or something else entirely.

The blonde woman smiled up at Zeke and then answered her phone once again. "Tribal Leader Grayhorse's office."

A week ago, they'd set Sally, Clive's best researcher, on the scent. A day later, in their D.C. office, Sally had isolated some possibilities. Zeke had joined the discussion via speakerphone.

"There's not much happening in the Dakotas except oil," she'd said during their briefing. "But the oil is big enough to get everyone's attention."

Clive nodded. "How big?"

"Scandalously big," said Sally, dramatically. She used a wispy voice and, on occasion, Marilyn's signature pout.

They waited a moment.

"Like half a trillion dollars, based on the latest estimate."

"The latest estimate…?" asked Clive.

"The USGS did a study… Well, an update to an earlier study. They determined that there's at least 7.4 billion barrels of crude that can be taken out of the Bakken Formation. Times about seventy dollars per barrel…"

"Five hundred eighteen billion dollars," said Zeke under his breath.

"That's for the entire formation, mind you. Part of it is in Montana, part in South Dakota and then there's quite a bit in Saskatchewan. Plus North Dakota."

"Wow. The good folks must be lining up to get paid…" said Clive.

"So, who's at the top of the food chain?" asked Zeke. "Who can't afford to lose what they have? Their position, their power, their control."

"Some of the pioneer families," Sally commented. "And politicians."

"Pioneer?" asked Clive. "Like wagon trains?"

"Actually, most of the pioneers arrived in North Dakota by train. Immigrant trains. And some arrived by steamboats and barges," Sally said helpfully.

"Hmm," Clive said. "Immigrant trains?"

"The trains were stationed on Ellis Island back at the end of the nineteenth century," said Sally, warming to the topic. "Immigrants from Europe could get off the boat and go directly to a train that would transport them out west to St. Paul and then to the Dakota Territory. A lot of them did just that."

"What was the draw?" asked Clive.

"Free land," said Zeke. "Homestead claims. The government was giving away 160-acre tracts to people who would farm it and commit to build, cultivate and stay on the land for five years. Lincoln started it when he signed the Homestead Act into law right after the Civil War."

"And all this land was sitting on an oil field the whole time?" asked Clive.

Sally nodded. "But it wasn't an issue. They were all using steam, back then… Steam engines and steamboats. Oil didn't become important until later on."

"OK, good. And who else can't afford to lose what they have?" asked Zeke.

"Some of the tribal leadership has done very well since the oil boom," said Sally. "The reservation is located on the oil formation. So, they've come into more money than they ever imagined."

"I'd say so," said Clive. "Plenty of motivation to keep the spigot flowing."

* * *

"I found something else," said Sally. "In my research."

"Do tell," said Clive.

"It's about the women. There are over 5,700 cases of missing Native American women that have been reported to the National Crime Information Center. And a lot more of the cases don't get reported," she continued.

"Hmm," Clive said.

"It gets worse. In some places, the murder rate of Native American women is ten times higher than the national average for all races."

Zeke, on his phone, said, "Who's responsible?"

"Not always their own people," said Sally. "Two thirds of the sexual assaults on Native American women are committed by white and other non-Native American people. And now that you have so many men moving into the area for the oil jobs..."

"The incidents just increase," said Zeke.

* * *

"Mr. Reid?" Zeke heard. He stood and turned in the direction of the sound.

"I'm Henry Wolsnoki, Tribal Leader Grayhorse's Chief of Staff." He offered Zeke a warm handshake.

"Mr. Wolsnoki, how are you? Edward Reid," Zeke said.

In investigating the North Dakota deaths, Zeke had decided

to take a look at those who had the most to lose. And starting in the Tribal Leaders' offices in New Town seemed right.

William Grayhorse was one of four Tribal Leaders who led the Sioux nation in North Dakota. Based on the available pictures, he was an imposing man, thick and tall with black hair that fell to the middle of his back. He typically wore it in a long single braid, decorated with native beads and feathers. In the newspaper photos he always smiled, showing large, white teeth.

Some quick research showed that Grayhorse had facilitated the way for big oil to establish its presence in northwest North Dakota and on the Fort Berthold reservation.

Posing as Edward Reid, a reporter for a national weekly magazine, Zeke had arranged for an interview with the Tribal Leader. The response had come back from William Grayhorse's offices and a schedule was set.

"We're excited about the interview," said Wolsnoki. "I'm glad we were able to pull it together this quickly."

"Yes, thanks," said Zeke, smiling sincerely.

"You're interested in the effects of the oil boom on education in our state, then?"

"Yes. It's a follow-up piece to an article I wrote about the financial impact of fracking on another state's educational system," said Zeke.

"Where was that?" asked Wolsnoki.

"Pennsylvania."

Wolsnoki nodded. "You'll find we're much less political up here. Let's use my office to prepare. Grayhorse will be able to join us at the end. Let's get started."

* * *

The office was a small room decorated primarily with pictures of Native Americans on the walls and on the credenza.

For the next hour and ten minutes, Zeke queried the Tribal Leader's Chief of Staff about the direct and indirect impact of North Dakota's windfall on the state's education system. He lobbed softball questions at Wolsnoki, who smiled through the interview and answered the questions patiently. Zeke took copious notes. They talked about pending legislation, pools of funding, the impact of the oil industry on North Dakota's economy and the future of the Bakken Formation's revenues.

They also discussed the impact of the oil boom on the Native American reservations in this part of the state.

"Well, you know, that's a topic that's close to my heart. I'm actually about a quarter Sioux."

Zeke said, "Really? With a name like 'Wolsnoki'?"

"My great-grandfather's contribution. He arrived in the Dakotas in the late 1800s, right off the boat from Europe. Married a Sioux woman a year or two later, and the Wolsnokis have been here ever since."

Zeke nodded and made a note.

"Who administers the revenues?" he asked.

"Well, we have a number of programs set up, you know, funded from the oil money."

"Sure."

"The money comes into the state through the 11.5% severance tax on the gross value of all the oil produced. That's why North Dakota has a billion dollar budget surplus," added Wolsnoki.

"Impressive."

"You did your homework. You know that North Dakota produces more oil than any other state, save one."

"Texas," said Zeke, absently. "Yes. So who administers this state's budget? That's a huge surplus."

"Well, the Governor's office is ultimately responsible for that. We have a budget committee, of course, and the Tribal Councils have a lot of input..."

* * *

The interview was winding down. Henry Wolsnoki kept looking at his watch and fidgeting. Zeke sat and watched.

"Tribal Leader Grayhorse should be here in a moment," Wolsnoki said, looking at the door.

"No problem."

A moment later, the door to Henry Wolsnoki's office opened and a tall, black haired man with a thick torso and squinted eyes walked in. From the skin on his hands and throat Zeke guessed he was about sixty. He wore traditional Native American Indian clothing, jeans and a leather vest over a colorful shirt, but with Parigi croc driving slippers on his feet.

Wolsnoki stood up. Zeke followed his example.

"Tribal Leader William Grayhorse," said Wolsnoki. "This is Edward Reid. He's writing an article for his national magazine about education in North Dakota. The results of our fracking efforts."

The men shook hands and the Tribal Leader pulled a chair up to the table. They all sat.

"I'm sure Henry has filled you in. Answered your questions," said Grayhorse.

"He's been very accommodating and generous with his time," said Zeke.

For a quick moment, Wolsnoki looked almost demure.

"It must make you proud to be able to do so much good," said Zeke. "To help so many children."

Grayhorse nodded slightly. "After the years of abuse my people took, it's something."

Zeke nodded empathetically.

"And I would hope for much more for my people." He paused. Then he added, "It's a shame the abuse we took. My people have been pushed around, robbed, moved from place to place, and taken advantage of. Whenever there was something found on the land that had value, well, we were moved by the government again."

Zeke nodded. "I can see where that would be a contentious issue."

"It has never been right. It makes me proud that we won at Little Big Horn. You know, that battleground is less than 300 miles from here. And it happened 142 years ago," Grayhorse said with pride in his voice. "But we've lost everything since then."

* * *

Zeke dialed the secure number.

"7428," said Sally, reversing the last two digits. The number changed daily.

"Mandy, how are you?" asked Zeke, using a simple word code. He confirmed security by using a name that started with the same letter as the day of the week. In this case, it was Monday.

"Hey, long time no see," said Sally, teasing.

"Is Eric in today?" asked Zeke. Eric was Clive's code name within The Agency.

"He's over at the FBI offices."

"I want to chat with him as soon as I can," Zeke continued. "About the state of the State."

"North Dakota?" she asked.

"Yep. I just had an interesting meeting with one of the Tribal Leaders. I could see him being involved with the murder. We just need to find the motive."

"Oh my, sounds like corruption in public office," said Sally.

"Nah, that doesn't happen," said Zeke.

"When are you planning to be back in Washington?"

"In a day or two, maybe," said Zeke.

"Oh, good, you can take me to Valor," she said. "I'll make reservations."

"Valor?" asked Zeke.

"Valor Brew Pub. Just opened to great reviews!"

"Downtown? Near the office?" he asked.

"About a ten minute Uber ride. Great food, though, they say. Totally worth it."

"What kind of fare?" asked Zeke.

"American. Like totally American. The owners and the staff are all ex-military."

"OK, count me in," said Zeke.

* * *

"Old boy, how're things up in the hinterlands?" asked Clive, calling Zeke back on a secure line.

Zeke smiled. "Reporting in, sir."

"Your interview went well, I presume," said Clive.

"It did. The Tribal Chief seems to have a pretty big chip on his shoulder," said Zeke. "He thinks he's hiding it well, but it dates back to the late 1700s. It's literally in his DNA. It blinds him."

"Do you think he has something to do with the Indian girl's murder?"

"I don't know," said Zeke. "But his anger seems to be directed toward the white men, not the Indians. There could be something larger in play, though. Lots of money up here."

"Indeed. What are you planning to do?" asked Clive.

"I have a couple more things to look at up here, and then I think I'll fly back to D.C. Need to spend some time on the money laundering thing."

"I have some thoughts about that," said Clive. "We may want to come at it from a different angle. When you get back here we'll talk."

* * *

Zeke parked his rental car along the road in Van Hook and walked back to Cheryl Black's house. It was mid-morning, but the air was crisp, hinting at autumn and the winter to come.

He knocked on the front door and waited. In a minute, a pale, gray haired woman holding a lit cigarette opened the door. She was dressed in a pink housecoat and slipper-socks.

"Yeah?" she asked. The volume on the television was turned up high.

"Looking for Cheryl Black," said Zeke, speaking over the TV. It sounded like a game show.

"Yeah." The woman turned away and shut the door. Zeke was glad for the relative quiet. A minute later, Cheryl Black opened the door and stepped out.

"We won't be able to hear each other in there," she said as she came down the steps. "*Family Feud* is on."

They walked to a small, wrought iron table with two chairs near the middle of the front yard. Cheryl sat and Zeke followed her lead.

"How can I help you? Have you found anything out about Casey's killer?"

"Was Casey some kind of an activist?" Zeke parried the question.

"No, not really. We're all unhappy about the oil and the problems it causes. Spills. Clean up. Contamination. All that sort of stuff. But Casey wasn't a radical or anything."

"What about the Keystone oil pipeline?" asked Zeke. "That was underway when she was killed."

"Yeah, it was being built then. They built it in phases. She wasn't happy about it, but I don't think she got killed because of that. Most people around here were against it," said Cheryl.

"Do you know if Casey had any Indian blood in her?"

"She did. Our family is one-half Lakota. Well, she and I are. Were..." Cheryl teared up for a moment. Then she reached in her pocket and took out her cigarette pack. She shook out another cigarette and lit it.

"Would Casey have run with the same crowd as Jenny Lakota?" asked Zeke.

"Sort of. She was older than Jenny, so it wasn't at the same time. But like I said, Casey was a free spirit. She didn't much care about the rules. But she was a good girl."

"What do you mean, the rules?"

"Well, Mr. Traynor, from the time she was in middle school, she dated the older boys. Then when she graduated, older men. They were part of that group that went to Sturgis every year. She liked the leather and the bikes and the pot and the Williston White."

"She liked the meth?" asked Zeke.

"Yeah. I told her she needed to stop, but... Well, Casey didn't really listen to anybody."

"But she did have a boyfriend?" asked Zeke.

"When she was in high school, she dated a guy. He was really into the Indian thing, long black hair, leather vest, Indian jewelry, tattoos and symbols on his clothes. He even rode an Indian-brand motorcycle. But then he got killed."

"How long was this before Casey died?" asked Zeke.

Cheryl said, "It really hurts to talk about her like this."

"I know, Cheryl."

"So it was maybe four or five years before she died. It was a big deal. The guy's name was Franklin, Franklin Three-Bears, but everybody called him Tonto. He was about four years older than her. Somebody killed him. They think it was a rival gang."

"Whatever happened?" asked Zeke.

"They arrested someone for it. Two guys, actually. They kept Casey in jail under protection, since she was a witness to the killing. They kept moving her around from town to town, jail to jail, until the trial, which took most of a year."

"Who were the guys?" asked Zeke.

"Two low-life bikers and druggies, called themselves Junior and Flattop."

"Still in jail, I guess?"

"Yeah, they're in the State Pen in Bismarck. There was something about drugs and money, and then these two squirrels shot Tonto in a drive-by. Casey was with him when it happened," she said, distant now.

"You said Tonto was all about being an Indian. Was he an activist?" asked Zeke.

Cheryl Black fidgeted for a moment. Then she drew on the last of the cigarette and tossed it into a flowerbed.

"Not in a normal sense," said Cheryl. "But yeah, he was about Indian rights and stuff."

"Where did Casey get her drugs?" asked Zeke. "Her pot and her meth?"

"From her friends, I guess. She always seemed to have some extra. She sold a little bit, too."

"To whom?" asked Zeke.

"Mostly to people she knew, people she grew up with," said Cheryl.

"Mostly to Native Americans?" asked Zeke.

"Well, those were the people she knew from school and from around here."

"What about her boyfriends?" asked Zeke.

"Well, she had a type, I guess you could say. Most of her friends were local guys from the Res, Indians, like Tonto."

CHAPTER 18

It made him sick. Just sick.

All that oil money, all those jobs and nothing for the Lakotas. Nothing but the same scraps they'd been fed for generations.

He read about it in the papers almost every day. The media put a spin on everything, of course, making it seem reasonable and fair, while it was anything but that. His office phone buzzed, an internal call.

"You have a call on line one," said his secretary. "Can you take it?"

He thought for a moment, almost declined, then said, "Yeah, OK."

"Hello?" he held the handset to his ear.

"I read about you in the papers," the voice said. "Saw your picture, cutting a ribbon or something, right?"

"Yeah, that was me. So?" he said.

"So how's this thing with the money going down?"

"Not on this phone." He looked around his office as if there were a gaggle of reporters surrounding him. No one was there.

"OK, call me back later then."

He hung up and dialed a different number from memory.

"I'm coming by after work tonight," he said. "Will you be there?"

"Where else would I be?" asked the woman.

"And Otaktay?"

"Yes, he'll be here, too." She nodded into the phone.

"I need to use the burner phone," he said, looking around his office again.

"OK. Will you stay for dinner?" she asked.

"I don't know. Maybe. No, I'd better not. Another time."

* * *

At five twenty-two, exactly, Henry Wolsnoki turned the old knob and pushed the front door open. The little house was dark, with flashing light coming from the television in the living room. He walked to the open doorway and looked in. Otaktay was sitting on the floor watching a reality show about hoarders on the large flatscreen television.

He called to the boy, who looked up and nodded, and then looked back to the screen.

"Where's Gramm?" he asked.

The boy pointed toward the kitchen.

Henry continued through the small house and stepped into the kitchen. She was there, shelling what looked like northern corn. It was one of his favorites.

Henry gave her a quick hug. "How are you, Gramm?" he asked. Everyone called her Gramm.

She looked at him. "I'm tired," she said. "I'm tired of the killing."

He nodded. Then he said, "Do you have the phone?"

She reached into her apron and handed him the burner phone.

* * *

"I'm calling you back," said Henry Wolsnoki. He waited.

"Is this a safe line?"

"Yes. But still, be careful what you say," said Henry. He had stepped out the backdoor, away from the kitchen.

"So how's this thing with the money going down?" asked the man.

Henry thought for a moment, then chose his words carefully.

"It's on track. We'll be allocating funds at the next meeting. The governor's anxious to get this behind him before the next election. He wants to take credit for it."

"Of course he does," said the man. "Will we get our share?"

"Sure. Once the money's allocated, it's a matter of invoicing the state for your work, and you should have a check within two weeks."

"We're tired of waiting," said the man. "This took way longer than you told us it would. They're not happy."

Henry wiped his brow. "I know. We had to reset everything

and start over. The tribal chiefs were making a lot of noise. We had to give them some money to shut them up."

"Yeah. That's your problem, though."

"I know. But don't worry. Tell them the money will be there shortly," said Henry. "A couple of weeks."

"We'll be looking for interest on that, for the delay," said the man.

Henry was quiet.

"You don't want us to get too vocal about this." It was a statement, not a question.

* * *

"You work for the men who oppress us," said his mother, when he returned to the kitchen. "You work for the oil companies." She was still shelling the corn, but her expression was one of anger.

"I can do more from the inside," said Henry Wolsnoki. "I can help our people better if I have some say, some control."

"The oil killed my daughter, your wife," said the woman.

It was a discussion they'd had many times. His mother was a purest, a Lakota from the old school who had heard the lies of the white man and had no trust in their promises. Her son had been educated at the University of Minnesota, Morris. He'd gone there on a minority scholarship, and then had been hired into government work with the Tribal Leaders in New Town, rising quickly to a position that he still maintained.

"Well, tell me then. What are you doing from the inside?" she asked him.

* * *

"I'm flying back tomorrow," said Zeke. "I met with the Tribal Leader and talked with Cheryl Black again. There isn't much more I can do here until we come up with something tangible."

"Is the picture getting clearer?" asked Clive from the other end of the secure line. He sounded distracted.

"Bits and pieces," said Zeke. "And we'll want to talk about the Pawnshop deaths."

"Kimmy's been organizing," said Clive. "Researching, analyzing and organizing. She and Sally will suss it out, I'd say."

"None better… They'll figure it out alright. That reminds me. I owe Sally dinner when I get back."

"She has somewhere in mind?" asked Clive.

"She mentioned the Valor Brew Pub. Been there?"

"I've heard of it. It's probably too, uh, Colonial for me," said Clive, a bit tongue in cheek.

"What have we been doing on the Pawnshop deaths, then?"

"Yes, well, we're researching each of the seven victims…I'd prefer to call them victims," said Clive. "The data's not all in, yet, but we know something's amiss…"

"Sure," said Zeke.

"And we've looked at most of their bank accounts, business receipts, credit card slips, all of that."

Zeke was quiet.

"And each one had pretty much tripled his gross income since franchising with Pawn 4 All."

"Which implies a hefty net profit," said Zeke.

"It does, particularly since their operating expenses hadn't changed. Except for the franchise fee, of course."

"So the suicides don't make any sense."

"They never really do, do they?" said Clive. "But yes, I highly doubt they were suicides. Murder is the word that comes to mind."

* * *

Zeke entered Clive Greene's office and slid into a leather club chair.

"How was your flight?" asked Clive.

Sally was sitting beside him, with Kimmy one chair down.

"Uneventful. Boarded. Took off. Landed. And here I am," said Zeke. "Just like the other two and a half million people who flew domestically today."

"Yes, they seem to have it down to a science, don't they?"

"Did we find anything more on the deaths?" asked Zeke. "The pawnshop owners?"

"Yes, well, that's what we mean to ascertain," said Clive. "I've got the files set out in the conference room." Then, to Sally, "We could all use some Earl Gray, I'd think. Do you mind?"

"Oh, I'm going to dinner with Zeke this week. Of course I don't mind," she responded in her wispy voice.

Zeke smiled as Sally left the room.

Kimmy said, "Don't tell me, the Valor Brew Pub?"

Zeke nodded. "All American place." Then to Clive, "What have you seen so far?"

"Well, I've looked the files over quickly. But Sally and Kimmy have spent some more time with them. Between us all, we should be able to extract something. A pattern, a schedule, a modus operandi…something."

"Let's get to it, then," said Zeke.

* * *

Several hours later, Zeke, Kimmy, Sally and Clive were staring at grids on the whiteboard and rubbing their eyes.

"That was proper Devonshire tea," said Clive. "Time for a break then?" The Earl Gray teapot was empty, and the plate of scones had vanished.

"Before we do, let's just take a minute and summarize," said Zeke, focused on the files.

"OK," said Clive.

Kimmy nodded.

"We've got seven deaths. Several different methods. Men and women. Most in different cities. The only obvious connection is that all seven had a Pawn 4 All franchise," Zeke said. "Some married, some divorced or otherwise single. Most straight, one gay. Almost everyone on the list was between 40 and 70 years old, except the two that had inherited their pawnshops when their parent or parents died. They were in their mid-thirties. But you'd expect that for business owners."

"Right," said Clive, nodding and following the list as Zeke outlined it on the board.

"Locationally, they were all in the northeast, Baltimore on

up to New York. To be expected since that's where the Pawn 4 All business is primarily situated," Zeke continued. "In Morristown, New Jersey."

Nods from Clive and Sally.

"We don't have complete forensic accounting from the FBI, but it appears that these little pawnshops went from 'getting by' to 'gold mine' pretty quickly once they bought a franchise," said Zeke.

"Indeed," said Clive. "That was the money laundering, no doubt."

Zeke nodded. "So let's assume that seven deaths of owners in a year or less are too many to be a coincidence. We think it was murder, and we haven't seen anything to change that hypothesis. Let's assume that all seven of the pawnshops were laundering money. We'll confirm that with the FBI since they have the financial statements, but it's probably right."

Kimmy nodded.

"What comes to mind first?" asked Zeke.

"It's clear to me that someone was skimming," said Clive. "No doubt."

* * *

"Let's start by looking at the murders," said Clive. "We've got background on each of the victims." He was flipping through the seven FBI files.

"Let's arrange them chronologically and see how they track with Pawn 4 All's growth pattern."

"OK." Clive made a note.

"But to get to the bottom of this, we'll need some face time at the Pawn 4 All headquarters. Someone has to be pulling the strings, ordering the deaths and such," said Zeke. "One or more someones. If it's not the Pawn 4 All management, we need to eliminate them as suspects."

"How do you want to do it?" asked Clive.

"Let's approach them as pawnshop owners, looking for a possible franchise agreement. Something big enough to get us in front of the officers. We should be able to see what's happening better from there."

"Right," said Clive. "I'll ask Sally to fill out a franchise application and get it to them."

"Good," said Zeke. "But let's make this even more attractive to them. Let's go in as the owners of a small chain of pawnshops. The way they've been expanding, it should make them drool."

"Right. Good. They'll most likely still be looking for places to keep the money flowing."

Zeke nodded. "What do we know about the people in charge of Pawn 4 All?"

Clive picked up a folder and opened it. "Chester Knowles," said Clive, closing it and sliding the folder across the table to Zeke. "He's the CEO."

"How long has Pawn 4 All been franchising?" asked Zeke.

"Quite a while, but not all successfully. Evidently, they started in the 1990s. Struggled for the first few years, but it caught on during the last recession, it seems."

"What's the back story on Chester Knowles?" Zeke asked.

"He was pretty much a small time pawnshop owner before Pawn 4 All. Had a couple shops in Baltimore. He was charged with receiving stolen goods a couple of times, but the charges were dropped. Lack of proof. One time, there was a break in the chain of custody, you know, for the evidence against him," Clive said.

Zeke looked through the folder. There was a DMV photograph of a man wearing a white shirt and tie, with close cropped blond hair and a small moustache. His features were small, and his expression was intense.

"So we'll assume that somewhere in the early 2000s our Mr. Knowles connected with someone who had a lot of dirty money that they wanted cleaned, laundered," said Zeke.

"Indeed," said Clive. "Person or persons. For that kind of money you're probably talking about the drug trade, or maybe sports gambling. Certainly organized crime, I'd wager."

"That's a safe bet." Zeke smiled to himself.

* * *

"Kimmy's been coordinating with the FBI while you've been away," said Clive. He was seated in his library-like office, talking with Zeke and Kimmy. He was spooning sugar into a cup from the teacart next to his chair. "She's been in daily touch with FBI Agents Matthews and Robbins, setting it up and coordinating the operation."

Kimmy said, "It's set to go down soon, in the next few

weeks. As soon as Donovan has the details in order."

"How many locations?" asked Zeke.

"She'll end up with warrants for about one hundred," said Kimmy. "Pretty impressive."

"Are they ready? The FBI?" asked Zeke.

"We'll see," said Kimmy, standing up and stretching. "But it seems like they will be."

"What's our role?" asked Zeke.

"Same as Donovan said before," said Clive. "We're to assist and monitor their central coordination. But no hands on."

"How will they execute it?" asked Zeke, curious now.

"Like Donovan said, they'll be using local law enforcement to serve the warrants and search the premises. But instead of taking what they seize to their property room, it'll all be kept under the FBI's purview in the warehouses they've rented."

"Basically, one in each major city involved?" asked Zeke.

Kimmy nodded.

"What exactly are they looking for?" asked Zeke.

"The FBI? They're interested in the accounting. Computers, ledger books, printouts, client lists, bank statements, that sort of thing," said Kimmy. "As well as making arrests."

"Publicity?" asked Zeke.

"Sure. As much as they can get."

Clive added, "They'll tip off the press, I'm sure, and have them waiting at the station when they bring in the paddy wagons."

Zeke smiled at the reference. "Is Donovan on a witch hunt?"

Kimmy smiled and pulled her legs up into her chair. "She is."

"What more do we know about the money laundering?"

"That's interesting, Zeke," Kimmy continued. "I spent some time with the FBI guys. They say they see some patterns in the operations. Like the franchises are all processing the laundered money the same way. They'll know more after the take-down, but they seem to favor the idea that someone is orchestrating and coordinating the whole thing. Across all the shops."

Chapter 19

Francis Donovan sipped her coffee and looked around the room. "How can I help you, gentlemen?" she asked again.

They were sitting in Clive's office, a library-styled room with antique furniture and a large window overlooking Pennsylvania Avenue. It was raining lightly outside, a gray and silver day.

Donovan was flanked by three of her FBI agents who had joined Zeke and Clive in the meeting.

"The coordinated raid is just about ready to go, I expect," said Clive.

"As would be expected," said Donovan. "We're prepared to serve arrest warrants on most of the principals."

"The franchisees, yes," said Clive.

"We'll miss a few. But things happen. We'll sweep them up afterward."

Clive said, "Zeke noticed something that we thought you'd want us to look into."

"Yes? What's that?" Donovan asked.

"We've been working out the suicide, Bart Conrad's death just before we went to his shop. We wanted to share our thoughts with you in person," said Clive. "We may have found something."

Zeke nodded in agreement.

Donovan looked at Clive with a direct gaze, as if she were measuring him. "Do tell."

"Well, we wondered about several things about Pawn 4 All. Not so much from the perspective of the entire operation, as you have that under control," Clive continued. "But rather about the incident at Cassidy's Pawn."

"The pawnshop you visited during your earlier warrant service," said Donovan.

"Our thought," Clive continued, "is that a suicide taking place in that narrow time frame seems queer. That's why we contacted your team and asked them to review the files."

"Looking for what?" asked Donovan, still distant, cautious.

"For other peculiar deaths of proprietors of pawnshops, particularly Pawn 4 All stores."

Donovan sat still for a moment. "What did they find?" she asked.

* * *

"They found a pattern of deaths that is very suspicious," Zeke said.

"Pawnshop owner's deaths?" asked Donovan.

"Yes. There have been seven deaths of pawnshop proprietors

in the past year or so. The local cops labeled some suicide, some murder during a robbery, and one a 'murder for hire' by the owner's wife. But we think they're wrong," Zeke continued.

"Similarities?" asked Donovan.

"Yes. You wouldn't see them unless you set the files side by side. And Pawn 4 All covers a huge geography, about one hundred thirty locations over a large number of jurisdictions. So it was subtle, tough to find," Zeke continued.

Donovan nodded and waited.

"We thought something was wrong from the start. Why would Bert Conrad kill himself on the very day that we were serving his warrant? And why would he even do so at all? There didn't seem to be any family problems, and his business was profitable. That was partially due to the money laundry he was running, but it'd been going on successfully for months. He franchised with Pawn 4 All early last year," said Zeke.

"Did he have a wife? A family?" asked Donovan.

"Ex-wife, no children. But they'd been divorced for six years," said one of the FBI agents. "He lived in a condo downtown."

"Also," Zeke continued, "it looked like he shot himself with a suppressed gun. Why would you bother with that, if you were checking out anyway?"

"A silencer," Donovan said, nodding again.

"Plus, there was a very good chance that his mother would find him. That's just the opposite of what a suicide victim would want."

She nodded again, slowly.

"But we keep going back to the seven deaths. That's too high a percentage to be random," said Zeke.

"So what's your theory?" asked Donovan. She made a small note on her pad and waited.

"Not yet sure about the motivation," said Clive, "but it certainly looks like a pattern. We'd like to look into the connections between the victims."

"But we don't want to do anything to step on your investigation or to get in your way," said Zeke.

"Not a problem," said Donavan. "We'll keep going, making our case, getting the money laundering arrests, as planned. You see if you can find a link in those deaths."

* * *

"Well, your bona fides check out," said Jack Thurmond. "And you've got the experience. We'd certainly consider selling you a franchise."

He looked across the table at Clive and Zeke, who were casually dressed and eating the last of their lunches. Zeke looked back at him and nodded.

"We've been in this business for a while," Clive said.

The men were meeting at a trendy restaurant in Morristown, New Jersey, the headquarters location for the Pawn 4 All franchise business.

"We're interested in expanding into your territories, actually," Thurmond continued. "Through our franchises, of course." He'd finished his Caesar Salad and spoke as the other men finished burgers and drank light beer. He was smiling to himself.

"I think we'd do well with the organizational aspects of the franchise," said Clive. "Plus it would be nice to have the regional advertising. Especially television."

"Yes, we're able to leverage our size and advertising budget to fund a fairly aggressive outreach program," said Thurmond. "Eighteen percent of all of the franchise fees we collect go back into television advertising. Our franchisees are very happy about that."

Clive nodded wisely. "Yes, I can see why."

"Well, I'm sold," said Zeke, who'd identified himself as Darrel Ryder. He'd adopted a slight western accent and took to calling everyone, "Partner." He pronounced it, "Pardner."

"How did you two meet?" asked Thurmond. It was intended as a polite question, although the man had very few social skills. Numbers were his only friends.

"Well, that's an interesting story..." Zeke started.

"Maybe for another time," said Clive, looking at his watch. Thurmond knew him as Henry Chamberlain, a British transplant. "It's quite a long story, actually."

Thurmond said, "I took the liberty of bringing the franchise paperwork."

"Good, good," nodded Clive. "We'll have our attorney look it over, and we'll sign it and get it back to you. Along with the check." He took the manila envelope from Thurmond's outstretched hand. "Shouldn't take but a day or two. We'll have them Fedex it to you."

Thurmond was nodding, too. "Good. You'll find it's all pretty standard stuff.

"And this agreement will cover all seven of our locations? Norfolk, Chesapeake, Virginia Beach, Fayetteville, Jacksonville, Savannah and Charleston?"

"It does. But I have a question," said Thurmond.

"Sure, Pardner," said Zeke. He smiled.

"Why did you expand your business into all these secondary towns? Were you looking for failing pawnshops to buy?"

"Oh, no," said Clive. "Just the opposite. We're specialists in our demographic. Each of our shops is located in a town with a military component, a base or at least a presence. We find that customers in the military are the most profitable for our particular business model."

* * *

"But you said you guys have a resource that would fit well with our operation and could make us more profitable. I'd like to know more about that," said Zeke.

Thurmond always hesitated at this point in the negotiations. Even though 'Chamberlain' and 'Ryder' had been well vetted by his team, this was a critical step, a point of no return.

He said, awkwardly, "Sure. Yes. Well, in addition to franchising the pawnshops, you know, 'Pawn 4 All', in addition to that, we have some clients who are...well, let's say they're willing to pay to have their money cleaned."

Zeke and Clive exchanged a glance. It wasn't lost on Thurmond, who Zeke realized was holding his breath.

"Money laundering?" asked Zeke.

"In a sense," said Thurmond. "But it's limited to a very few clients. Our franchisees say it increases their average profits by 25%, all told."

"Yeah, we'd be up for that," said Zeke, nodding slowly.

"Is that what happened to that guy who committed suicide?" asked Clive. They'd discussed Conrad's death with Thurmond in the course of their negotiations for the franchise. It had made the evening news on two networks.

"No, nothing like that," said Thurmond, looking away.

"Well, give us the details," said Clive.

"After you sign," said Thurmond. "We'll talk about it after you sign the franchise papers."

* * *

"Everything looks like it's in order," said Jack Thurmond, scanning the signed agreement. "Let me get you gentlemen a copy." Thurmond called, "Marge?"

A middle-aged woman with brown hair and the beginnings of secretarial spread stepped into the room.

"Can I get a copy of this, Marge?"

She took the stack of papers and quickly disappeared.

"We didn't want our attorney to Fedex this, Pardner," said Zeke, acting as Darryl Ryder. "We're very interested in the, uh, other source of income you alluded to, so we thought we'd bring back the paperwork and perhaps have a chance to discuss it further…"

"Now, tell us, old man," said Clive, acting again as Henry Chamberlain, "about the money we'll be laundering."

Zeke smiled a sincere smile at Thurmond and maintained eye contact.

"Yes, well, it's a part of the business, you might say. We have a corporate client that needs some of their revenues 'washed', and they're willing to pay for it. So, you'll receive an extra hundred thousand a month, you'll work it into your bookkeeping, and you get to keep 25% of it," said Thurmond.

"How exactly does that work?" asked Zeke.

"Well, we'll get the hundred thousand from our client," said Thurmond, "And you'll launder it, build it into your receipts and such. Then, each month, we'll deposit it into your bank account at Union First Bank of New Jersey. You'll show most of it as paid out for invoices you'll receive and for merchandise you buy. But you're not really buying anything. The money that goes through the process comes out clean, you pay some bills and you get to keep 25% of what we deposit for you. Simple. We'll get into the details on your next visit here to our headquarters for the training."

"Will that be for all of our locations?" asked Clive.

"Eventually," said Thurmond. "We'd like to start with one, show you the process and then build on it over the next few months. It's a solid system."

"Sounds like it, Pardner," said Zeke.

"And, when you're ready to expand, we can arrange

favorable financing for you and Mr. Ryder, Mr. Chamberlain."

"Let me guess. First Union Bank of New Jersey," Clive said.

* * *

"How was Morristown?" Sally asked as Zeke entered her office.

"Easy. It's only an hour flight from D.C., and a short drive from Newark," said Zeke.

They were at dinner at the Valor Brew Pub. Zeke had chosen a seat against a sidewall where he could see the front and the back entrances.

"Sally, I need a favor," Zeke said.

"Of course you do," said Sally, sounding slightly ethereal. "I had that feeling..."

The restaurant was a long, narrow space with brick walls and a stamped concrete floor. It had a bar on one side and a long row of two-top tables on the other.

Sally had ordered the Flank Steak, and Zeke was working on a plate of avocado toast on grilled garlic bread.

Zeke said, "We're almost directly across the street from the Marine Barracks."

"We are?" asked Sally. "That makes me feel safe."

"It's the oldest post in the Marine Corps," said Zeke.

She nodded.

"What's the favor?" asked Sally.

"I need you to check on the former Sheriff of Monroe County with your law enforcement friends. A guy named Billy Forester, down in the Keys. Something doesn't add up. He was involved in a gang of locals, back when my folks died," said Zeke. "When they were killed. I don't know if there's a connection. But I'd like to find out more about that."

Sally took a bite of her chicken and closed her eyes, enjoying the taste as she chewed. Then she said, "You want me to check with some of my FBI sources?"

"Some of yours and some of Clive's, I think," said Zeke. "Whatever it takes. This was thirty years ago, so I can't imagine it's still classified..."

* * *

The next day, Zeke stopped by Sally's workspace.

"How're you doing with the Keys research?" he asked.

"I've been burning the midnight oil," Sally said. She was dressed in a hunter green turtleneck sweater that accentuated her shape and contrasted nicely with her green eyes. "We need to go back to Valor."

"The food was good," Zeke agreed. "I enjoyed that. What do you have on Billy Forester?"

Sally swiveled, picked up a thick file from her desk, swiveled back and handed it to Zeke.

"In addition to the normal background check, I did some digging." Her voice sounded wispy again. "I called a friend at the FBI and found that Billy Forester was under investigation for something back then."

"Back then?" asked Zeke.

"In the late 1980s. An FBI informant told them that Forester was involved in the cocaine trafficking that was going on in the Keys. Said he was head of the group responsible for getting the dope into the country, mostly by fishing boat."

"If that's true, there would have been a link between Forester and someone in South America, maybe Colombia," said Zeke.

Sally nodded. "It's possible the fishermen you told me about, down in Florida, were all involved."

"Either that, or they were just following gang orders, doing their assignment and unaware of the bigger connections," she said.

"That would be safer for Forester," said Zeke.

CHAPTER 20

"So you're here in the Keys for the weekend?" asked Zeke.

"The government calls it 'flex time'. But I'm combining it with Veterans' Day and...yep, I'm here for a long weekend," said Tracy. "Wouldn't want you to forget about me..."

"Not much chance of that," said Zeke, feigning seriousness.

They were sitting on the outside veranda of Zeke's rental cottage in Marathon, watching the sun reflect off the bright blue water. An obscure Jimmy Buffett song was playing in the living room behind them.

"You're getting this swimsuit thing down pretty well," said Zeke. "Looks nice." Tracy was wearing a red two-piece bikini, visible under a thin white cover-up. She was barefoot, with her feet pulled up into the oversized beach chair. Her nails were painted the same shade of red as her bikini.

"Mmm," she said. She closed her eyes for a moment and took a deep breath of the warm salt air. The only sounds were the lapping ocean and occasionally the hoarse, croaking call of an excited egret. "I could live here."

Zeke sat in a matching chair. He wore Billabong board shorts and Rainbow flip-flops.

After a pause, he said, "I think we're getting closer to the truth."

"About your parents' deaths?"

"Yes. The fisherman named some names and I've been running down their whereabouts. Some of them are dead or disabled, but a couple are still around. Old, but still around."

"What's your plan?" asked Tracy. Her dark eyes were wide and brilliant and listening attentively.

"I plan to spend every possible moment with you," said Zeke. "Enjoying all of this goodness."

Tracy smiled. "That suits me just fine," she purred.

"We'd better go inside, though," said Zeke. "You don't want to burn."

Tracy adjusted her legs in the chair and closed her eyes. "OK. In a minute," she said.

* * *

"Sometimes you make sounds like an egret," said Zeke.

Tracy said, "What?"

They were naked, lying under a ceiling fan and across the four-poster bed, covered only with a light sheet. Sunlight invaded the small bedroom.

"Nothing," said Zeke. "That was an excellent idea."

"I think it was your idea, originally," said Tracy.

Zeke looked at her.

"No, it was a collaboration," she said thoughtfully. "And a successful one."

Zeke kissed her gently on the lips.

"Don't start anything, now..." she said. He kissed her again, gently.

"That's not fair," she whispered. And then she kissed him back.

* * *

"'Skinny' Gonzalez. Jerry Cabot. Billy Forester. Captain Brown. I think they're all septuagenarians," said Zeke.

"Sounds like the over-the-hill gang," said Tracy.

"Really. But apparently they were bad-ass thirty or forty years ago. Caused all kinds of trouble up and down the Keys back then. Trying to keep it for themselves," said Zeke.

"But wouldn't they have prospered from the tourism?" asked Tracy.

"They were obsessive. Too territorial. And parochial. They missed the bigger picture. Just wanted it to stay like it was, or something like that."

"What are we going to do? Track down a handful of senior citizens and hold them accountable?" asked Tracy.

Zeke looked at her. "I think that's exactly what we're going to do."

Tracy thought about it for a minute. Then she said, "OK, I'm in. Where do we start?"

* * *

"This guy, Brown, the way Parks described him, may be the weakest link of the group," said Zeke.

"What did he say?" asked Tracy. They were driving Zeke's BMW north on US Highway 1, heading toward Key Largo. It was a spectacular day.

"Said Brown was 'sorta half in and half out,' and that he wasn't as committed as the rest. Sounded like he's sort of independent."

"Why do you think he'd be the weakest link?" Tracy asked.

"Partly elimination. Billy Forester, the former sheriff, I imagine he's got a lot of confidence and a lot of connections, still. So he'll be tougher to rattle."

"I can see that," she said.

"And one old guy, Jerry Cabot, is in a nursing home in Miami. Has some sort of dementia, according to Parks," said Zeke.

"OK, and?" Tracy asked.

"There's a guy living on Little Torch Key by the name of Skinny Gonzalez. They say he has a pile of money now. So he may have a lot to lose…"

Tracy nodded.

"We'll leave Skinny Gonzalez for later. But one guy's in Key Largo, living with his daughter. Sounds like he would be the one to talk with first. And the daughter could be leverage." Zeke was thinking aloud now.

Zack Brown's "Knee Deep" was streaming from the BMW's speakers, belying the seriousness of Zeke's plan. Tracy sang along quietly.

"What's his full name?" asked Tracy.

"Captain Brown," said Zeke.

"Is that a rank?" asked Tracy, momentarily confused.

"Nope. His parents named him 'Captain'. Don't have a clue why," said Zeke. "Parks said he's old school. His family's been here for a couple generations."

"How'd you get his address?" asked Tracy.

"I called my new friend Susie Franklin at the Monroe County Sheriff's office. She was happy to help."

Tracy nodded to herself in rhythm to the beat and said, "This is as intense as I've seen you. Are you sure you're OK?"

* * *

"You're the guy who broke in on Owen Parks and his boy, aren't ya?" said the man. "He called me and said you'd probably be by. Didn't expect you so soon, though."

He was a short, stout man with muscular forearms and small, round ears that stood out perpendicular to his head. He was bald with a few wisps of white hair around his ears.

Zeke gave him a smile. "If you're Captain Brown, then yep, I'm that guy."

Brown turned stiffly and looked toward the small house. Then he looked back at Zeke.

"I don't think I can help you, though," he continued. He looked at Tracy.

"Is this the girl who was with you when you did it?" he asked.

"No, actually that was a different girl. She was muscle."

Brown looked at Zeke, then he nodded.

"Parks is an ass," he said. "Small-minded. Doesn't want change. Won't spend any money. Always griping about something."

Zeke nodded. "There was an explosion near here. Thirty years ago. My parents were killed in it. I want to know who was responsible." Short, declarative sentences sometimes worked best.

Captain Brown shook his head.

"Down in Marathon. A motorsailer named the *West Wind* went up in flames. I'm sure you heard about it," Zeke continued.

Something flashed behind the older man's eyes, a hint of recognition. He said, "That was a long time ago."

"Yes, it was," said Zeke.

The house was a modest one-story, elevated on pylons and fronting on a secondary street. It had a shell driveway and a barrel tile roof and jalousie windows. It looked like it was from a different era.

A woman who may have been about fifty came out down the front steps and stood next to Captain Brown. "Everything OK?"

Brown said, "This here's Zeke Traynor. The girl is muscle. He's here about an explosion that happened when you were twenty or so."

The woman's face tightened like a fist for a moment, and she said, "An explosion?"

"In Marathon. It was aboard a boat. My parents were

killed," said Zeke.

"This here's Stella," said Captain Brown, indifferently. "My daughter."

"Hi, Stella," said Tracy. She introduced herself. Then she said, "But I'm not the muscle. That's a case of mistaken identity."

Stella looked confused, but rallied and said to Captain Brown, "Can I have a cigarette?"

He took what remained of a soft pack from his front pants pocket and gave it to her. She liberated one and deftly lit it with a disposable lighter.

Captain Brown took the pack back and slid it back into his pocket. "I don't really know much about that. Just what I read in the paper, and what folks were saying."

Zeke said, "What were folks saying?"

"Just that it was a horrible accident. A fuel line problem or something. And it left their boy an orphan with no family." Brown stopped. "Wait, that was you..."

"Who was behind it?" asked Zeke.

Brown looked away. Then he rubbed his nose absently. "Don't rightly know anything about that," he said.

"Was Skinny Gonzalez involved?" asked Zeke.

Captain Brown looked up sharply.

"Snyder?" asked Zeke.

Brown looked anxious. "He's dead."

"What about Jerry Cabot?" asked Zeke.

Brown started shaking his head. "I don't know anything for sure. But I know those boys had some crazy ideas back then. Wanted to keep the tourists out of the Keys. They tried to warn people off."

"But you didn't agree with that plan?" asked Zeke, friendlier now.

"Well, I wasn't what you'd call 'all in' with their ideas. They included me some, but part of that was because of my dad. He was pretty political in Monroe County. Was a Commissioner a few times. Ran for Mayor once, like that."

"You said 'Those boys'. Who were you talking about?"

"Oh, well, Parks and Crabby. Real name's Jerry. Jerry's in a nursing home I think. Up in Miami. He's been there since he had that stroke a few years ago."

"OK, who else?"

"Well, you mentioned Skinny. And Snyder."

"I did," said Zeke. "And?"

Captain Brown stood mute, looking at the ground.

"If your dad was in local politics, he probably knew the sheriff. That's an elected position down here, right?"

Brown nodded his head slightly, probably in answer to the second question.

Zeke said, "Owen Parks said Billy Forester was involved with your group, too."

Brown looked up quickly.

"Parks said Billy pretty much ran the group back then," said Zeke.

Captain Brown looked stunned. He looked at Tracy, a blank expression on his face. Then he started shaking his head. "No, no, that's not right… But I don't remember things so well now," he said.

* * *

In the car, Zeke asked Tracy for her input.

"I don't know, really," she said. "He was faking the memory loss, I'm sure," she said.

"He was. His responses were lucid and on point until that last part about Billy Forester. Then he pretended to switch it off."

Zeke's smartphone rang, and he answered it.

"Hello, Sally," he said. "What's up?"

"I may have found a connection, Zeke," she said. "I think I know why your folks were killed."

CHAPTER 21

Zeke and Tracy drove south after their meeting with Captain Brown, following the road to Little Torch Key in the Lower Keys. They stopped at a famous oceanside restaurant for a fish sandwich and a beer each before continuing over the Seven Mile Bridge.

"The island's named after the Sea Torchwood trees that grew here," said Zeke as they turned right off the Overseas Highway onto the land spit. "They've been mostly cleared out for houses and mobile homes, though."

Tracy said, "This place is like a different world."

Zeke nodded and drove along a secondary road paved with sand and crushed shells. They passed mobile home after mobile home, propped up on blocks in yards that held old vehicles, small sun-faded fishing boats and miscellaneous yard furnishings, chairs and tables and lounges, most piled in a corner of the yard.

"This is certainly a working class neighborhood," said Tracy.

Toward the north end of the island, Zeke followed the road as it curled to the right and emptied in front of an oceanfront estate. The yard was contained by a black wrought iron fence and a matching double gate, which prevented access to the paver stone driveway and immaculately landscaped front yard.

The house was palatial, an impressive two-story affair on stilts with a green and beige front and copper appointments over the entry and the dormers. Through the first floor stilts they could see an unobstructed view of the Florida Bay, just yards from the back door. An Italian-style marble staircase curled up a story from the front of the house to the grand front door.

"Nice digs," said Zeke.

"They certainly are," said Tracy. "Is this the place?"

"According to Susie it is," said Zeke.

There was a security alarm decal on a post outside the gate, and a call box with a button and speaker at typical drivers-window height. Zeke pushed the button and waited.

Two minutes later the speaker cackled and a tinny voice said, "Yes?" Zeke couldn't tell whether it was male or female.

"It's Zeke Traynor," he said. "I called for an appointment."

"Sure, come on in," said the voice. "Park out front and come up the front stairs."

* * *

It turned out that the voice belonged to a tall, lithe, tanned girl who appeared to be in her late twenties or early thirties.

She pulled the heavy mahogany door open and smiled at the visitors.

"Hello," she said. "I'm Cassy Gonzalez." She seemed straightforward and innocent. Her accent was subtle.

Zeke introduced himself and Tracy, and they stepped into a foyer with a light marble floor and a wall of windows looking east at the water.

"Wow," said Tracy.

They were ushered into a sitting room at the back of the house that shared the same ocean view. They sat in overstuffed leather chairs facing the windows.

Cassy Gonzalez said, "You called to talk with my grandfather. About the Keys, you said, thirty years ago? I'm afraid I wasn't born then." She smiled. "But he's here. I'll get him."

Zeke said, "Thank you, Cassy."

A few moments later, she returned, wheeling an elderly man into the room. His wheelchair was silent with thick, oversized tires, like a beach bike. He had a plaid blanket covering his lap.

"This is Grandpa," she said simply.

Skinny Gonzalez was small and very thin, and he looked like he was dying. His skin was pale and drawn, and his face tight as if he were in chronic pain.

"Who are you?" he said. His voice was a whisper. He had a pronounced Spanish accent.

"We're Federal agents," said Zeke, exaggerating slightly. "Investigating the boat explosion that killed two people thirty years ago in Marathon."

Skinny Gonzalez looked at him, but he didn't say anything.

His lips pulled back over his teeth in a permanent grimace.

"I'm sure Owen Parks called and talked with you, so you're up to speed on what we're doing," Zeke continued.

"Are you going to pull a gun on me, too?" Gonzalez asked. "Threaten to kill an old man?"

"Do we need to?" asked Zeke.

Gonzalez took a deep breath. "Look, my granddaughter is too trusting. She shouldn't have let you in here."

"I think you wanted us to come in so you can figure out what we know and what evidence we have," said Zeke. "I think you're that clever."

"Parks said your parents were killed in that explosion," said Gonzalez. "That true?" He wasn't belligerent, but he was suddenly more aggressive.

Zeke nodded. He noticed that Tracy had opened the clasp on her purse for better access to her weapon.

"Well, I don't know anything about how that all went down," said Gonzalez. "I heard about it. But I was building lobster traps that day. I wasn't anywhere near Marathon."

"That's probably true," said Zeke. "But I think you and your friends planned the attack, and then Owen Parks and his boy carried out the plan."

"I think you're crazy," said Gonzalez. "Why would we do something like that?"

"The FBI says there was an ongoing investigation of Billy Forester back then. They think he was running drugs, cocaine. A lot of conchs got into that in the late 1980s. Those records show that the FBI had a couple of witnesses. A married couple."

"Your parents?" asked Cassy Gonzalez. "You're saying they were the witnesses?"

* * *

"Have you heard of the Medellin Cartel?" asked Zeke when he and Tracy were alone. They were driving back to their cottage.

"Vaguely," said Tracy. "I think that name was brought up in my Secret Service training. Why?"

"Pablo Escobar was one of the leaders. The cartel's business, their purpose was to bring cocaine into the United States."

"Were they successful?"

"Wildly successful," said Zeke. "At one point, there was more cocaine coming in to the States than there was coffee. Escobar was nicknamed the 'King of Cocaine' and had a net worth of about $30 billion. He was the wealthiest criminal in history."

"Whoa," said Tracy, looking at Zeke.

"Yeah," said Zeke. "It was a huge machine. They were shipping almost 80 tons of cocaine to the United States monthly."

Tracy opened her mouth, then shut it again.

"And they killed anyone who got in their way."

"What happened to Señor Pablo?"

"He was in charge of the Cartel until he was gunned down by the Colombian National Police in 1993," said Zeke. "But he was near the height of his power in 1989, when my folks died."

"That's huge," she said.

"It was incredible. He used a scorched earth approach.

Basically, if you were with him, you could get rich. If you were against him, you were as good as dead. 'Silver or Lead,' he used to say. Those were the options."

"And you think Billy Forester was working for this Escobar," said Tracy.

"There's a chance. And by extension it's possible that this entire 'gang of conchs' were working for Pablo. The Keys were a major entry point for drugs back then."

"Makes sense. Your folks might have seen something and reported it. They could have been witnesses," she continued.

Zeke nodded. "Sally confirmed it with the FBI. My folks were the witnesses for the Feds. And someone went after them."

* * *

"Sally, how've you been?" asked Zeke, over the secured phone line.

"I've been naughty," said the blonde researcher. "Since you asked."

"Of course you have," said Zeke. "I know you've checked with the FBI, but can we also run a credit check on Billy Forester? Former sheriff of Monroe County?"

Using the Agency's vernacular, a credit check included a search of criminal records, military records, financial statements, employment history and much more, including an actual credit check.

"Sure can. That would be 'William Forester'. He must be a key player."

"I believe that may be so," said Zeke. "He presently lives in Marathon." He gave her the address.

"Will do. I'll let you know when it's ready."

"Thanks, Sally," said Zeke.

* * *

"I wondered when you'd get to me," said Billy Forester.

"I'm sure you've been tracking our progress. Owen Parks. Captain Brown. Skinny Gonzalez. Our trajectory was toward you the whole time," said Zeke.

Forester was about six feet tall and looked to be in his sixties. His gray hair was cut short, close to his head in what looked like a quasi-military fashion, and his bearing was erect. Overall, he looked like a retired bird colonel.

Zeke was standing on Forester's dock, while Forester was working on his fishing boat. Zeke had found the former Sheriff doing something to one of the vessel's two fighting chairs.

Forester looked at Zeke and shrugged. "You're digging around in something that happened thirty years ago. There's no physical evidence of any crime. And I don't think you have any witnesses. At least none that would testify…"

"Why do you say that?" asked Zeke.

"Look, I was sorry to hear about your folks. Sincerely. But there's nothing to be done about it now."

"Is this your place?" asked Zeke, looking behind him at the waterfront mansion that dominated the double lot.

"It is. I made some good investments along the way. I was in public service for thirty-five years. And the county has a pretty good retirement system."

"You were a part of the gang that killed my parents," said Zeke.

"How old were you when they died?"

"I was eight," said Zeke.

"Like I said, I was sorry to hear about that. But I can't help you."

* * *

"So how does the story sound to you, so far?" asked Zeke.

Tracy thought about it for a moment.

"Well, like the puzzle is missing some pieces," she said.

"I agree," said Zeke. They were sitting in the living room of the Marathon cottage, looking at the water and talking. Zeke had just returned from his visit with Billy Forester.

"There seem to be a number of things that don't fit quite right," he continued.

"Like, why would you try to terrorize tourists to keep them away?" said Tracy. "Who would think a bomb would do that? Even a dud?"

Zeke was nodding. "And why was the *West Wind* targeted?" asked Zeke. "This wasn't random. Owen Parks let that out. He finally implied to me that Billy Forester chose the target."

"But he didn't say why?" asked Tracy.

"I doubt that he knew why," said Zeke. "He kept referring to the conch gang in military terms. 'I was just following orders,' 'I was a soldier,' things like that. Could be the soldiers didn't know the strategy behind the plan."

Tracy said, "But you do. It was the FBI connection."

* * *

"The word that keeps coming to my mind is 'frisky'," said Zeke. "You're still frisky."

"I thought you needed a distraction," said Tracy. She was sitting on the small couch next to Zeke, wearing one of his long sleeve shirts and nothing else.

"Well, you certainly had my full attention. And I'm growing fonder and fonder of that tattoo."

Tracy said, "It's in a great spot. Makes me shiver when you kiss it."

She had a small tattoo on her neck, just below her ear.

"I know," said Zeke.

Tracy stretched, content.

Zeke said, "I'll pour us some wine, and we can watch the sunset."

"Over the ocean. Nice," she said.

* * *

"Most people react to situations in a similar way," said Zeke, after they'd arranged their chairs on the cottage deck. "It's based on both their experiences, and on their observations. We all watch how other people react to something, and we often mimic it. Particularly if it's someone we respect."

"Sure," said Tracy.

"So as I interviewed the remaining members of the Conch Gang…"

"Is that what we're calling them?" asked Tracy. "I was thinking something like 'The Cocoon Boys'."

Zeke smiled. "Whatever you like," he said. "But there wasn't a lot of consistency in their responses. It was like they were isolated from each other. Given different information. Everybody had a little bit different view of what was going on.

"Hmm," she said.

"Parks knew about the mechanics of the operation, but I doubt that he knew the real motivation. He didn't have a leadership perspective," said Zeke.

"You said he was more like a soldier," said Tracy. "Taking orders."

"Yes, he was, I'm sure. It probably scared the hell out of him when the bomb went off."

"And the others?" she asked.

"Well, I doubt that Captain Brown was involved in their murders. He didn't know that they were FBI witnesses, and both Parks and Gonzalez said he was on the periphery of the organization. Not someone in whom you'd confide all your secrets. Particularly your illegal secrets," said Zeke.

"So he was probably low level in the organization?" asked Tracy.

"They probably kept him in because of his father's connections. And maybe even as leverage on his father, if they ever needed it," said Zeke.

"It seems to be taking shape," said Tracy.

"But Billy Forester was in a leadership role. He probably had the most to lose. And he was in a position to run the operation."

"As sheriff? You mean he could have coordinated the operation to keep the tourists and the mainland fishermen out of the Keys?" asked Tracy.

"Sure. Plus, his digs right now are way above 'public servant' level. His boat alone has got to be worth $700,000."

* * *

"So, are you heading back to the northeast soon?" asked Tracy. "I hate to leave, but my flight out is tomorrow afternoon."

"It's a quick flight to Atlanta," said Zeke. "You can visit every weekend, if you'd like."

"I can," she said. The sun was glimmering, looking as if it were settling slowly into the blue ocean. "That would be nice."

"To answer, yes, I'll be heading back to Morristown, New Jersey next week. We've got something going with the FBI on a money laundry operation," said Zeke.

"Is Morristown anything like this?" Tracy asked.

Zeke looked around. Then he looked at Tracy and shook his head. "No, it's not. It's a whole other world."

* * *

"We can't have this coming back on us," Julia Conners said. "There's too much at stake. That's why we pay so well. For distance."

The two men stood across from her, looking down at her desk. They were relaxed and unshaken.

"Why don't you let us do our job, and you do yours?" said the body builder. They were in Conners' office at Pawns 4 All headquarters. They had completed their last assignment and were reporting in.

The second man, more disheveled in appearance, said to his partner, "I think she's micro-managing." Then to Julia he said, "Didn't they teach you about that in Business School? Micro-managing? It's a bad thing."

Julia Conners looked from one man to the other. They were a true contrast, the shorter man immaculate in his appearance from his suit to his shoes to his coiffed hair to his designer glasses. He was fit and athletic looking. The slightly taller man was disorganized and disheveled. *The odd couple,* she thought.

She ignored the comment. "Mr. Kirby brought you in for a reason. I suggest we focus on the next part of the program."

"OK with me," said the second man. The bodybuilder nodded.

"We caught another one skimming," she continued.

"Checks and balances," said the slightly taller man. "You need checks and balances. You can't afford to wait until the audit to discover this sort of thing."

"Working on that," said Conners. "But in the meantime, this one's got to go."

She recited a name and an address from memory. The bodybuilder nodded again. He asked, "When?"

"As soon as you can, Harry," said Conners. "As soon as is

reasonable. We need to demonstrate that we're taking action."

"Demonstrate to whom?" asked the slightly taller man.

"To your boss, Wilbur," she said.

* * *

Jack Thurmond stepped out of his office onto the plush hallway carpeting and walked to the waiting area. He was frowning a bit, possibly with the news of their Baltimore franchisee's death.

Clive and Zeke stood as he approached. Clive extended his hand and Jack shook it.

"Glad you could make it, Mr. Chamberlain," said Thurmond to Clive. "I want you to meet our staff and our leadership."

"Nice office space, Pardner," said Zeke, louder than he needed to and glancing around the open area. Floor to ceiling windows looked out over Morristown Green.

"Thank you, Mr. Ryder," said Thurmond, still distracted. "We've reserved a conference room. This way, please." He started walking toward an interior hallway.

"I noticed that this is the Union First Bank of New Jersey building. Has Pawn 4 All been associated with the bank for long?" asked Zeke.

"We have," said Thurmond, over his shoulder. "They funded our start-up. Then, a few years ago, they funded our expansion plans... We have a very good relationship with the bank."

Zeke agreed. He'd reviewed their financial statements for the past four years. During that time their gross revenues had increased exponentially.

The men entered the large conference room and took seats around the table. There were a dozen empty chairs, and they clustered their seating around one end of the table. Thurmond sat on the end, with Clive and Zeke next to him.

"I'm having water and coffee brought in," said Thurmond. "And tea for you, Mr. Chamberlain."

"Well, thank you," said Clive.

"Today, we'd like to get you oriented with our processes," said Thurmond, "and give you the assistance you'll need to transition your operations to Pawn 4 All franchises."

"That's good, Pardner," said Zeke. "And we're looking forward to meeting Mr. Kirby and the others."

* * *

After a few hours of procedural meetings with middle managers in the Pawn 4 All headquarters, Zeke and Clive were led back to the waiting area. The receptionist, a blonde twenty-something with smooth skin, said, "I'll let Mr. Thurmond know that you're back. Please have a seat." She dialed a number.

Zeke and Clive sat again, waiting for Jack Thurmond. There seemed to be a lot of activity in the office, people coming and going, stopping by the receptionist's desk, picking up files and escorting apparent visitors back and forth.

A nearby office door opened and a woman walked out. She looked to be in her forties, with brown hair tied in a complex bun and wearing a red business suit with a mid-thigh matching skirt. Her makeup was subtle, expertly applied, and she had a golden tan.

"...all the involvement we can afford right now," she said, finishing her sentence as she walked by Clive and Zeke. Two men followed her from the office. The first was obviously a bodybuilder, a short man with biceps that pushed against the fabric of his dress shirt, and a weightlifter's tight buttocks under his suit pants. Zeke noticed that he walked on the balls of his feet. It looked awkward.

"We've got to take care of this, though," he said, shaking his head as he followed her.

The second man was single-file behind the body builder. He was average height and slightly pudgy around the middle. His brown suit was a sloppy fit, and his green shirt contrasted poorly with it. As he passed in front of Zeke and Clive, he looked at each of them with a cold, blank stare. His expression was one of boredom and disinterest.

When they had gone, Zeke stood and stretched and walked to the door of the office they had exited. The name on the door read, "Julia Conners, Vice President- Risk Management."

A few minutes later, Thurmond came out of his office.

"Good timing," he said. "I want to get you in to meet our President, Mr. Kirby."

* * *

"Great to meet you," said Kirby, and he shook Clive's hand heartily. "My pleasure."

Zeke and Clive had been ushered into Kirby's office by Thurmond, and after the introductions, they took the available chairs across from Kirby's desk.

"Well, I'll share with you that we're very pleased to have you two as franchisees," he said jovially. "Glad to have you in the Pawn 4 All family!"

Chester Kirby looked like a miniature person, maybe three-quarter size. He wore a thousand dollar suit and a three hundred dollar haircut. Zeke noticed that he smelled of Pour un Homme by Caron.

"We're glad to be here, Pardner," Zeke said, as Clive nodded, showing a smile.

"What do you think of the operation?" Knowles asked.

"Well, Jack has been taking good care of us," said Clive. "We've met a lot of your staff, and we're impressed."

"Thank you, Mr. Chamberlain," said Knowles, smiling. "Did you have any questions so far?"

"Well, no, the operational part of it seems pretty solid," said Zeke. "But we'd like to know more about how the, eh, money thing works."

"Mr. Ryder, that's a great question," said Knowles, almost patronizing. "I'm sure Jack has given you the 30,000 foot overview."

Thurmond nodded.

"The specifics, the details, will be covered later this afternoon. You'll meet our VP of Risk Management, Julia Conners. She runs that part of the operation."

"We're heading there next," said Thurmond.

CHAPTER 22

The door to Julia Conners' office was slightly ajar, and Zeke heard her talking on the phone as they approached. Jack Thurmond stuck his head in the door and mouthed something to Julia, probably, "We're here," and stepped back out into the hallway.

"She's wrapping up a phone call," Thurmond said apologetically. "Just be a minute."

"I must say, your operation is pretty impressive," said Clive. "From your processes to the support staff, even to your training. It's blinding."

Thurmond looked confused.

"He means it's excellent, Pardner," said Zeke by way of interpretation. "Very impressive."

Thurmond's face cleared. "Well, we've been at it for a while."

In character, Zeke put his hand on Thurmond's shoulder and squeezed. Thurmond visibly drew back from his touch.

Julia Conners called out, "Come in, Jack."

The three men entered the large office and stood together in front of Julia Conners' desk. Thurmond introduced Ryder and Chamberlain, and they shook hands with the woman. She had a dazzling smile, and her jewelry matched her red jacket and skirt. Her handshake was firm, exuding confidence.

"This office is in charge of risk management," said Julia, still smiling. "We assure that the company avoids potential problems."

She has a crisp, sharp voice, no nonsense, thought Zeke. Her manner was self-assured, even a little condescending, but in a rather kind way.

"What type of problems have you seen, Miss Conners?" asked Clive.

"We handle most anything that threatens our franchisees," she said. "It might be media, or legislative. We've had problems with security and the police. One operator was being harassed by neighboring businesses. Essentially, anything that disrupts operations."

"Interesting. Just how do you handle things like that?" asked Zeke.

Conners looked at Zeke and smiled. "It seems like every individual problem has a unique solution," she said. "We have in-house attorneys and lawyers on retainer, of course. And public relations people to handle the media. Our Security personnel are some of the best anywhere, and they've been trained to work with local law enforcement." She paused. "But my job is to get out in front of it, to prevent the threats from even happening. Keep things working smoothly."

Thurmond nodded. "And Julia's done an excellent job with that," he said.

* * *

Harry and Wilbur were dressed casually, wearing jeans and windbreakers; Wilbur had on a Baltimore Orioles ball cap and Harry a knit watch cap. They pulled the door and entered the pawnshop from Fayette Street.

"After you," said Harry.

There was one other customer in the shop, apparently negotiating with the clerk about something. The two men wandered around the shop while looking at displayed jewelry and firearms. They walked slowly, from case to case, inspecting the merchandise.

"Be with you in a minute," the clerk said in a loud voice. Harry waved at him. "No problem."

A few minutes later the customer left.

"How can I help you, gentlemen?" asked the clerk. He was a rangy guy with long arms and a barrel chest, standing behind a display case counter. He was wearing a .38 Special in a holster on his belt.

"We're looking for Bryce Carroll," said Wilbur. "He's expecting us." His smile never made it to his eyes.

"Bryce was here, but I think I heard him go out for a minute," said the man, looking over his shoulder toward the back of the shop. "Hey, Bryce. You there?" he shouted.

There was no answer.

Turning back to the two men, the clerk said, "Yeah, he must've gone out the back. He parks back there. I'm sure he'll be here in a few…"

"That's fine," said Henry, bouncing on the balls of his feet. We'll wait for him."

"OK with me," said the clerk.

* * *

The dashboard clock read 2:40 as Zeke pulled the rental car up to the Pawn 4 All pawnshop and parked in the lot. There was one other car in the lot, a silver Aston Martin Rapide S that could only belong to one man. Clive stepped out of the passenger side as Zeke opened his door.

Yellow crime scene tape was pulled across the front door of the shop, and an official-looking notice was attached to the door with gray duct tape. The notice explained the penalties associated with disturbing a crime scene.

"You know, Baltimore feels like a pawnshop city," said Clive, looking around. "Something about the downtown area."

"You have access, I assume," said Zeke.

Clive nodded and held up a key. He unlocked the front door and they stepped inside, careful to pull the door closed and bolt it behind them.

"Where did it happen?" asked Zeke.

"In the office, in the back," said Clive.

"Was there surveillance in the building?" asked Zeke.

"Yes, but mostly in the front, the customer area."

"Have you seen it?" Zeke asked.

"Yes," said Clive. "There wasn't much there."

"Was there any traffic just before he died?" asked Zeke.

"Well, yes, it looked like two men entered the shop," said Clive. "They looked around at the display cases for a while. They spoke to the sales clerk for a moment, then one of them asked him a question, while the other one went to the back of the shop for about fifteen seconds."

"Providing secondary access?" asked Zeke.

"Unlocking the back door, I'd guess," said Clive.

"Can we identify them from the video?" asked Zeke.

"No, not really. They were wearing hats, one was a ball cap, and they kept their heads down, as if they were looking for something in the cases."

"But...?" Zeke asked.

"That's the thing. Most people go to a pawnshop to sell something or to acquire something specific. A guitar, maybe, or a piece of electronic equipment," said Clive. "In this case, these two wandered around the store and looked at most everything."

"You think they were checking for security? Or to be sure the place was fairly empty?" asked Zeke.

"Maybe both. It wasn't a quiet death, I assure you. There aren't silencers for shotguns," said Clive.

* * *

"Actually, there are, now. The Salvo 12 was developed by a Utah firm. It pretty much mutes the sound of a shotgun."

"Sometimes I forget about your eidetic memory," said Clive.

"Do tell."

"They're not cheap. About a thousand dollars," Zeke continued. "They're made for 12 gauge shotguns. But that would do the job."

"I don't recall that a suppressor was found on the pawnshop premises," Clive said, mostly to himself. "But the men on the security video didn't have a shotgun. Surely we would have seen that."

"They wouldn't need one. This was a pawnshop, so there were plenty of guns around. They'd just need to bring the suppressor," said Zeke.

"Hmm," said Clive.

"Did the video show the visitors with a rifle?" asked Zeke.

"No, but the cameras are mostly focused in the front of the shop. So there are a number of blind spots once you get further into the place," Clive said.

"They could have wandered for a bit, checking things out, confirmed that Bryce Carroll was in the back, picked up a shotgun, fitted it with their suppressor, loaded it and confronted Carroll. It wouldn't have taken thirty seconds from the time they finished their browsing to the time Carroll was dead," Zeke said. "Did they leave through the front door?"

"According to the clerk, they must have exited through the back door. He didn't see them again after they disappeared," said Clive. "The sales clerk said he'd heard something by the front of the shop and he looked that way for a second. When he looked back, the men were gone."

"Did he go after them?" Zeke asked.

"He called after them, but he didn't want to leave the front of the store empty. He said he went toward the back of the shop and said something along the lines of, 'Hey, you're not allowed back there,'" said Clive. "Something innocuous and ineffective."

"When did they find Carroll's body?"

"After about ten minutes, the store clerk decided to check on Carroll. When he did, he found the owner dead," said Clive.

Zeke nodded. "Sounds like it was done by pros," he said.

* * *

Zeke and Clive spent the next hour in the pawnshop, examining the crime scene. The layout of the building was more conducive to a retail operation than it was to security, with separation between the front and back areas and no line of sight available.

"It seems that Carroll was back here, sitting at this desk," Clive noted. "The killers, we're pretty sure it was the two men who'd come into the shop earlier, must have come back from the showroom area, picked up the shotgun, attached the suppressor, loaded it and walked right over to Carroll and shot him. Then they spent a minute or two making it look like a suicide. They put the gun in his hands and staged the scene."

"What about GSR?" asked Zeke, talking about the gunshot residue that would have been on Carroll's hands had he pulled the trigger.

"It was there," said Clive.

"I saw that in the file," said Zeke. "It was the main reason the M.E. declared it a suicide."

They must have planted it somehow," said Clive.

"It can be transferred, actually," said Zeke. "And fairly easily."

Clive was listening.

"Say the shooter put gloves on before entering the rear door. Maybe cotton gloves, maybe latex, either would work. After he's shot the victim, there would be GSR on the gun. When he puts the gun in Carroll's hands, some of that GSR would be transferred," said Zeke.

Clive nodded. "But not as much as if he'd shot the gun himself," he said.

"Right. But then the killer rubs his gloved hands on Carroll's hands, front and back, furthering the GSR transfer. And suddenly, everyone thinks it's a suicide."

"Do we have anything on their business? Revenues, profits, inventory…?" asked Zeke.

"Donovan pulled their financials for me," said Clive. "It looks like they were fairly profitable, running a franchise that made money."

Zeke looked around. "This was no suicide," he said.

CHAPTER 23

Sally stuck her head in Clive's office. "Zeke, hey, I've got something to share with you."

"I'll be right over," said Zeke. He and Clive had been talking about the Pawn 4 All operation, deciding on a next step.

"Let me check with Sally, and we'll pick up here when I get back. Shouldn't be ten minutes," said Zeke.

"No worries," said Clive. "It'll give me a minute to make a quick call."

Zeke walked a couple doors down the hall and entered Sally's office. She was standing at a file cabinet, wearing a yellow high-collar blouse with shoulder pads, a knee-length skirt and seamed stockings. Her hair was pulled into a ponytail with a bright yellow ribbon.

"Knock, knock," said Zeke.

When she turned to greet him, her skirt twirled. She said, "You were right."

"I was?" asked Zeke.

Nodding, Sally said, "I talked with a friend at FBI headquarters. He checked with the Florida SAC in Miami, who had someone research it. Turns out your folks were key witnesses in the prosecution of the former sheriff, Billy Forester."

"I met Billy Forester," said Zeke.

Sally nodded. "The file says they were eye witnesses to him bringing drugs into the Keys on a Cigarette. One of those Go-Fast boats, I think they call them."

Zeke nodded. "They used to be called 'Rum Runners' a long time ago. Did it say where or when they saw Billy?"

"I have a copy of the file here," said Sally. "I'll let you read through it."

"The FBI file?" asked Zeke.

"It's amazing what you can get when you ask," said Sally.

"When you ask," said Zeke, thoughtfully. "What else is in it?"

"Enough to make you head back to the Keys. I'll book you a flight."

* * *

Zeke walked around the house, jumped over a wire fence and stepped onto the wooden dock. He heard metallic clanking sounds coming from the interior of Billy Forester's moored yacht.

"I'm back, Billy," he called out.

The noise stopped, and a moment later the former sheriff stepped out on deck. He was sweaty, dressed only in dirty cargo shorts and holding a greasy wrench.

"You again," he said.

"Yes, sir," said Zeke. "I was just admiring your boat."

"She's a beauty, isn't she?" said Forester, looking over his shoulder. "Probably my favorite thing in the world."

"I know. You always seem to be working on it. Must be your passion."

"It is that. You let yourself in?"

"The door was open," Zeke lied.

"I told you there's nothing to be done about your folks," said Forester, carefully. "Why'd you come back here?" He was watching Zeke's hands. *Watching for a weapon,* thought Zeke.

"Information," said Zeke. "I got more information."

Forester looked at Zeke. "I think you'd better leave," he said.

"I'll bet you do," said Zeke. "But not yet. I have a story I know you'll be interested in."

Forester shrugged, obviously not concerned. He sat in one of the fighting chairs on the boat's back deck and nodded slightly. "OK, I'm listening."

Zeke sat on a small bench on the dock, across from Forester.

"So does the name Pablo Escobar mean anything to you, Billy?"

* * *

"You had your gang of conchs convinced that you were scaring off tourists and fishermen from the mainland. You pushed their buttons, because you knew that would keep them involved and compliant," said Zeke.

"Why would we care?" asked Forester.

"Your gang of fishermen cared because a few years earlier the State passed a law prohibiting gill fishing. Their catch was suddenly reduced to a tenth of what they'd been bringing in, and they couldn't pay their bills or feed their families. They were starving," said Zeke.

"I remember that time, but I had nothing to do with the law being passed," said Forester.

"That's true, but it brought you all together against a common cause," said Zeke. "And your gang was motivated to do something to make some money."

"So?"

"And you had boats," said Zeke. "Every one of the conch gang had a fishing boat."

Forester said, "I'm still listening."

"So you hooked up with Pablo Escobar, and you started using the fishing boats to bring in his cocaine," said Zeke. "Much more profitable than fishing, right?"

Forester looked at him and yawned. "I was in law enforcement for a long time. Trouble with this story is that nothing's been proven."

"Right," said Zeke. "So what happened? Did the *West Wind* spot one of your gang making a run? Did my folks happen across you unloading the cocaine? Or perhaps they accidentally found your warehouse? It could have been anything like that," said Zeke.

Forester looked at him. "That's some wild speculation," he said, sitting forward in his chair.

"It is," said Zeke. "I'm thinking that my dad saw something having to do with the drugs, and he called the police. But not the Monroe County sheriff's office. He would have called the DEA. In this case, there was a joint task force of the DEA and FBI working together in the Keys to take down Escobar. It was pretty much at the height of Pablo's power."

Billy Forester said nothing.

"Or maybe my dad saw Escobar kill someone. It doesn't matter, really. So, the way it happened, the Feds had my dad as a witness against Escobar. They kept him a secret, waiting for the trial, but along the way someone told Escobar about my dad and the *West Wind*. Maybe someone on the task force taking bribes. Or maybe it was you, Billy. That's the kind of information that you might uncover, right?"

Billy Forester shook his head slightly, dismissing it all.

"My guess is that Escobar told you to get rid of the threat. So you enlisted your gang of conchs to blow up the boat, putting a spin on the bombing, maybe as 'taking action against the tourists' that your men were already mad about. And you targeted the *West Wind*, because Escobar told you to."

"You have a pretty big imagination," said Forester. "Did you come up with this all by yourself?"

"I had a little bit of help from Parks and the FBI," said Zeke. "But I think it's essentially true. Care to comment on any of it?"

"OK, it's time for you to go," said Forester. "You can't come onto a man's property and accuse him of something like that. That's not right." He was working himself up, showing some outrage, leaning toward anger. "I'll forgive you because your parents died, but…get your ass off my property!"

* * *

"You know, you've seemed distracted lately," said Tracy. "Which is a shame while we're together in this great place."

"I haven't been much fun, have I?" asked Zeke.

"I wouldn't say that. But this thing about your parents being killed…"

"Is sort of a damper. I know. And I'm sorry."

"It's all right."

"Somehow I went from needing to know, to needing closure. Once I realized what had happened, that they'd been killed, I had to do something," he said.

"That's just who you are, Zeke. It's why I love you," said Tracy.

"Hmm," said Zeke.

"What?"

"You just sort of slipped that in there, didn't you?" Zeke said, smiling at her.

"I did. It seemed like the right time."

"Well, I love you, too," he said quietly. "But you already know that."

"It's nice to hear, though," Tracy said. "What are you going to do now?"

"Well, I'd be a fool not to follow you into the bedroom," said Zeke.

"You would," said Tracy. "But I meant, what are you going to do about your parents' deaths?"

"I've been thinking about that," said Zeke.

* * *

"Zeke, I just received an e-mail file from a friend at the FBI. He sent a link to a live stream. Thought you'd be interested in this one," said Sally.

"Are you supposed to have that?" Zeke asked.

"Well, it's a gray area…" Sally started.

"…but Clive Greene's name lubricates the wheels of information gathering," he said.

Sally giggled. "I'm sending it to your e-mail."

Zeke typed in the web address and the password and opened the live stream on his laptop. The video began with a shot of Billy Forester, who was standing inside the open front door of his waterfront mansion, talking with someone standing outside.

"Look, I was in law enforcement for over thirty years," said Billy.

The camera must have been on the visitor's lapel. The visitor turned slightly to include his partner in the recording. Zeke recognized the man as an FBI agent.

"We know," said the agent. He was large and black and appeared to be fit.

"What's your name?" Forester asked the agent.

"Agent Williams," said the large man.

"Did you play ball?" asked Forester.

"What do you think?" Williams responded.

The man with the hidden camera said, "I'm Agent Colfax. We'll need to come in, now."

"Well, Civil Rights and all," said Forester. "You'll want to get a search warrant, I think." He smiled easily.

On the live stream, Agent Williams nodded sheepishly.

"That would be good," said the one who'd introduced himself as Agent Colfax.

"Well, you see, Billy," said Agent Williams, "the arrest warrant that we have here is actually better. It's kinda like having a trump card. Open the door."

* * *

Zeke watched through the one-way glass as Billy Forester shifted in the metal chair. Then he shifted again and smiled toward the mirror behind which there was a video camera, recording away. He yawned and sat back and twiddled his thumbs. The handcuffs made it difficult to look casual.

A few minutes later the door opened and Agents Williams and Colfax crowded into the small room. They were accompanied by a slight, young looking man wearing a white guayabera shirt and beige slacks.

"Hello, boys," said Billy jovially. "I'm glad you didn't forget about me."

Zeke smiled. The FBI agents had arrested Forester and taken him to their offices in the Federal Building on Simonton

Street in Key West, where Zeke had joined them.

The younger man said, "I'm going to read you your rights again, Billy."

"I think I know what they are," said Billy. "No need to be redundant. But what did you arrest me for?"

"Forgive me, but I'm an attorney. We'll do this by the book. And for the camera." He looked at Agent Williams who took the cue and Mirandized Billy Forester a second time, for the camera.

"OK, good, now tell me, who are you?" said Forester.

"I'm the Federal Prosecuting Attorney for the Southern District of Florida." The younger man spoke with a slight Hispanic accent, maybe two generations away from a Spanish-speaking household. "My name is Ortiz."

Forester nodded slowly, his smile gone. "Federal Prosecuting Attorney," he said. He looked at the two agents. "I don't know what you think happened, to bring in the big guns, but..."

"Let's start with your friend, Skinny Gonzalez," said Ortiz.

"Not really my friend," said Forester.

"How about 'Business Partner'?"

"What..." Forester started.

"We know all about Skinny," said Ortiz. "We've had a file on him since he arrived from Colombia in the 1980s."

Forester was silent.

"When Escobar sent him to keep an eye on you, Billy," Ortiz continued. "When you were running his cocaine."

Ortiz continued. "We all know that Pablo didn't turn his cocaine import business over to you, Billy. He wasn't a trusting guy. So Skinny relocated to the Keys to make sure everything was above board. As above board as cocaine smuggling could be, anyway."

Forester furrowed his brow and said, "This is all ancient history, Mr. Ortiz. Why are you even interested in it now? Escobar was killed in Colombia in the early 1990s. And the five-year statute of limitations on Federal drug conspiracy charges ran out years ago."

"It did," said Ortiz. "But there is no statute of limitations on a first-degree murder charge."

Billy Forester suddenly looked furtive.

"The witnesses against Escobar. The Traynors. You killed them with the bomb."

Billy said, "You have no proof of that..."

Ortiz smiled. "Skinny Gonzalez is going to testify," he said.

"Why?" asked Billy.

"To keep his granddaughter out of prison," said Ortiz. "We booked her as an accessory after the fact."

"For murder? That's a stretch. She wasn't even born back then," said Forester.

"No, not for murder," said Ortiz. "For smuggling drugs. We closed down their operation yesterday."

* * *

"You did what?" asked Tracy Johnson, shocked.

"It wasn't a big thing," said Zeke. "I just took the transom drain plug out and shut off the bilge pump."

"And his boat sank?" asked Tracy. "Right there at the dock?"

"It wouldn't have taken long," said Zeke. "Maybe overnight. I thought it prudent to disappear before it went down."

"Oh, my. Can they catch you?"

"Not likely. Four times as many boats sink at dock each year as sink while under way. And most sink because of 'operator error.'"

"What causes it?" asked Tracy.

"Generally, it's too much beer."

"No, silly, what causes the boats to sink?"

"I suspect that usually someone forgets to put the drain plug back in and floats the boat with the hole open. The bilge pump keeps pumping the water out for a while, but eventually, it gives out. Bilge pumps aren't designed to run 24/7."

"Did you really do that? Sink his boat?" asked Tracy.

"No, I didn't," Zeke confessed. "But that man loved that boat, and it gave me some pleasure, thinking about doing it."

"I understand," said Tracy. "Do you have closure now? About your folks' deaths?"

"Not really. I'm glad that we know what really happened. And I'm glad the guilty parties didn't get away with it. But I don't feel closure. Just melancholy when I think about it, I guess."

"I have just the cure for that," said Tracy. "Let me make you lunch and we can talk."

* * *

"Guess how I'm feeling?" asked Tracy with feigned innocence.

"Hmm," said Zeke. "I suppose I'd narrow it down to something between 'frisky' and 'randy' based on what I'm seeing."

Tracy was dressed in a loose, short beach cover-up, and nothing else. She'd pulled the cotton belt tight, which accentuated her small waist. She sipped a Seabreeze unselfconsciously while Zeke worked on a single malt and soda.

She had pulled a large leather chair around in the cottage, inside the sliding glass doors and facing the ocean. They were sharing it, side by side. The sun was approaching the blue horizon.

"You smell good," said Zeke. "That's Ex Nihilo. Devil Tender, right?"

"You know it is," said Tracy. "You said you liked it, so I brought it along."

"'Out of Nothing.' I do like it," said Zeke. "I'm glad you have it with you."

"So what's next?" asked Tracy, taking a small sip.

"As soon as we finish these beverages, I'll be chasing you back to the bedroom," said Zeke with a sparkle in his eye.

"Won't happen," said Tracy.

"How would you stop me? I know you're not carrying your gun in that outfit. It would show," said Zeke, pretending to look.

Tracy smiled. "No, silly. You won't be chasing me. 'Cuz I'll be chasing you!"

Chapter 24

Chester Kirby sat comfortably in the back seat of the black limo and smiled a winning smile at his three companions. They had been driving in New Jersey traffic for forty minutes and were still a half hour from their destination.

"I need to charter one of those helicopters," he said to no one in particular. "Just to get around. Especially in New York."

The limo was headed for a newly renovated brownstone located in Alphabet City, a few blocks from Tompkins Park. Kirby had received a call from his partner, who owned the entire building as well as the two next door. He had requested a meeting, and the car had been dispatched to pick him up.

The man closest to Kirby, the oldest son of his partner, said, "My father's concerned about these losses."

Kirby nodded sincerely. "I am, too. More than anyone. But we've got it under control."

"We've been doing business for a long time," said the man. "I believe it's been good for both sides."

Kirby nodded and smiled nervously. "It has, Ghafran.

We're very pleased with this ongoing relationship. And I assure you, you won't see any of the losses. We're absorbing all of that."

* * *

At the brownstone, Kirby joined the men on the sidewalk as the limo pulled away from the curb. They walked up the front steps, in through the ornate door, and took the recently replaced elevator to the fifth floor. They knocked and entered an opulent space that occupied the entire floor with wide views in every direction. The suite was decorated with antique furnishings arranged in several small groupings. The art on the wall was obviously expensive. Kirby noticed a picture that might have been painted by Gustave Courbet.

"Hello, Chester, my friend. How are you?"

Kirby turned to see Ferman Khoury entering the room through an interior door. He walked directly to Kirby and the two men shook hands.

"I'm well," said Kirby, "It's good to see you again, Ferman."

The Lebanese man signaled for tea to be brought in, and the men arranged themselves around a low table set with cups, saucers, and a small pitcher of heavy cream.

"Ghafran mentioned that you were disappointed in the recent losses," Kirby started, still slightly nervous. "I assured him that none of them will make their way back to you."

"That is reassuring, Chester," said Ferman. "I wouldn't want to take such a loss. You promised me that this investment would be risk-free."

"Yes, absolutely, Ferman. We're taking the losses. And we're fixing the problem, so it won't happen again."

"Using my men," said Ferman. "Wilbur and Harry."

"It seemed most expedient to do so," said Chester, not certain where this was going.

"How will you stop this from happening in the future? Other pawnshop owners may get greedy, also."

"Yes," said Chester. "We're working on that, too. Our Risk Management people have that as their first priority."

"Your Risk Management people?"

"Yes, Julia Conners. I hired her to manage this problem, to make it go away."

"She is the one with ties to Sinn Fein?" asked Ferman.

"She is," said Kirby. "Her husband was killed by the Brits some years ago. She's an angry one."

"I see. Is there an action plan?" asked Ferman.

"Yes, most definitely. We're having the bank do random audits." He ticked the points off on his fingers. "We've increased scrutiny for our franchisee applicants. We've gone back and reviewed the files for each franchisee, looking for prior arrests or trouble with the law. And we're weeding out anyone we catch skimming. Zero tolerance."

"That is all reassuring, Chester," said Ferman. He sipped his tea. "We go back a long way, almost since I started selling the weapons internationally. Both of our businesses have grown quickly and are very profitable. But I can't risk my entire operation just to clean my money. You know I will hold you personally responsible for any failures." This last was a statement more than a question.

Kirby squirmed in his chair, and said, "I understand, Ferman."

* * *

"So how can we help you today, Mr. Ryder? Mr. Chamberlain?"

The sign on his large, wooden desk read, Cal Harmon, President of the Union First Bank of New Jersey.

"We recently bought Pawn 4 All franchises, Pardner," said Zeke. "Chester Knowles asked us to transfer our accounts to your bank."

Clive nodded.

The big man was going to flab, and he had sharp, beady eyes like a weasel. But his manner was cordial, even engaging.

"We handle the bulk of Chester's business accounts," Harmon said. "Not just bank accounts, but loans for expansion, cash flow management, real estate acquisitions, that sort of thing."

"Well, we wanted to meet the man in charge," Clive said. "We're actually franchising all seven of our locations."

"Certainly, Mr. Chamberlain, I'm always glad to meet our new clients. And I think you'll find the transition to Union First seamless."

"Yes, that would be good," said Clive.

"It's our understanding that Pawn 4 All is interested in expanding further," said Zeke. "Mr. Kirby said so. I thought we could help with that."

Cal Harmon looked surprised. He looked at his office door, as if to verify that it was closed. Then he said, "Well, uh, yes." He'd clearly made a decision in those few seconds.

"Is something wrong?" asked Clive.

"Well, no," said Harmon. "We try to avoid talking about our customers' business here in the bank. Or in Chester's offices. We don't want to be overheard, you know." He smiled warmly, his mental balance back.

Clive looked around at the closed door. "We do have a couple questions we were hoping you could help us with," he said.

Harmon said, "Well, I guess there's no harm in that, this one time…"

* * *

"I hope that answers your technical questions about Union First's role in all of this," said Harmon. "But, as I said, we tend to follow Mr. Kirby's lead."

"I understand," said Clive. "And thank you for explaining the details."

"One thing, though, Mr. Harmon," said Zeke.

"Yes, Mr. Ryder?" asked the banker.

"Where does the extra money come from?" asked Zeke.

Cal Harmon sat still for a moment, thinking. Then he said, "Well, I don't know. Perhaps that's a question better answered by Chester Kirby…"

"OK, we'll do that," said Zeke. Then, looking at his watch, he said, "Well, we've taken enough of your time."

* * *

"I wanted to circle back and thank you for your assistance in this takedown," said Agent-in-Charge, Francis Donovan.

Zeke and Clive were sitting at a low table in Clive's office, talking with the FBI agent on the speakerphone. Kimmy was standing next to them, bouncing slightly with her kinetic energy.

She's in perpetual motion, thought Zeke.

"How did the operation go?" asked Clive.

"Very well. We were able to close down over one hundred Pawn 4 All shops, and we arrested as many owners in the process."

"That's great," said Zeke. "What about the franchise operation? The headquarters?"

"Yes, that, too. We've got Chester Kirby and Jack Thurmond in custody, along with a handful of their middle managers. Now's when they start giving each other up, rolling on each other to get reduced prison sentences," said Donovan.

"And the remaining franchises?" asked Clive. "You said there were about 130, if I remember correctly."

"That's right. We have paper for the rest of them, and agents camped out to arrest them as soon as they show up. Most of them aren't aware of the operation yet, so I expect we'll get most of them," said Donovan. There was pride in her voice.

"Nice job, Donovan," said Clive.

"All that remains, then, is the Union First bank," said Zeke. "Is Cal Harmon involved in the money laundering?"

"The Federal Prosecuting Attorney says it's possible," said

Donovan. “We executed a warrant for Harmon and the bank records, thanks to your work. We’ll get to the bottom of it.”

Zeke said, “What about the owner suicides? The killings? Did you come across anything that could help us figure out that part of it?”

Donovan said, “Not yet. But if anything comes up in our interviews, we’ll definitely pass it along.”

* * *

“Damn it,” said Julia Conners. “I’ll have to go underground. I can’t risk being picked up by law enforcement. If someone rolls and gives me up…”

She was talking with Ferman Khoury, the Lebanese gunrunner, at his brownstone in New York.

“Is there a link back to my operation?” he asked.

“That could only be Kirby or myself,” said Julia. “And neither of us would give you up, Ferman.”

“Tell me again what’s going on,” said Khoury.

“Someone organized the arrest of a number of our franchisees. It started yesterday. They used local cops in each city to scoop up the owners. The papers they served said it’s about money laundering.” She hesitated before saying anything more, then looked at Khoury.

“How did this happen?” he asked.

“I don’t know,” she said. “It was a total surprise.”

“What’s changed recently? What have you noticed that may be related to this?”

"Nothing really. Business as usual. We took on a small chain of pawnshops in several new territories, but nothing extraordinary," said Julia. "And we'd almost finished dealing with the money skimmers."

Khoury said, "Yes, that was very stupid on their part. They were being compensated very well for their efforts."

"Human greed," said Julia. "We've eliminated the problem shop owners. But the bigger problem…law enforcement…"

"How well do you know these new franchisees? The ones with the 'small chain' you mentioned?" asked Khoury.

"Not well. None of us do. But Chester has been feeling the pressure to expand, to handle more illegal cash. He's been on a tear to add more shops since the summer," said Julia. "When these guys showed up with multiple shops in their chain, he was just about salivating."

"Where is their file?" asked Khoury.

"Actually, it's in my briefcase. I was working on some of the 'security' details for the Risk Management plan for their shops when the arrests started," she said. "I had to get out quick."

"Give the file to me. I'll have Harry and Wilbur see if there's any connection between the new franchisees and the arrests."

* * *

"We've found them," said Harry into the cell phone in the Office Tavern Grill, a Morristown bar. "Some of the fingerprints on the franchise paperwork they submitted track back to a Clive Greene. My friend in the New York PD ran the fingerprints for me." He was smug.

"And what do we know about this Clive Greene?" asked Ferman Khoury.

"It's a thin file, boss. Like it's secure or something. But we were able to dig around and find a home address. And his office, called The Agency, is on Pennsylvania Avenue in Washington."

"A neighbor of the President, then," said Ferman from his New York brownstone. "Good, you know what to do."

Harry hung up the phone and turned to Wilbur, who was on the barstool next to him drinking a dirty martini. Wilbur glanced at him and Harry nodded in the affirmative.

"How do we do this?" asked Wilbur, with one eye on a television broadcasting the Giants game.

Harry started to speak, but Wilbur cut him off with, "First down!" Harry sipped his small batch Bourbon and decided to wait for a commercial.

* * *

"We head to D.C. tomorrow," said Harry. "We've got his home address, so we'll follow him there from his office after work.

Wilbur said, "OK. Do you want to wait until he gets there? Or take him on the road?"

"Let's play that by ear," said Harry. "When we get to D.C., we'll follow him home, do a test run. Then we can decide."

"Where does he live?" asked Wilbur.

"In a condo. In Silver Spring. About thirty minutes outside of Washington. I looked it up on Google Maps."

CHAPTER 25

Clive drove his silver Aston Martin north on 16th Street NW until he left the District of Columbia, and then he turned left toward Silver Spring. Mozart's Concerto No. 24 was playing on his Bang and Olufsen speakers, and he lost himself in the emotionally charged piece. The Beosound Rapide sound system provided a wonderful platform for the performance.

Zeke sat quietly in the passenger seat, enjoying the music.

Clive's condominium building was five stories high and constructed of equal parts of modern silver metal siding and tinted glass. Plantings and trees complimented the building's small yard and balconies, and video cameras were carefully concealed on the exterior of the building.

Clive drove his vehicle into the underground parking area and slotted it in between a current year BMW sedan and a slightly older blue Bentley. He sat for a moment as the music reached a crescendo, and then he shut off the car and said, "Let's go."

Zeke nodded and, guns in hand, they opened their doors.

Clive noticed several of his neighbors exiting their vehicles and heading toward the elevators. The usual end-of-the-workday crowd. He stepped on the elevator and assured himself that the fifth floor button had been pushed.

* * *

"The FBI alerted him?" asked Kimmy, who had been staking out the condo.

"Yes, Clive's records are all electronically flagged. When someone checks on him—his criminal record, military record, fingerprints—the system sends a message to the appropriate authorities," said Zeke. "It's standard for anyone with his security clearance."

They were sitting on a square sofa in Clive's large living room.

Alerted by the FBI of the NYPD's search of Clive's fingerprints a week ago, the three of them had developed a protection plan. Just now, Clive was acting as bait.

"I thought they might try to get inside and 'greet' me when I arrived," said Clive.

Zeke nodded.

"Well, we know that we've made waves, gotten their attention," said Clive, sitting down across from them. "Apparently, Julia Conner disappeared. Kirby, Thurmond and the rest are wrapped up, and in the FBI's care, however."

"Conner was the only link to those two we saw in her office. They were so out of place, I'm betting they're the hired guns," said Zeke.

"Based on their looks?" asked Kimmy.

"And their dead eyes. And their superior attitudes," said Zeke.

Clive nodded.

"Their eyes never changed," said Zeke. "There was no real emotion, no real fear there. I don't think they cared about anything."

Kimmy said, "I know people like that. It's like they've learned how to imitate people, but they don't feel any of it. They'd as soon kill you as not."

* * *

"Better in public?" asked Kimmy.

They were descending the elevator in Clive's condominium building, after deciding to go to dinner...and to further expose Clive to the killers.

"It works in our favor," said Clive. "They'll have fewer opportunities. And it'll be more difficult to execute, and difficult to escape. More possible collateral damage, though."

"I'm not certain they care about that," said Zeke.

The elevator stopped at the first parking level and the door opened. Zeke stepped out, and then Kimmy, followed a moment later by Clive. It was quiet in the garage, and they saw no one.

"I think I fancy Italian tonight," said Clive. "OK with you?"

Kimmy, distracted and watching for movement in the garage, nodded.

Zeke said, "Sure."

A few moments later, Clive backed the Aston Martin out

of its assigned space and exited the condominium garage. "You have a preference?" he asked.

"Let's eat at Antonio's," said Kimmy from the back seat. "It's the most secure building and the easiest to protect you, Clive." They'd been over this before.

Clive nodded and pointed the car east.

* * *

Traffic was thinning out and the sky was gray, settling into the twilight hour as Clive turned onto the four-lane highway that led to downtown Silver Spring.

"There's a black Hummer following us, four cars back," said Clive. His handgun suddenly appeared on his lap.

"I've got it," said Zeke. "It picked us up when we left the garage."

Kimmy hummed a quiet tune.

"Tinted window and push bars. That could be our friends," said Zeke.

Suddenly the black vehicle accelerated and passed two cars before it pulled in behind the Aston Martin, crowding the vehicle. A moment later, the Hummer banged into the rear of Clive's car and pushed it along for twenty yards. Then it disengaged, fell back a few feet, and, accelerating, rammed the British car again, hard. Then they fell back a second time.

"Somebody's trying to get our attention," said Kimmy. She turned in her seat and gauged the speed of the approaching vehicle.

Clive waited until the last second and then, suddenly, turned hard left into a parking lot before slamming on the brakes. There were just a few other vehicles at this end of the lot.

"I'm out," Kimmy said. She opened the door and rolled, coming up behind a garbage dumpster, a concrete block enclosure.

Clive accelerated again and spun the car ninety degrees and stopped, facing the Hummer. It had backed up, turned and followed Clive into the lot.

Now the two cars were face to face.

Zeke opened the passenger door and pointed his semiautomatic at the Hummer and snapped off three shots. The powerful slugs cracked the front window of the vehicle and pocked the front fender.

Fifteen feet away, the passenger door of the Hummer opened and Wilbur stepped out with a long rifle. Zeke recognized it as an M4 carbine, a U.S. Military weapon.

Wilbur leveled the weapon, propping it on the hinge between the door and the hood.

Zeke shot into the door twice, with little effect.

It's armored, he thought.

Immediately, Zeke dropped to the ground, sighted and placed shots in both of Wilbur's ankles. The M4 clattered to the ground, followed by the killer.

Clive, also on the ground now to avoid the automatic fire, finished the man with a double tap to the head and neck when he fell.

Suddenly, it was quiet as the smoke cleared and the smell

of burning gunpowder floated off. Then the driver's door of the Hummer opened and someone stepped out.

He was covered in a full set of body armor and carried an M4 carbine identical to the one Wilbur had used. He wore a helmet with a visor, and wore arm and leg armor, as well. He leveled the carbine.

That's Harry, thought Zeke. *I recognize his body size and shape.*

Zeke and Clive had retreated to the rear of the Rapide S and were angling to escape, using the car as a shield. Clive fired four shots, three of which hit Harry's chest and arm and spun him to his right, ruining his aim.

But then Harry recovered, turned and took aim at the two men. They had moved farther away, back toward the cover of the garbage dumpster.

Zeke heard the screaming of accelerating tires as a soccer Mom's passenger van flew into the fray. Without hesitation, the van sped toward the armored man from behind.

Harry, encumbered by the weight and bulk of his body armor, turned and apparently realized that he couldn't outrun the vehicle. He was attempting to climb back into the Hummer when the van plowed directly into the driver's side door, crushing him into the doorframe.

The van driver backed up a couple of feet and accelerated again, this time squeezing the life from the killer. The van's wheels spun for a while, continuing the pressure, as blood ran down into the parking lot. Then the van stopped, and Kimmy stepped out.

She walked over to the armored man and picked up his carbine, which had fallen to the ground. Then she turned back to Zeke and Clive and announced, "All clear."

* * *

"Well, that's it, I suppose," said Clive. "You both kept me alive."

"Our pleasure," said Kimmy. She was sipping some organic green tea and bouncing lightly on one of Clive's stuffed office chairs. Her feet didn't reach the floor when she sat.

"No problem," said Zeke. "It's what we do."

Clive said, "Well, thank you." Then, somewhat awkward in the moment, he said to Zeke, "What's next?"

"I'm heading up to North Dakota tomorrow," said Zeke. "Going to meet up with Tillman Cord and see about wrapping up the Jenny Lakota thing."

Clive Greene nodded and sipped his Earl Grey tea. Rumor was that he had it imported from Calabria, Italy.

"Well, then, fare well," said Clive.

* * *

"This investigation doesn't seem to be going anywhere," said Tillman Cord, angrily. He was leaning forward across the table, and his black bolo tie was swinging comically as he spoke.

"Let's go over what we have, then," said Zeke. "Let's review."

Zeke had flown to Williston and driven to New Town for

the next, and hopefully final, phase of the Jenny Lakota investigation.

Cord nodded and sat down.

"There are a number of unanswered questions," said Zeke, "all of which lead to more questions."

"OK," said Cord. "You go first."

"No particular order?" Zeke asked.

"OK…"

"Let's talk about the Jenny Lakota crime scene."

Cord nodded.

"She was skinned, and she was skinned while on the railroad track,"

"…according to the M.E." Cord added.

"Yes. But she wasn't tied or bound. She just sat there while it was happening."

"Apparently," Cord said.

"And the killer got her to sit still?" asked Zeke.

"The horse tranquilizers," Cord remembered.

"Right. Xylazine," said Zeke. "That kept her still and quiet. But how would the killer get her to take the drug?"

Cord thought for a moment. "She took it orally and by injection, according to the M.E. So someone she trusted gave it to her, I imagine."

"Yes, that," said Zeke. "Or she took it thinking it was something else."

"Like meth. She could have bought some pills thinking they were meth," said Cord, speaking as he thought.

"Probably capsules, if that's the case," said Zeke. "It wouldn't be hard to put powdered Xylazine in capsules and pass them off as Crystal Meth."

"Do we know if Jenny Lakota had a meth problem?" asked Cord.

"Sure. Remember what Angel said? I think she was trying to tell us that Jenny used drugs."

"I'm sure Angel does, too," said Cord. "But yes, if she had a habit, it makes sense that Jenny would take capsules if she thought it was meth."

"What about the injection?" asked Cord.

"That wouldn't be hard if she was already reacting to the capsule, right?" asked Zeke. "So the killer could juice her up, keep her quiet and compliant."

"So, someone she knows. Sam Bearcat?" asked Zeke.

"Or a mutual friend? Maybe one of his axe-throwing buddies?"

"Or one of Jenny's friends. She grew up in New Town," said Zeke.

"OK, that's good. We just need to find out who supplied her," said Cord.

* * *

"What other questions?" asked Cord.

"Well, I was wondering about Will Carter, the truck driver," said Zeke. "There's got to be more to it than he's telling us."

Cord nodded.

"He said he was in the bar, the Salty Dog, talking with Chip

Wellers and drinking beer. Had a couple of shots, too," said Zeke.

Cord opened his notebook and flipped through some pages. Then he nodded. "Right."

"Then, and they both confirmed this, Jenny Lakota came over and started flirting with Carter. He said he bought her a drink and Chip Weller said she was loud and very friendly with Carter. Sort of egging on the boyfriend," said Zeke.

"You believe them?" asked Cord.

Zeke nodded and kept going. "So why did Jenny pick Carter? Seems like a stretch that she'd approach a stranger in a bar, flirt a bunch, then leave, and a little bit later end up having sex with him in a trailer."

"Even if money was involved?" said Tillman Cord.

"Maybe," said Zeke. "But there's money and drugs that run through this whole thing."

"Yes to that," said Cord.

"And think about what Wellers told us. Jenny left the bar, and Carter finished his drink and left shortly after. The exact words were 'When he saw her leave he finished his beer and then took off.'"

"Seemed pretty convenient when he said it," said Cord. "The timing, I mean."

"No one at the bar really knew Carter," said Zeke. "He was a truck driver and an occasional patron, according to Sandy, the bartender."

Cord looked at his notes and nodded again.

"But—and here's the question—Did they have a prior

relationship? Will Carter and Jenny Lakota?" asked Zeke.

"Carter could have been moving drugs," said Cord. "Being a truck driver and independent like he is, he could be distributing, taking it down to Bismarck."

"So they could have known each other from that," said Zeke, agreeing.

"And it could account for the sudden rush, the two of them going to the Lakeside Trailer Park," said Cord.

"Most likely it wasn't their first get together. Remember what Carter said about Jenny 'liking them big'?" Zeke said.

"Well, this is productive," said Cord.

"I know," said Zeke. "How about another one?"

"Another question?"

Zeke nodded.

"OK, shoot," said Cord.

"We've got two girls who were killed with a similar weapon, if not the same weapon, a few years apart. Casey Black and Jenny Lakota."

"Right," said Cord, listening harder now.

"And we have no clear motive in either case. It wasn't money, as both girls were pretty much broke. And no one inherited anything, from what we know."

"That's true, we checked that," said Cord, referring to the FBI.

"And it wasn't love. I don't think Sam Bearcat killed Jenny, particularly in that fashion. He was too far out of it, plus she was his meal ticket," said Zeke.

"Right," said Tillman Cord.

"And Casey's sister said that Casey's last boyfriend had been killed by a rival gang. It didn't sound like she was dating anyone exclusively when she was killed," said Zeke.

"Yet it seems like it wasn't done in anger. More like a ritual or something," said Cord.

"Exactly," said Zeke. "Like a ritual sacrifice."

CHAPTER 26

"You have any more of those questions?" asked Tillman Cord.

"Maybe," said Zeke. "How about this: If it was a ritual killing, what was the killer trying to say? And what was the killer's motivation?"

"Hmm," said Cord.

"There's an incredible amount of money moving through this state," said Zeke. "The State Government can't spend it fast enough. They have a billion dollar surplus."

"Wow," said Cord. "That's more than enough to motivate most people."

"So here's a question you'll like," said Zeke. "What if the killing or killings, assuming they're related, were to cover something up? Or to protect someone from being discovered?"

"So someone killed Jenny Lakota to keep a secret?" said Cord. "I guess that's possible. But what secret would she possibly know of that would be worth her life?"

"Maybe she saw something or someone doing something

illegal. It wouldn't be the first time," said Zeke.

"No, it wouldn't. But two girls stumbling onto a secret, a few years apart, and then being killed…that seems like a pretty big coincidence, doesn't it?" said Cord.

"Or perhaps the killings were a punishment, retribution for something the girls did in the past, something they were involved in," said Zeke.

"That could be," said Cord. "But it'd have to be a pretty big thing for her to end up like she did. Which could have been a warning to some other people."

"Could have been," said Zeke.

* * *

At nine fifteen that evening, Tillman Cord and Zeke parked their car and walked across the street toward the Salty Dog. Both men wore leather jackets over dark shirts and pants. The night was cool.

It was Sunday and they'd decided to check out the bar and watch the locals for a few minutes.

"So we're watching for anyone we can connect with the drugs," said Cord. "The meth." He said it as a statement.

"Yes," said Zeke. "We want to find some leverage and see about following the drugs back to their source."

"Williston White," said Cord to himself.

"And maybe find out more about what happened to Jenny Lakota that night," said Zeke.

They opened the door and walked into the busy building.

The bar area was full, shoulder to shoulder with some patrons sitting at nearby tables. Everyone was talking and watching the Vikings playing football.

Zeke went to the bar and ordered a couple of beers from Sandy. It seemed like she was always working.

Two men were taking turns throwing axes at the target on the far wall. Half a dozen of their friends stood around watching the action. They were all drinking Bud Light from longneck bottles.

Alcohol and axes, thought Zeke. *What could go wrong?*

Zeke and Cord sat at a small table with a view of the front door, the bar area, and the poolroom where the axe contest was unfolding. Zeke looked around and noticed a few familiar faces, including Chip Wellers, the guy who had been talking with Will Carter on the night Jenny was killed. Will Carter wasn't around.

He didn't see Cindi, either, the first girl from the green trailer, but Angel was there, sitting at a table talking with three roughnecks, making jokes and touching their hands and arms when she laughed.

"She's working the crowd," Zeke said to Cord.

Cord nodded. "Wants to get paid tonight," he said, absently.

Occasionally, they heard a loud 'thump' as the hand axe found its way into the wooden target. Cord said, "How far you reckon those boys are throwing that axe?"

"Regulation is 12 to 15 feet," said Zeke. "There's a box marked out on the floor with tape. They need to stay in the box when they throw."

"You've done that? Thrown axes?" asked Cord.

Zeke smiled cryptically.

A man walked through the front door and stopped for a moment, looking around the room for someone. He had unkempt stringy brown hair and a fuzzy beard, and he was wearing work clothes, canvas pants and a long-sleeved brown shirt with the name 'Kent' above his left pocket. His boots were scuffed black steel-toed DeWalts.

The axe throwers were concentrating on tallying their scores. One of them looked up at Kent, who waved and walked over to the contestants.

Zeke said, "Might be a buy."

"Or he's next in line to toss the hatchet," said Cord.

"I'm pretty sure he's a tweeker," said Zeke.

"A methhead? How do you know?" asked Cord.

"Well, first because he bypassed the bar. Most people come in and get their drink first thing. And do you see the cystic acne on his jawline? Also, his teeth are starting to rot. Signs of a serious tweeker. Watch."

Kent was talking with one of the contestants, a taller man with a small potbelly and thin arms. The man nodded. He was maybe forty, Zeke judged.

Kent looked around the room, and then, apparently unalarmed, took some bills out of his pocket, palmed them and gave them to the man. The man set a small glassine envelope on the table, picked up his beer and walked five steps away. He started talking with someone else.

Zeke saw Kent slide the envelope over and slip it into his

pants pocket. He looked around the room again and headed for the front door.

* * *

"You're the ones who arrested Sam Bearcat," said a gravelly voice from just over Cord's shoulder. "Put him in prison."

Cord turned and looked at the man with a dead-eye cop stare. Zeke smiled and nodded.

"We didn't actually," said Zeke. "It was the Tribal Officers. They arrested him before the FBI could get a warrant issued. It was pre-emptive."

"Pre-bullshit. I heard it was you that caused it," the man persisted. He was a large man with long arms and a thick neck. He'd been one of those watching the axe throwing. His head was hairless except for his black eyebrows, and he had tattoos peeking out from under his shirt. His right shirt-sleeve was rolled up to his elbow, revealing a forearm of colorful tattoos. His arm muscles looked formidable.

This guy could have carried Jenny's body, no sweat, thought Zeke. He said, "We're about the only ones looking for the killer. Everyone else assumes it was Sam."

"So you say," said the large man. He stepped in closer behind Cord, crowding the table.

Zeke stood up and took a step away from his chair.

Cord said, "Be sure that you want to do that. I'm the FBI."

The large man said, "Why would I care about that?"

Cord tried to stand also, but he couldn't leverage his chair back past the man.

"We're actually here looking for a connection to the meth," said Zeke. "And we came across Kent, earlier."

The large man thought for a minute.

"Kent ain't hurting anybody," he said. "You're looking in the wrong place."

"Kent's hurting himself," said Zeke. "He's actually killing himself."

"Maybe you two should beat it," said the man. "Before things get worse." He looked over at his friends, four men standing at the axe throwing station, their attention on Zeke and Cord. One man, the smallest of the four, held the axe loosely in his hand, swinging it in a small arc.

Zeke said, "You may want to rethink that."

"Hey, Ronnie, what're you guys talking about over there?" asked one of Ronnie's friends. "You need some help?"

"Naw," said Ronnie. "These two were just leaving."

"You're obviously used to people doing what you tell them to," Zeke said to Ronnie. "How long since you had to enforce it? High school?"

"It wasn't college," said Cord. "This mutt didn't get anywhere near a college."

Ronnie apparently didn't like that remark, and he put his paw on Cord's right shoulder. Zeke noticed he was squeezing, hard.

Zeke reached quickly and grabbed the large man's ring finger with his left hand and his thumb with his right hand. Using his body weight as leverage, he swung his body under his arms, twisting and locking the large man's elbow suddenly. Zeke pressured the arm into a horizontal position and maneuvered Ronnie's wrist in a two-handed standing wristlock, taking the man to one knee.

"Ow, shit," said Ronnie. Zeke tweaked the wrist, forcing the big man's face farther toward the ground. Then he looked over at the small man.

The small man looked indecisive for a moment, but then he rallied and set himself to throw the axe. He took a step back as his arm rose above his shoulder, an overhand movement forward, like throwing a baseball, and a release as his arm hit the horizontal plane. Then he followed through with his right hand.

Good form, thought Zeke, as the axe flew toward him. He had already dropped Ronnie's hand and was lifting his leather jacket from the back of his chair, holding it between himself and the axe. The axe hit the leather with a dull, flat sound and fell to the floor.

In four steps, Zeke reached the small man, who a moment later was face up on the floor trying to catch his breath. A sharp jab to his solar plexus had incapacitated him, and a leg sweep knocked his feet from under him. His three friends drifted away.

Simultaneously, Cord drew his service revolver and pointed it at Ronnie. Then he levered the man's wrists up behind him. The cuffs were barely large enough to click closed around his wrists.

* * *

Zeke saw Angel watching as Ronnie and the small man were removed from the Salty Dog by five Tribal Officers. Bruce Doekiller stayed behind to take statements from the patrons.

Most all of the activity in the bar had stopped. The televisions were muted and the jukebox was unplugged. The men who had been watching the axe throwing contest wandered away from the area and tried to blend into the crowd by the bar.

The oilfield workers that Angel had been talking to decided to leave after Doekiller examined their I.D.'s and took their statements. Zeke overheard one of the men say something about moving on to the Four Bears Casino.

"You sure know how to screw up a nice night," said a girl's voice. Zeke turned to see Angel Wilson standing behind him, one fist on her hip and a sarcastic look on her face. "Buy me a beer."

Zeke smiled to himself and nodded. "Sure."

Cord said to Angel, "Sit down here. I want to talk with you for a minute."

The girl looked around, as if for help, her eyes scanning the room. She said to Cord, "What, me?"

"Yes, you. Right there," he said.

Angel looked like she wasn't going to sit, defiant, but then she shrugged to herself and sat in an empty chair next to Zeke.

Cord said, "You're doing meth too."

Angel shrugged again. "Just a snort once in a while, if

somebody has it available." She rubbed her nose a little bit.

Zeke knew that she was lying, both from the body language and from the physiology of the drug. "You're into it more than that, Angel," said Zeke.

"Why do you say that?"

"Meth destroys the limbic system in the brain, the part that affects emotion and behavior. Meth addicts tend to become single-minded and paranoid, and they're usually short on empathy and reasoning power. That's what I'm seeing right now in you, Angel."

Angel looked away, thinking.

"I'm not an addict," she said.

"We can take you in and find out," said Cord.

"I don't care what you think," she said. She looked sullen. Then she looked at Zeke and said, "Hey, how about that beer you promised me?"

* * *

"No doubt Kent is way into the meth," said Zeke. "Injections, based on the advanced symptoms I saw."

Clive from D.C., through the speaker of Zeke's smart phone, said, "How does that help us?"

"It's a part of the fabric of this area, the culture," said Zeke.

"Well, I was looking for leverage," said Cord, who was sitting across from Zeke in his hotel room. "Trying to get one of the girls, Cindi or Angel, to act as bait for the killer. I thought we might flush him out."

"How did that go?" asked Clive.

"Well, we'll see. We went to the Salty Dog and found Angel Wilson there. She looked like she was hitting on a couple of oilmen," said Zeke. "Trying to drum up some business."

"Huh," said Clive. "The wheels of commerce."

"But when Zeke took down one of the locals, the entire place got chilly," said Cord. "The local tribal cops came, and the customers started drifting for the doors. The buzz was pretty much killed, at that point."

"What about the girl?" asked Clive. "Do you think you can leverage her?"

"Sure I can," said Cord. "We lock her in a cell for a day, she'll do just about anything for a fix."

"How are you planning to use her?" asked Clive. "As bait, I mean."

"There are a couple of options. Let's talk with her," Zeke said.

* * *

"You want me to what?" asked Angel Wilson, once again sitting in the living room of her mother's house, smoking a cigarette. Cord and Zeke were standing in front of a couch, which was covered with laundry waiting to be folded.

"We want you to flush out the killer," said Cord.

"Hell, no," said Angel defiantly. "No way I'm getting anywhere near that psycho..." She sucked on the cigarette until the ash burned bright.

Zeke smiled.

Cord said, "Then I guess we'll have to take you in, Angel."

"For what?"

"You pick. Prostitution. Using meth. Selling drugs. How about drunk and disorderly?" asked Cord. He took a pair of handcuffs out of his pocket.

"You can't make that stick," said Angel.

"I don't need to," said Cord. "We're going to separate you from your drug of choice for a couple days, see what that does for your attitude."

Angel looked startled.

"And while we're at it, we're going to arrest your friend, Pete," said Cord. "You said he was your friend, but we checked with the tribal officers. He's your dealer and your pimp."

Angel looked at them for a minute. Then she said, "What do I have to do?"

* * *

To Zeke, Angel Wilson looked anxious. She hadn't had a pop for several hours, the whole time she was in the police station talking with Zeke and Kimmy and Tillman Cord. Now she was tapping her fingers on the tabletop and frequently squirming in her chair. Her attention was divided, as if she were having second thoughts.

"You can do this, Angel," said Kimmy. She'd arrived in New Town that afternoon, to assist with their plan at Zeke's request.

The girl said nothing. Then, "Listen, I need to use the bathroom."

Cord looked at Zeke, and Zeke nodded slightly. *She'll do better without the anxiety,* he thought. Angel got up and put her purse strap over her shoulder. Cord signaled and a female Tribal Officer opened the door and Angel left the room with her.

"You know she's going to snort some meth, right?" asked Cord.

"Sure. I'd expect no less," said Zeke.

Cord nodded. "Can she pull it off?"

"We'll stay close, right with her," said Kimmy.

"Just between us, I'm pretty confident that the killer has been reacting more than anything else," said Zeke. "I doubt that there's a plan or agenda. But when the right stimulus is applied, the killer kills."

"And what's the stimulus?" asked Kimmy. She was moving around the room now, watching the Tribal Officers working through the glass door. They were using a vacant office in the Three Affiliated Tribes Police Department.

"I've looked at the Casey Black killing, and at the Jenny Lakota killing," said Zeke. "There are commonalities, but there are also a number of differences. But there seems to be a pattern. In both cases the killing took place shortly after the dead girl did something that disrespected her heritage."

"Heritage?" asked Kimmy. "Her Native American heritage? Like what?"

"Like sex or drugs. Selling sex or drugs," said Zeke. "Jenny Lakota was heavy into dealing meth. She was addicted, and she was selling it for her boyfriend, Sam Bearcat. She also visited number seven at the Lakeside Trailer Park enough to be a regular. Somebody decided to stop her."

"And with Casey?" asked Cord.

"She was killed shortly after the Dakota Access Pipeline Protest, trying to stop part of the pipeline from being built."

"Pipeline?" asked Kimmy. She was listening, but bent over, watching out the glass in the door.

"In 2016, it was a grass roots protest that began at the Standing Rock Reservation," said Zeke.

"Where's that?" asked Kimmy.

"It's on the South Dakota border," Zeke said. "It actually straddles the two states."

"So what happened there?" she asked.

"The Feds didn't do such a good job with that one. About 500 people were arrested for protesting, and about 300 were injured. The Feds treated it like the protestors were terrorists."

"And Casey was one of those?" asked Kimmy, looking at Zeke and obviously warming to the topic.

Zeke nodded. "She and her motorcycle buddies were in the middle of it. She was on the news several times, interviewed by the national news stations, before she was arrested."

"What did she do that disrespected her heritage?" asked Kimmy.

"The FBI says she was dealing, transporting and selling drugs. She used the protest as a reason to go back and forth, peddling the meth at Standing Rock Reservation," said Zeke.

The door opened and Angel Wilson stepped back into the room. She looked much more relaxed to Zeke.

"It's time for you to help us catch Jenny's killer," he said.

"How?" the girl asked.

"We're going to go looking for him. I think he'll be looking for you already, Angel," said Zeke.

Angel looked around the room, warily. "I don't think…"

"But you want to stay out of jail, right, Angel?" asked Cord.

"Well, yeah," she said.

"Like we said, unless you want to go to prison for a while, you'll need to help us."

"You're a bastard," she said to Cord.

"OK, let's go," Zeke said.

* * *

Zeke and Kimmy sat in the car outside the Salty Dog and waited. Angel was inside, trolling, she called it, trying to find a guy to buy her a drink, or better, give her a pop. She had a small, one-way device with a microphone and GPS sewn into her jacket, courtesy of the FBI. It looked like a button.

Zeke looked at his watch. It was eleven fifteen.

"Do you think the killer will show up?" asked Kimmy.

Zeke nodded. "Tonight's a good night for it. It's Saturday, and both of the dead girls were killed on a Saturday night. Well, Sunday morning, actually."

Kimmy nodded.

"And there's been a lot of local noise about Angel. The word's out that she was involved with the drug sales. And that she was arrested. Her coming here would set off alarms. And she's been a regular at Lakeside..."

"If they're watching," said Cord.

"They are. But if not this weekend, it'll be next. It's a matter of the killer's reaction time."

"You told her to do what she normally does?" asked Kimmy. "To pick up a guy in the bar and take him home?"

"She's living in her mother's house now, and the trailer's closed up tight. I suspect she'll try to get the guy to go back to his place," said Zeke.

"It's another variable," said Kimmy.

Zeke nodded.

They waited some more.

At twenty minutes before eleven the front door of the Salty Dog opened and Angel Wilson stepped out. Right behind her Zeke saw a big man with longish hair and wearing a cowboy hat.

Through the microphone Zeke heard the man say, "What say we go to my place?"

Angel said, "OK. Do you have anything there?"

"I have just what you need," said the man. "Just stocked up."

The couple stood in front of the building as if uncertain what to do next. Then they turned and started walking north.

Zeke started the car and followed them from a distance.

* * *

It turned out that the man's house was a block and a half north of the Salty Dog. It was a dirty white, one-story bungalow with a detached garage at the back of the house. The trim was painted brown, and the place looked like a dump. One wall of the garage was sagging, slowly collapsing in on itself.

Angel and the man walked through the yard to the front door.

"This is it. Come on in," Zeke and Kimmy heard the man say over the small speaker. The sound was tinny.

"OK," said Angel. They heard a door close.

"You wanna party?" asked the man.

"Sure, why not," said Angel. "But…can I have some…"

"Sure, of course," said the man. "Here you go."

Zeke looked at Kimmy. "Time to turn down the volume?" he asked.

"I thought you'd never ask," said Kimmy.

CHAPTER 27

Angel Wilson stepped out of the white house and looked both ways. There was no one in sight. Zeke and Kimmy had parked their car around a corner and were watching the front of the house from behind a solid, low fence three doors down.

"There she is," said Kimmy, quietly, turning the volume up on the mic.

Angel straightened her blouse, buttoned her coat and took a step away from them toward Main Street. She said, "I hope you turned the mic off while I was inside."

Zeke smiled.

"I'm heading toward the tracks, like we planned," said the girl.

The mic picked up her monologue and transmitted it to Zeke's and Kimmy's earpieces.

Angel cut through the back yard and ended up on First Street, a half block from the Salty Dog. Zeke and Kimmy left their car parked and followed her in the dark.

At the Salty Dog, Angel stopped and looked around. Then

she unbuttoned her jacket, patted her hair and stepped into the bar. Zeke heard the bar sounds clearly and dialed the volume down a bit.

"Here's where she trolls the bar for the killer," said Zeke. There was sudden chaotic noise from inside the bar coming through their speaker.

After ten minutes and a few flirty conversations, Angel stepped back outside, still alone.

She said out loud, "So here's where I hang around outside and wait for someone to come out or to show up. OK?" They watched her light a cigarette.

A few moments later she said, "Bobby, hey, what are you doing here?"

Zeke heard a mumbled response and then Angel said, "Well, it's pretty late to be out, isn't it? Are you heading home?"

Then suddenly they heard a clear voice. A man's voice. "I'll walk you home, Angel."

She said, "No, I'd better not."

The man said, "Suit yourself. But hey, I have something you'll like." There was a zipping sound. "Try one of these. It's stupid fresh."

"That means good, right?" asked Kimmy in a low voice.

Zeke nodded, thinking. Then he broke into a hurried jog.

* * *

Bobby, it turned out, was formidable. From a distance in the dark he looked like a linebacker. He was big with large features, black eyes and straight black hair pulled into a single ponytail.

Angel was hiding something when Zeke arrived, having a little trouble because she had to use both hands to open her coat pocket, and she fumbled a bit with the hypodermic needle.

"What was that?" asked Zeke. He was focused on the girl but was watching Bobby on his periphery.

"Just something to get me over," she said.

Bobby nodded and said, "Who're you?"

"I'm Angel's escort tonight," said Zeke, smiling. "Want to be sure she gets home safely."

Bobby looked at him and squinted. He said, "What?"

"Can't have her running into an Indian killer like Jenny Lakota did," Zeke continued. "Did you know Jenny Lakota, Bobby?"

"How do you know my name?" asked the man. He was squinting again.

"Jenny told me all about you," said Zeke.

The man looked confused for a moment. Then he said, "No, she didn't."

"He went to the same school I did," said Angel, starting to slur her words. "New Town High School. He's a couple years younger…" She seemed to lose the rest of the sentence.

Zeke looked at Bobby. "What was in that syringe, Bobby?"

"What?" asked the man.

"What did you give her? It wasn't meth…"

Angel suddenly slumped down, sitting on the sidewalk, and Bobby turned abruptly and walked away.

* * *

Kimmy appeared a moment later, as Zeke was trying to revive Angel. She'd passed out and wasn't responding to his efforts.

"Is it Xylazine?" asked Kimmy, looking around the immediate neighborhood.

"Most likely. Same as Jenny. She's fortunate we were here. And Bobby looks as if he could easily pick her up and carry her to the tracks."

"He probably did, with Jenny. Probably wanted to with Angel," said Kimmy.

"Let's get her to a hospital," said Zeke, dialing his phone. "We'll find Bobby later."

* * *

"You dropped the girl at the hospital?" asked Lieutenant Mankato in his slow, deliberate voice.

"On our way here, yes," said Zeke. "We asked the officer on duty in the E.R., to keep a close eye on her." He and Kimmy were sitting across from Mankato in matching wooden chairs. Kimmy's feet just missed the floor, and she swung them as they talked.

"What happened to her?"

"Best we can guess," said Zeke, "someone named Bobby substituted something, probably Xylazine, for the meth she thought she was taking. She injected it subcutaneously, which may mean she's a more advanced addict than we thought."

"Or maybe it was just for convenience," said Kimmy.

"How do you mean?" asked the Lieutenant.

"Well, if this Bobby handed her a loaded syringe, and it sounded like he did, she'd have to inject it," Kimmy explained.

"Someone substituted something for the meth?" asked Mankato.

"We think he did. And we think he was going to kill her," said Zeke.

"Did you see the killer, then?" asked Mankato.

"I did," said Zeke. "If he's the killer. Eighteen to twenty years old, about six foot three, weighs maybe two fifteen. He looked like a linebacker to me, but that could be genetics. And he was definitely Native American. Brown eyes, black hair in a long, single ponytail."

"Sounds like a number of local guys," said Mankato, thinking. "Can you look through some mug shots, try to identify him?"

"Sure," said Zeke. "But this wasn't a stranger to Angel. She was nervous enough tonight that she wouldn't have taken anything from a stranger. Judging by the way they talked, she definitely knew the guy."

"Then why would he want to kill her?" asked Mankato.

Zeke nodded. "I wondered that, too. But I've seen this guy before. Somewhere. Same hair and eyes, same facial structure. It wasn't exact, and I saw him in the dark tonight, but there's something there."

Kimmy said, "Hey, I thought you had an eidetic memory."

Zeke nodded.

Mankato said, "One of those photographic memories, like on TV?"

Zeke said, "Not exactly. But I do tend to remember most everything. At least the important things."

Mankato looked at Zeke for a long minute and then said, "I've got an officer heading for the hospital to keep an eye on Angel. But we've got to find this guy, this Bobby."

* * *

Angel Wilson was passed out in the hospital bed. A doctor was standing nearby, checking her chart. Tribal Officer Bruce Doekiller was sitting in a chair in the room.

"How long do you think she'll be out?" Zeke asked the doctor.

"Can't say. If she took Xylazine it could be hours, or all night, depending on the dosage. She's a small girl, so it would hit her pretty hard." The doctor's name was Bill Ryan, and he had a grandfatherly manner about him.

"We think this could very well be related to the two earlier killings, of Jenny Lakota and Casey Black," said Zeke.

Zeke noticed Doekiller listening intently while pretending to be absorbed in his hunting magazine.

"Can you connect them?" asked the doctor.

"Maybe. All three of the girls were turning tricks for money, and all were using drugs. They were most likely selling meth, too. They could all be considered disrespectful of their heritage, of the values the tribe upholds."

"Hmm," said the doctor. "Seems pretty extreme, killing off people who don't agree with your ideas."

"Making a statement, perhaps," said Zeke.

Angel snored quietly.

Kimmy asked, "Where did the killer get the drugs? It's a controlled substance, right?"

"It is not," said Dr. Ryan. "It's an analgesic, and it's used in veterinary medicine as a sedative…and a muscle relaxant."

"So it's widely available?" asked Kimmy.

"Sure. You just need a vet prescription. That's not that hard to get around here," said Ryan.

"Is there a vet on the reservation?" asked Zeke.

"Sure, there are a couple," said the doctor.

* * *

Zeke snapped his fingers. "I know where I've seen Bobby before," he said.

He and Kimmy were sipping bad coffee in the hospital cafeteria. Angel was still sleeping quietly with Doekiller keeping watch in her room.

"Really? Where?" she asked.

"When I interviewed Henry Wolsnoki, the Tribal Officer's Chief of Staff. We were in his office, and he had some family pictures on his credenza. A number of them, actually."

"And one was of Bobby?" asked Kimmy. She stood and walked three steps to a large, gray garbage can and tossed her paper coffee cup, still full, into the trash. "Life's too short," she said.

Zeke was thinking. "Actually, several were of Bobby, but at different ages. Not current pictures. That's why I felt that I recognized him when we saw him. From the photographs."

"So there's a connection?" asked Kimmy.

"Seems to be," said Zeke. "A possible killer connected to the Tribal Leader's Administrator. We'll want to check into that."

"Next stop?" asked Kimmy.

"I think the local police. We'll pick up Tillman Cord and visit Lieutenant Mankato when he gets in tomorrow morning." He thought for a moment. "Meantime, let's get some sleep."

* * *

"What's the motivation?" asked Cord.

"For the murders?" asked Zeke. "It could be something about the drugs, selling drugs to Indian girls," said Zeke. "Or the sex."

"But?"

"But I have a hunch it's about the tribe."

Cord said, "That's still pretty dramatic, flaying the girl. Had to be a statement there, right?"

"Seems like it," said Zeke. "It might be something about disrespect."

"Disrespecting the tribe? These girls were, well, not the most well behaved citizens…"

"And then there's the money," said Zeke.

Kimmy smiled. They were sitting together in the Better B Café, a sprawling family restaurant that apparently specialized in breakfasts and lunches. The place was busy with ranchers, oil workers, mechanics, and truck drivers, plus a handful of retirees were crowded around one large corner table. It seemed like everyone was drinking coffee this morning.

"Money?" asked Cord. "We haven't come across any money in this investigation."

"Nevertheless, it's there. And it's a big factor," said Zeke.

Cord scratched his head. "Do tell."

* * *

"Well, it's easy to see the source," said Zeke. "It's the oil. Fracking. When such a disproportional amount of money is spread across a small number of people..."

"There's, what, about three-quarters of a million people here in the state?"

"And the State Government has a billion dollar surplus. Just sitting there, not being used. That's a lot of motivation for someone with unscrupulous tendencies."

"You think it's that big?" asked Cord. "That it reaches that far? The State Government?"

"Money and murder and big oil," said Zeke. "Probably so."

"How would they access the money, though?" thought Cord out loud. "How would the killings benefit the murderer, financially, I mean?"

"It could be a cover-up," said Kimmy. "Killing people who could give him away..."

"Possible," said Zeke. "But there's one way to find out."

"Well, then, let's go," said Cord.

* * *

Cord took the lead and knocked on the wooden door of the small home.

"FBI, open up," he called.

The house had seen better days. The exterior paint had been worn off the sides of the house from wind and weather, and the wooden deck of the porch was blistered with old, green paint interspersed with exposed wood. A few hundred yards away was a horse barn and a small corral. There were no other structures in sight.

Cord knocked again. "FBI, Bobby, open up."

They'd gotten Bobby's home address and job status from the Tribal Police. With the connection between the boy and Henry Wolsnoki, locals who knew the family history were able to direct Zeke and Cord to the small farmhouse, Henry's homestead when he was growing up.

"Too bad we couldn't get a warrant," said Cord.

"Not likely," said Zeke. "I believe Mr. Henry Wolsnoki is pretty well connected around here. Makes it tough to get cooperation from law enforcement."

"Or the courts," said Cord. "We'd be hard pressed to get a judge to sign off on the paper. The guys got too much juice."

"Could have used a Federal judge," said Zeke. "You being the FBI and all."

Just then, the door opened. A small, thin woman wearing

a gingham dress and moccasins stood framed by the door. Her hair was gray and black, and was arranged in two long, braided pigtails, one on either side of her head. She looked to be about sixty.

"Hello, ma'am," said Cord. "We're here to talk with Bobby. Bobby Wolsnoki."

The woman looked at Cord for a moment, and then she sighed and turned around. Leaving the door open, she called into the small house, "Bobby? Bobby, the police are here to talk to you."

The men waited a minute on the porch. They heard a door slam, and Zeke said, "He's going out the back!"

"Kimmy's back there. Can she handle?…" Cord started.

Zeke nodded and said, "I'll go. You watch the front." The small woman had silently disappeared into the darkness of the house.

It took just a few seconds for Zeke to circle the perimeter of the small farmhouse and gain a view of the back yard. As he cleared the back corner of the house he saw Bobby pointing a shotgun at Kimmy, who was standing between him and the vehicles in the drive.

Zeke thought, *Bad idea, Bobby.*

Kimmy, dressed in a tie-dyed cotton skirt and a yellow sweater, looked a bit like a flower child. She was two feet in front of Bobby and about half his size. And she was smiling.

"Get outta my way," said Bobby. "Or I'll shoot ya." He waved the shotgun in a wide arc.

Kimmy looked at him. "Are you high, Bobby?" she asked.

"Are you doing meth right now?"

Bobby seemed disoriented. "What? No..."

Zeke stepped in behind the boy, quietly, and nodded to Kimmy, who started talking again, distracting him.

"Bobby, you don't want to do this. It'll shame your dad, and you'll go to jail..."

"Shut up!" Bobby said. "Shut up about my dad!"

Zeke moved closer to Bobby's left and leaned forward and said, in his ear, "Put it down, Bobby."

Surprised at Zeke's sudden proximity, Bobby swung the gun barrel to the left, toward the voice. Zeke slipped the barrel under his left arm as it came around, tightened down on it and pulled Bobby closer. Bobby held tight to the gun. One sharp blow to his larynx with the yoke of Zeke's right hand caused Bobby to let go of the gun and sit down in the grass, hard. He held his neck with both hands and gasped desperately for breath.

Cord said, "Damn. I've never seen a five foot naught girl face down a shotgun before..."

"She's deadly," said Zeke. "She has one speed and that's full throttle. Good thing I was there to go easy on the boy."

Cord looked at Kimmy, then at Bobby, still gasping and holding his throat.

"Well, let's get him down to the police station," he said.

CHAPTER 28

"He won't be in here for long," said Lieutenant Mankato. "His dad pretty much has a direct link to the Governor."

"Will that matter in an attempted murder?" asked Zeke.

Cord said, "With the FBI involved?"

Mankato sat for a moment, and then said, "Maybe, maybe not."

"We think he's the serial killer. I like him for killing Casey Black and for skinning Jenny Lakota. I have to talk with him," said Zeke. "As soon as possible."

"He's in my jail," started Lieutenant Mankato. "I think…"

Cord jumped in. "This is Federal, Lieutenant. We're just using your jail to house him. The Marshals will pay you rent for it. You know the routine."

The lieutenant nodded. "I guess I do."

"We'd like to talk with him before his dad gets involved and he lawyers up," said Cord, pushing. "Can we get some time with him this morning? Right away?"

"You just brought him in this morning," said Mankato.

"We're still processing him."

"It'll benefit everyone if you let us interrogate the boy," said Cord. "Zeke here was in counter-intelligence for the military. He knows about this sort of thing."

Zeke said, "You've been reading my file…"

Mankato looked surprised.

"And he's working with the FBI on this," Cord continued.

Kimmy nodded. "Zeke's very good."

Lieutenant Mankato sighed and said, "OK, I'll set it up."

* * *

"I don't know what you're talking about," said Bobby.

"It's a simple question," said Zeke. "Where did you get the Xylazine?" He thought, *And you're lying from the get-go.*

Bobby shook his head and closed his eyes, as if to shut out everything around him.

"Bobby, you have horses on the farm, don't you?" asked Zeke.

Bobby said, "What?"

He's deflecting, thought Zeke. *Buying time and avoiding the question.*

"Simple question," said Cord. "Do you have horses?"

Bobby looked at him and said, "Some."

"And you work at the vet office on the reservation? The Tribal Officers mentioned that."

Bobby nodded. "I work there sometimes."

"So you have access to muscle relaxers," said Cord. "Xylazine."

"I don't know. No, not really. That's a controlled substance, so how would I get that?" His tone was suddenly lower.

That's convoluted phrasing, thought Zeke. *He's trying to make this more confusing than it is.*

"Did your grandmother know about the killings?" Zeke said, asking an unexpected question.

"What?" asked Bobby. His blink rate increased as he looked at Zeke. Then he looked down and away.

"Bobby, did your dad know about the girls?"

Bobby looked at Zeke. "You don't kill other people's horses," he said.

Zeke nodded. "Did your grandmother know about the murders?"

"Leave my Gramm out of this!" he shouted suddenly.

He's still lying, thought Zeke. *About most everything.*

"Why did you kill the girls, Bobby?" asked Cord. "Who told you to do it?"

It had become clear that the boy's intelligence level was below average. He'd grown defensive, evasive, even paranoid, as the questioning continued.

"A murderer? That wasn't me," said the boy. "I'm a warrior."

Lieutenant Mankato opened the door to the interrogation room and said, "Can I see you for a minute?"

Zeke and Cord stepped out of the room.

"His attorney's here," said Mankato. "He said no more interview."

"That's OK, we're not getting anywhere in there anyhow," said Cord.

"Let's talk about it over a cup of coffee, Tillman," said Zeke.

* * *

The Better B Café's coffee was on par with the Salty Dog's, which meant it was hot and plentiful, but not very tasty. Zeke and Cord, joined by Kimmy, slid into an empty booth away from the other diners.

"You think his grandmother was involved somehow?" asked Cord. "What was the motivation?"

"Is Bobby smart enough to plan all this and then carry it out?" said Zeke, partially to himself.

"Probably not," said Cord. "But remember, he was coming down from a high on meth when we questioned him. Makes it tough to gauge what he's really like."

Zeke nodded.

"The first killing of Casey Black, the girl up north by the Evans Site, took place in 2016, almost three years ago," said Zeke.

Cord nodded.

"Bobby would have been, what, sixteen years old then?"

Cord said, "So, you're saying it's less likely he committed that killing."

Zeke nodded. "And I don't see a teenager like Bobby being motivated to kill because of 'acts of disrespect to the tribe.' Seems like that would be too political, too abstract to move a teen like him to action."

Cord said, "Maybe it was a hot button for him. Like one of

those school shooters that are cropping up all over the country..."

"Maybe," said Zeke. "But it could have been a hot button for someone else. Someone older and more traditional."

"His sibling? One of his parents?" asked Cord.

"Or his Gramm," said Zeke.

* * *

She sat crosslegged on the floor of the small room with the threadbare carpet, alone once again.

The Federal officers had taken the boy, Otaktay, as she had watched from a window. The woman put him in the back of the car and drove away. When they were gone, she sent Mika to stay with a neighbor.

It was once again a time for action. She had taken the knife from its hidey-hole, and she was holding it in both hands, a symbol of the violence and death to come.

She chanted to it, as she had done long before.

Suddenly, her phone rang.

"Hello?" she answered.

She heard the man's voice on the line, speaking Sioux first, then English. "Hau. Hello. You called me?"

"Yes," she said. "They've come and taken him."

"Otaktay?" asked the man.

"Yes."

He paused, thinking.

"What should we do?" she asked.

"I'll arrange for a lawyer for him. You must finish the work."

* * *

They were staying at the Four Bears Casino hotel, on the west side of the Little Missouri River, about four miles from New Town. The hotel was a wide three-story structure sitting next to the casino and event center. It was the only hotel near New Town.

Darkness was falling as Zeke, Kimmy and Cord left the restaurant and walked through the brisk North Dakota breeze. Kimmy pulled her jacket closed with both hands as they cut across the parking lot toward the hotel lobby.

"I'll catch up with you," said Kimmy. "I need to get something from the car."

"Do you want us to wait?" asked Zeke.

"No, I'll see you in the morning."

Cord said, "Yes, ma'am. We'll meet you downstairs for breakfast."

Kimmy found the rental car parked in the back of the hotel in a spot in the second row. She opened the trunk, pulled the gun safe toward her and opened it. Her Jericho 941 was there, along with Zeke's Walther and extra ammo for each. They'd left them there when they'd stopped by the Tribal Police Station. She slid her gun into her waistband, closed the safe and the trunk, and turned toward the hotel.

Kimmy saw a flash of light in a car window, a reflection of the parking lot lights on something shiny. She turned quickly and saw the falling blade of the skinner's knife slashing toward her, an inch from her face as she shrank back and twisted, keeping her right shoulder and arm out of range. The knife nicked her thigh as it came down, and then it whistled past her, ending its arc near the asphalt pavement.

"You must die! You abandoned your child! You are no daughter of mine!" the woman screamed.

As the knife hesitated, its momentum spent, Kimmy stepped forward onto the blade, flattening it onto the pavement and crushing her attacker's hand beneath the handle. Her attacker, she saw, was an Indian woman, old and wrinkled and crazed.

Her foot on the knife, Kimmy reached and grabbed the woman's braids and yanked her head forward. Her knuckles still beneath the knife handle, the old woman fell forward as Kimmy, with minimal motion, kneed her in the face. Then again, and again.

Blood flowed from the old woman's damaged nose and mouth. Kimmy scooped up the knife and handcuffed the woman.

"You whore!" screamed the old woman through bloody teeth. "You whore! I'll kill you! I'll kill all of you!"

* * *

The four Tribal Police vehicles and the ambulance all flashed their red and blue lights in a distracting random sequence.

"I heard the excitement," said Zeke. "Sorry I missed it." He and Cord had returned to the parking lot when Kimmy called

Zeke's cell phone and told them what had happened.

The EMT finished bandaging Kimmy's leg and said, "You were lucky." She picked up her medic case and said, "Come by the ER for a tetanus shot," and walked over to where two husky EMT's were patching up the woman.

Four Tribal Officers with their hands on their holstered guns watched as the handcuffed woman's swollen face was cleaned and bandaged. Three other officers maintained a perimeter, keeping curious hotel guests and staff at bay.

"It was nothing," said Kimmy.

"Are you losing a step?" asked Zeke, looking at her bandage.

Kimmy looked up at him, dead serious. "Uh, no," she said. "That would be a 'No'."

"Bobby's Gramm?" asked Zeke. It was hard to recognize the woman with her face bandaged.

Cord nodded. "She sounds crazy. We should talk with her now."

Zeke said, "OK," and they all walked over toward the woman. She was mumbling something unrecognizable, over and over. It sounded like a mantra.

"She's OK?" Zeke asked one of the EMT's.

"She'll live," he said as he worked.

"What's she saying?"

"It's the Lakota language," said the second EMT.

He has some Native American blood, thought Zeke.

"She's talking about killing whores," said the man.

Zeke looked at Kimmy. "Maybe I should handle this interview," he said. "She seems to be angry with women."

"Suits me," said Kimmy.

"It'll have to be tomorrow," said the first EMT. "We just sedated her."

* * *

"I'm wondering, now, about a number of things," said Zeke. "Rethinking it some."

"Yes, sir?" said Cord.

They were back in the Better B Café, drinking average coffee, talking through their findings and preparing for the interview.

"What Bobby's Gramm did, and the anger and emotion she was feeling, what's behind that?"

Cord nodded. "It did seem extreme…"

"And what about Bobby's mother? I wonder if there may have been an earlier killing."

"Bobby's mother killed?" asked Cord. "You think that's what the old woman was ranting about?"

"It could make sense," said Zeke.

"So you think the old woman killed Henry's wife and took Bobby in? Raised him?"

"It's possible," said Zeke. "Let's ask her about it."

* * *

The first thing Zeke noticed was the fire in her eyes. They burned with a fierce hatred, like an ageless flame in her soul.

The second thing he noticed was that she never blinked.

She said, "Uŋkčémna." She spat the word out of her mouth with venom.

Officer Doekiller, who was sitting in as a translator, said, "She says you smell like…well, feces."

Zeke thought, *Great way to start an interrogation.* He said, "What would make you so angry?"

The woman's eyes burned with hatred and her entire being, all her energy, was behind the force she leveled at Zeke. It was palpable. Zeke shook it off.

"They say your name is Paytah," said Zeke. "Officer Doekiller says that means 'Fire.' Is that right?"

The woman said nothing, staring past Zeke.

"Here's your chance," said Zeke. "Tell us why you're so angry. Who did this to you?"

Suddenly, the woman looked upward, as if searching for help from above. Zeke looked up, too. The ceiling of the interrogation room was wire mesh, painted black, and about a foot lower than the electrical conduits, lights and air conditioning ducts. Nothing there. Zeke shrugged.

"Your grandson, Bobby. He's killed some people," Zeke continued, looking for a maternal reaction. The woman leveled her gaze at him again. "He'll have to pay for that."

"I have no grandson named Bobby," she said, the anger suddenly gone from her face. "I have only Otaktay."

Zeke looked at Doekiller, who said, "It means Great Warrior."

The old woman didn't seem to have heard him.

"Where's Otaktay's mother?" asked Zeke. "Why is he with you?"

Now the woman looked away for the first time. Then she looked down at the table.

"Why is he with you?" Zeke asked softly.

"His father cannot take care of him," she said, simply. "He doesn't have the knowledge to bring the boy up. They were doing it wrong."

"Did you stop that?" asked Zeke.

"I had to. My daughter was a disgrace, a drug addict and a whore!"

"How long has he been with you?" asked Zeke.

"Forever," she said.

Zeke changed tactics. "What happened last night? In the hotel parking lot? Why did you try to kill the woman, Kimmy?"

"She took Otaktay away. I had to get him back."

"And you used the knife?" asked Zeke.

"Yes."

"The police say it's probably the same knife that was used to kill Jenny Lakota," Zeke continued.

No response. Then, suddenly, "That Indian girl! She was a whore! She laid on her back for anyone! She was a cancer, she sold those drugs to other Indians…"

Zeke said, "Was that your daughter? Did you kill your daughter? Again and again…"

"She was with that man. She was in the stable with that man. I heard her, I heard him give her money. And the meth. She promised she would stop the meth. But she never did. She shamed me! She shamed us all!"

She was screaming, now.

Zeke said, "Your daughter. You killed your daughter."

"Yes, I killed her!"

"And you kept killing her," said Zeke. "You sent Bobby to do it, didn't you?"

She focused suddenly and said, "It had to be done. There was no other way to purge the evil."

CHAPTER 29

"Bobby Wolsnoki's mother was named Carol Wolsnoki, nee Carol Talking Owl. It looks like she married Henry Wolsnoki in 1995 and they had two children, a boy and a girl, born in New Town. The boy's birth certificate has him as 'Robert.'" Sally read some additional information to Zeke from the public records she'd found.

"Carol was killed, then?" he asked over the phone line.

"Yes, in April of 2008. They found her in a small barn on a local ranch. The stable owner was an Indian. He was killed, too, same time and place. The newspaper article says she used to ride horses there," Sally added.

"How did she die?" asked Zeke.

"Cut with a sharp knife," said Sally. "Her throat was slit. Same as the man."

"And the killer?" asked Zeke.

"They looked at Henry first, but he had a good alibi. He was in Washington when it happened, according to the police file notes."

"How'd you get access to those?" asked Zeke.

"Electronic magic," said Sally. "I'm sworn to secrecy, so don't ask."

"Did they arrest anyone for the murders?" asked Zeke.

"It looks like they didn't. In fact, it looks like the Tribal Police had trouble getting the FBI to pay any attention to it at all. An Indian woman is killed on the reservation. And it's still an open case, technically."

"Carol Talking Owl," said Zeke. "So the woman who attacked Kimmy was Henry's mother-in-law."

"Sounds right. What was her name?" asked Sally.

"Police say they booked her as Ramona Talking Owl. But she refuses to answer to anything except her Indian name."

"Which is?" asked Sally.

"Which is Paytah," said Zeke. "In Lakota, it means 'Fire'."

* * *

"She killed her own daughter? She must be nuts," said Tillman Cord.

They were sipping coffee and waiting in the Tribal Police station for Lieutenant Mankato to come out of a personnel meeting.

"Sally says Henry's wife became addicted to painkillers when the second baby, the baby girl was born," said Zeke. "Apparently there were complications with the birth. They gave her opiates of some sort for the pain. And according to the Tribal Officers, it just got worse over time. She couldn't get

Oxy, so she started using meth and became addicted…"

"So it's very possible she was trading sex for drugs or money. Possibly with the stable owner. And it's possible she was dealing to make money for her own meth. That would make sense, in light of the double homicide," said Cord.

Zeke nodded. "That would infuriate her mother. Perhaps it was the one thing that put Gramm over the edge… And then she killed her own daughter."

Cord said, "And then she started using Bobby? To kill?"

"Very possible. She's seriously deranged," said Cord.

"But maybe someone guided them," said Zeke. "Someone could have pointed them at their victims."

"That's possible," said Cord.

"Tillman, let's check on Henry Wolsnoki. It's possible that he's involved in this somehow," said Zeke.

* * *

"Henry Wolsnoki, I'm the FBI. You're under arrest," said Cord.

He and Zeke, along with two Tribal Officers, were standing in the lobby of the Tribal Leaders' offices when Wolsnoki stepped out of his office.

Bruce Doekiller stepped behind the man and secured his wrists in handcuffs.

"What? What are you doing?" the man sputtered. "Do you know who I am?"

Cord said, "Let's take this downtown, Henry. Unless you want everyone here to know your business."

"What's the charge?" the man persisted.

"OK, we'll do it your way. Embezzlement," said Cord.

Henry's jaw dropped. "What?"

"Stealing from the State of North Dakota. You should be ashamed." Then, to Doekiller, "Read him his rights."

* * *

"Who told you this?" said Henry Wolsnoki. "My family? They're not credible witnesses."

His attorney, Douglas Brown, sitting next to him, nodded. Zeke and Cord sat across the table from them.

Cord said, "Who is Edward Reasons?"

Wolsnoki looked up at him quickly.

That shocked him, thought Zeke.

"I don't recall," said Wolsnoki.

"We agreed to this, uh, meeting to clear things up," said Brown, sensing his client was losing ground. "We didn't agree to a fishing expedition."

Brown looked to be about forty, an average sized man with a pin stripe suit and a crisp white shirt. His red tie was clipped in place and his haircut was almost military. He was making notes on a legal pad.

"We're not fishing," said Cord. Then he said to Wolsnoki, "We interviewed your mother-in-law."

"I told you, she's not credible. She's delusional. Has been for years."

"Since her daughter died," said Zeke. "Your wife. We know."

"What does that have to do with anything?" asked Wolsnoki.

"Well, I got to thinking about it," said Zeke. "And we asked the Medical Examiner to compare the knife your mother had when she attacked Kimmy with the wounds on your wife. And on Casey Black. She had to do some forensic analysis, but fortunately the M.E.'s file was pretty detailed, very complete. It had photos and measurements of each cut and stab on both women."

Henry Wolsnoki said nothing.

"And they were a match."

"We found several interesting things," said Cord. "It's standard procedure to get a search warrant for a killer's home. Or, in this case, two attempted killers' home."

Wolsnoki was quiet, listening.

"We found a phone, a burner, in the house," said Zeke. "Your fingerprints were all over it. And it had one phone number in the caller list. Edward Reasons."

"So without the fishing, let me ask again," said Tillman Cord. "Who is Edward Reasons?"

"I didn't make any call..." started Wolsnoki.

"Time to shut up, Henry," said Douglas Brown.

* * *

"Edwards Reasons is a highway contractor," said Cord. "He's been involved in most of the new major road projects and Interstate repairs in North Dakota."

"And he's been paying off Henry Wolsnoki?" asked Zeke.

"He has. Henry had the responsibility for approving invoices at the Tribal Leaders' level. Since Reasons' company is already established in the State's accounting system as a vendor, it was pretty easy for him to submit additional, fictitious invoices for consulting work, and having them approved by Henry," said Cord. "Then he split the money with Henry. Not much to it."

"How long has it been going on?" asked Zeke.

"Looks like maybe three years," said Cord.

"So he started stealing money after his wife died. Was he trying to get even with the State for her death?" asked Zeke. "Or just trying to get what he thought was his share of the money?"

"Hard to tell," said Cord. "I just think the whole family's crazy."

"They are. The old woman, Gramm, never recovered from her daughter's drug addiction. That put her over the edge, and she killed her. And then she started killing Indian girls, as if she were still killing her daughter…"

"Indian girls who were selling drugs and sex, out of control and disrespecting the Nation," said Zeke. "She saw herself as an instrument of the Tribes."

"And when she couldn't do it anymore, when she was too old, she passed it on to her grandson," said Cord.

"Henry's boy, Bobby. Yes," said Zeke. "Like you said, the whole family's crazy."

* * *

"You certainly know how to treat a girl, Mr. Traynor," said Tracy.

Zeke smiled to himself.

"Does this mean we're going steady?" he asked.

"Hmm. That's a pretty big commitment, sir. I'd have to think about that."

They were alone on the porch of Zeke's cottage in the Keys, feeling the heat of the afternoon sun on their shoulders and their faces. Zeke was sitting on the wide porch rail and Tracy sat on a chaise lounge nearby.

"This place is great," she said.

"It's a special place," said Zeke.

Tracy looked up at him.

"It's where we first started going steady," he said, smiling.

"You look good in board shorts and nothing else," said Tracy. "We could move down here and forget about law enforcement."

"There are worse things," said Zeke. "Could you see me as a fisherman?"

"Honestly? I could see you as a pirate," said Tracy.

Zeke thought for a minute. "I owe you an apology," he said.

"Oh?"

"I've been distracted. I got caught up emotionally in finding my parents' murderer, and I've been ignoring you. I'm sorry."

"You haven't been ignoring me," said Tracy. "I feel very much appreciated."

"Well, I've been preoccupied. It took away from you and me."

"Just for a little while," said Tracy. "And it was necessary. It was important."

"Yes, I remember. You were the one who encouraged me to pursue it."

"You pretty much remember everything. It's annoying, sometimes," said Tracy with a smile in her voice.

"But we're done with that," said Zeke. "And now I can turn my undivided attention back to you."

"Uh-oh," said Tracy. "I'd better sleep with one eye open."

Zeke thought for a moment. "Who said anything about sleep?"

# # #

Other Zeke Traynor Mysteries available at
http://amzn.to/2DL2jyF

If you enjoyed Zeke's latest adventure, please consider leaving a brief review on Amazon.com.

And sign up for the author's e-mails at:
http://eepurl.com/b5JIkf

About the Author

Jeff Siebold loves a good mystery. A life long reader, he has embarked on a personal journey in creativity designed to contribute to the delight of mystery readers everywhere. He plans to continue writing as long as there are stories to be told!

Jeff and his wife Karin live on a barrier island in North Carolina, not far from the Cape Fear River (made famous by one of his favorite authors, John D. MacDonald). They have three college-aged children and two unruly dogs.

Made in the USA
Columbia, SC
15 June 2020

11125273R00202